THE TRAITOR SPY

ALSO BY MARION BLACKWOOD

Marion Blackwood has written lots of books across multiple series, and new books are constantly added to her catalogue. To see the most recently updated list of books, please visit: www.marionblackwood.com

CONTENT WARNINGS

The *Court of Elves* series contains violence, morally questionable actions, and later books in the series also contain some more detailed sexual content. If you have specific triggers, you can find the full list of content warnings at: www.marionblackwood.com/content-warnings

THE TRAITOR SPY

COURT OF ELVES: BOOK ONE

MARION BLACKWOOD

Copyright © 2021 by Marion Blackwood

All rights reserved. No part of this book may be reproduced in any form or by any electronic or mechanical means, including information storage and retrieval systems, without permission in writing from the publisher, except by reviewers, who may quote brief passages in a review. For more information, contact info@marionblackwood.com

ISBN 978-91-986387-9-0 (hardcover)
ISBN 978-91-986386-9-1 (paperback)
ISBN 978-91-986386-8-4 (ebook)

Editing by Julia Gibbs

This is a work of fiction. Names, characters, places, and incidents either are the product of the author's imagination or are used fictitiously. Any resemblance to actual persons, living or dead, events, or locales is entirely coincidental.

www.marionblackwood.com

For everyone who has given too much

CHAPTER 1

*H*aving ambition was incredibly dangerous for a slave. But no matter how much I wished it were otherwise, I did possess that particular character trait. I wanted more. More than just keeping my head down and doing as I was told. I wanted enough money to buy my freedom one day. So with that goal in mind, I continued adding to my secret treasure trove. One blackmail ransom at a time.

Moonlight cast the dark stone building in silvery light. The candles in the upstairs window had been blown out half an hour ago, and with them, the sounds of muffled grunting had gone quiet. After making sure that the hood of my custom-tailored black jacket was secure, I snuck out of the shadows and approached the front door.

No rust covered the metal lock and the door was plain but in excellent condition, as most things were in this part of the city. I placed a gloved hand on the handle and pushed down. Locked. To be fair, if I was doing what the humans in this house were doing, I would've locked the door too.

Unfortunately for them, that didn't stop someone like me. With a sly smile on my lips, I took a step forward and walked right through the sturdy slab of wood.

Being a half-elf sucked sometimes. It wasn't that people looked down on you because of it or considered mixed heritage unnatural–though there probably were people in the five courts that made up our continent who preferred the bloodlines to be pure–but neither humans nor elves really considered you one of their own either. Not to mention that the elven prince who ruled your territory could apparently just take you and force you into servitude regardless of what you and your family wanted. Which was what had happened to me. But one of the good things about not being entirely human was inheriting magic from the elven side of your bloodline. Being able to walk through walls made both my job and my side hustle a whole lot easier.

The hallway inside was lined with paintings. Stern-faced men in powerful poses stared down at me from within their metal frames as I slunk across the floorboards and approached the staircase at the back. Taking care to place my feet at the far end of each step, I made my way upstairs.

Another dark hallway met me. I noted a study behind an open door on my left but continued in the other direction, where I knew my target was. The door to the bedroom was closed. I could probably just have opened it but I didn't want to risk any creaking hinges, so instead I walked straight through this one too.

Every time I walked through walls, it always felt as though I was passing through a curtain of sheets, its soft silken fabric whispering against my skin, until I stepped out on the other side and the world was back to normal again.

I relished the feeling before it disappeared when I cleared

the door. Glancing around, I found myself inside a tastefully decorated bedroom with a large double bed against the far wall and a set of dark wooden drawers to my left. Discarded clothes littered the floor. I arched an eyebrow at the sleeping humans as I stepped over a set of purple lace undergarments and made for the right-hand nightstand.

Bundled into the cream-colored sheets, a blond woman lay curled up against a heavyset man. Their chests rose and fell in tandem. I spared them only a swift glance to make sure they were still sleeping before turning my attention back to the small table on the woman's side of the bed. Jewelry glittered in the moonlight that filtered in through the window. The pieces were pretty, I had to give her that. But not valuable enough to sell for a decent profit, so I decided to stick to my original plan.

I chose a pair of earrings with drooping blue stones and carefully lifted them off the nightstand. After tucking them into one of the numerous hidden pockets in my jacket, I strode towards the still closed door and disappeared back into the hallway in the same manner I had come.

The door to the study on the other side of the corridor was still open so I simply strolled through it and plopped down in the ornate chair. Swinging my feet onto the massive oak desk, I crossed my ankles and leaned back in what I deemed a sufficiently cocky pose. After checking that my braided hair was still invisible beneath the heavy hood, I pulled down the black mask sewn into the top of it and adjusted it across my face. Once my disguise was firmly in place, I reached over and knocked a ceramic pot filled with writing material off the desk.

Pale brown shards skittered across the floorboards as it crashed down and a terrible clattering filled the dark study.

From across the hall, shocked gasps rang out. I remained lounging in the chair while a pair of stamping feet rushed towards me. Flickering candlelight painted the walls with shadows, first in the bedroom and then in the hallway.

"What is the meaning of this?" bellowed the man who owned this house as he stalked into the study. Light from the candle in his hand danced across my dark-clad body as he snatched up a fire poker and brandished it in my direction. "Get out of my house!"

"In a minute." I smiled even though he couldn't see it behind the black mask. "But first, you're going to give me some money."

His rather substantial stomach flapped under his unbuttoned white shirt as he harrumphed. "And why would I do that?"

"Because that is not your wife in the bedroom."

Silence descended on the room. Panic fought against anger in the man's pale eyes as he flicked a glance at the bedroom behind him. Then, he squared his shoulders and raised the poker higher.

"If I kill you, no one will ever know."

I didn't even bother drawing the knife strapped to my thigh or the sword across my back because, well, you can't blackmail a dead man. So instead, I just shrugged. "You could do that. But before you do, ask your mistress if her earrings are still on the bedside table."

He stared me down for another few seconds before bellowing the question to the woman in the bedroom. When her frantic voice replied that they were indeed gone, the man of the house narrowed his eyes at me but lowered the poker slightly.

"My wife would probably just think that they were her own earrings."

I scoffed. "Women know their own jewelry. Trust me."

"I could say that I bought them for her."

"Which she will definitely believe when she finds only one earring and it's also wedged behind a drawer, or under the bed or something."

Rage flickered over his face but his shoulders slumped in defeat as he rammed the fire poker back in its place. "What do you want?"

"And we have finally circled back to the beginning of this conversation." Swinging my feet off his desk, I stood up. "Money."

Wooden floorboards quivered in fear as he stomped over to the wall and lifted off a painting to reveal a metal safe. It would have been so much easier if I could have just reached in and taken the money inside the safe myself, but unfortunately, I can't phase through objects that way. It's either all of me, or none of me.

"How much?" he ground out as he yanked open the small metal door.

"How much is your honor worth?"

First rule of blackmail: never bid against yourself. I had no idea how much money he had in that safe, so the best course of action was always to make the mark decide the amount. Out of fear, they usually ended up giving me more than I would have demanded.

Paper rustled and coins jingled as he pulled out what looked to be the majority of the cash stashed in there. I held out a hand but let him come to me. My fingers curled around the tall stack of paper notes as he placed it in my gloved hand.

"You can keep the coins," I said when he lifted the pouch. I couldn't very well sneak back into the Court of Stone with all that metal jingling in my pockets.

His fist tightened on the small sack but he nodded. "And the earrings?"

"I'll keep those as collateral." Sticking the blackmail ransom into one of my magic-imbued pockets, I breezed past the seething man. "Just in case you get it in your head to tell anyone about this."

"And how do I know that you won't plant the earrings anyway?"

A wicked laugh drifted past my black mask. "I guess you'll just have to trust me."

Vicious swearing followed me as I glided down the stairs but the disgruntled man stayed in his study. Sliding a hand into my pocket, I ran my thumb over the stack of notes as I walked straight through the sturdy front door and disappeared into the night again.

Not a bad night's work. This put me ever so slightly closer to my goal of buying my freedom from the elven prince who held my leash. The Prince of Stone. Pushing the mask back into my hood again, I set course for the sprawling castle of white stone that made up the heart of his court.

Now, all I had to do was make it back to my room and stash all my ill-gotten goods without anyone noticing. I cast a quick glance at the nearest clock tower. And I had to do it all before Prince Edric started his briefing. Which would be soon. Very soon.

Wind tore through my clothes as I sprinted up the cobblestone street with my heart hammering in my chest. No rest for the wicked. Especially not if you were a blackmailer. And a spy. I sucked in a lungful of cool night air as I crested the hill before the Court of Stone. This was going to be close.

CHAPTER 2

"Kenna!" A sharp knock followed the berating voice. "What are you doing? Hurry up."

"Coming!" I called back while shrugging out of my jacket.

It landed on the floor in a dark heap with the blackmail ransom and earrings still tucked into its pockets. Muffled clattering followed as I dropped my sword and knife on top of it. Yanking off the strap that secured my braid, I fluffed out my loose red curls until they cascaded down my back again. After one last look at the mess I'd made in the hidden compartment of my room, I walked back through the wall and into the room proper.

The one good thing about having lived in the Court of Stone for years was that I had at least been able to maneuver myself into the room I wanted. Not only was my room located perfectly for someone who wanted to sneak in and out of the castle by walking through the walls, it also had a walk-in closet that I had redesigned. Where the door used to be, there was now only a smooth white wall of stone. It was the perfect place to hide my secret fortune since I was the only one who could get inside.

Wood vibrated as knuckles rapped against my door again. "Kenna!"

I drew a deep breath to compose myself before opening the door. Turquoise eyes blinked at me in surprise as I slipped out and closed it behind me.

"Come on, Monette," I said before she could start asking questions. Looping my arm through hers, I pulled the gorgeous half-elf with me as I strode towards our meeting chamber. "He'll kill us if we're late."

"You're telling me? You are the one who's late." Monette's delicate nose crinkled in disapproval as she flicked her gaze down my body. "What are you wearing?"

Since I'd been short on time, I hadn't been able to change back into my usual clothes, so I was still wearing the black pants, shirt, and gloves that I opted for while conducting my extra-curricular activities.

"I was trying a new style," I lied smoothly.

I didn't like lying to my friend but no one could know about my little side hustle as a blackmailer.

Monette drew a hand through her shining blond hair while returning her gaze to the grand marble hallway ahead. "You look better in a dress."

"I'll change back after the briefing."

A pair of intricately carved stone doors had been left open at the end of the corridor. I detached my arm from Monette's as we entered the meeting chamber. Rows of white stone bookcases lined the walls and flickering candles painted the pale room, as well as its occupants, with dancing shadows. The only seat was a plain but sturdy marble throne on a dais by the left wall, but that particular piece of furniture was not meant for us, so I took up position next to a bookshelf instead. Silence hung over the room as the spies of the Court of Stone waited for the prince who commanded us.

The marble around us rumbled as Edric Mountaincleaver, the Prince of Stone, strode into the meeting chamber. His blond hair fluttered behind him as he swept towards the throne and drew himself up before it. As one, we bowed low. Dark gray pants and a white shirt whispered against stone as he settled himself onto the throne before twitching his fingers, motioning for us to rise. Eyes the color of gray granite stared down at us when we straightened.

Prince Edric was stunning, in the way that all elves were stunning, but there was also a roughness to his features. As if he had been carved from the mountain itself. His powerful muscles shifted beneath rolled-up sleeves as he raised his arms. Using his power of stone manipulation, he made the heavy double doors move without touching them. They slammed shut with a loud bang, making me flinch slightly. I shuddered to think of the damning wrath he might release upon me if he ever found out that I was blackmailing his citizens.

"What do you know about the Dagger of Orias?" Prince Edric asked without preamble.

"It is said to be able to pierce magical armor," a soft voice replied from the other side of the room.

"Correct." Edric's eyes hardened. "Rumor has it that the dagger has now been found. And that one of the other courts is in possession of it."

A ripple went through the crowd of spies. I braced a hand against the cool bookshelf and blew out a sigh as well. Next to me, Monette scrunched up her pale eyebrows.

"What?" she whispered.

"The dagger can be used to kill the King of Elves," I breathed back.

"Oh."

Edric silenced the room with a slash of his hand. "Explain to the ones who don't know about the dagger why it is bad that another court has found it."

"Because the one who has the dagger can use it to kill the King of Elves," Monette said.

The Prince of Stone nodded at her in approval. "Correct. Which is why we have to get it first."

"Is it really true?" a half-elf with short copper hair blurted out. "Is there actually something that can get through King Aldrich's stone skin?"

Felix. Out of all the spies in the Court of Stone, he was the least smooth one. Which was probably why he was only on transport duty.

When Edric's granite stare slid to Felix, he seemed to remember himself and cringed.

"I just meant that since King Aldrich used to be the Prince of Stone before he ascended to be King of Elves, that you might know if there was..." Felix trailed off and swallowed while the rest of the room silently begged him to stop talking. "I'm sorry. I apologize for the interruption, my prince."

"Yes, the Dagger of Orias can pierce King Aldrich's stone skin and kill him." Marble rumbled around us as Edric swept hard eyes across the room. "Any other questions?"

We all dropped our gaze and shook our head.

"Good." He gave us a curt nod. "These are your orders. Four of you will be sent to the other courts with the sole purpose of finding the dagger. The rest of you will continue working your previous assignments, but you will *all* keep your eyes and ears open for any information about the dagger. King Aldrich will make his next appearance at the fall equinox ball, which means that we have less than two weeks to find the dagger. Time is of the essence. And failure will not be tolerated. Am I clear?"

Every spy in the room nodded swiftly.

"Good," he said again. "Monette, Kenna, Ymas, and Tena. You will be sent to each of the courts."

My heart skipped a beat. The elf known only as 'the Void' usually handled the Court of Shadows because he was the only spy skilled enough to infiltrate it without getting caught. But since I hadn't seen him in this room and Edric hadn't called his name, it meant that someone else would be sent there this time.

"Monette," Prince Edric said. "The Court of Water."

A dazzling smile flashed across Monette's luscious lips and she clapped her hands excitedly. I tried to return the smile but my stomach twisted in nervous knots so it came out more like a grimace.

"Tena," Edric continued. "The Court of Fire."

Tena, the brown-haired half-elf at the front of the room, swallowed but nodded at her prince. The Court of Fire was brutal, but at least it was possible to infiltrate. Blood continued pounding in my ears and I had to grip the stone bookcase next to me for support. *Please not the Court of Shadows. Please not the Court of Shadows.* No sane person willingly crossed that court and even the other elven princes did their best to stay on the Prince of Shadows' good side.

"Kenna," Edric called. "The Court of Trees."

My breath whooshed out of me in a deep sigh of relief as I nodded at the prince in acknowledgement of the order. Across the room, Ymas blanched since that meant he would be sent to the Court of Shadows.

"Which means that Ymas gets the Court of Shadows," Prince Edric confirmed.

Ymas who, along with the Void, was one of the few pure-blooded elves who worked as spies for the Prince of Stone, schooled his features into a determined expression and nodded.

"Tena, Monette, Kenna, and Ymas, I will provide you with detailed instructions in the morning."

Once more, the four of us nodded in acknowledgement. He usually did that. Kept us on a strict need-to-know basis so that we only had information about our own assignments. Which was good, I supposed. If we were captured, we wouldn't be able to compromise the Court of Stone to any great extent.

After sweeping his granite stare across the room, Edric pushed to his feet. "That is all."

We all bowed low again as he strode towards the double doors. They swung open with a flick of his power. Only when he had left the meeting chamber did we straighten.

"Water and Trees!" Monette swatted me on the arm with the back of her hand and flashed me a smile. "That's perfect."

I drew my fingers through my hair before hooking the long curls behind my ears. "Yeah, we were lucky."

"Lucky? We're skilled. Finding this dagger is going to be a piece of cake."

Shaking my head, I followed her into the wide hallway. I wasn't sure if I agreed that it would be easy but I was at least very thankful that I had been assigned to one of the more pleasant courts. Though the news that the Dagger of Orias was in play made me nervous. If one of the other elven princes did use it to kill King Aldrich and steal the throne for himself, it would plunge all the courts into chaos. The king always chose his successor, but if he died without naming the prince who would succeed him, then we would have a war on our hands.

I pushed the grim thoughts aside as I reached my room. First, I had to clean up the mess I'd made as my blackmailer alter ego and change out of these clothes. Then, I would start planning my infiltration of the Court of Trees. No rest for the wicked, indeed.

CHAPTER 3

My stomach twisted and my body felt as though it was folding in on itself. Then the blur around me disappeared and a lush forest took its place. I sucked in a breath that sounded more like a gasp and shook my head to clear it of the disorienting feeling.

"Still not used to worldwalking, huh?" Felix grinned at me while releasing his grip on my waist.

I threw him an embarrassed smile in return.

Worldwalking was one of the more convenient magical skills that elves could possess because it gave you the ability to move between two different places in the blink of an eye. But far from everyone had that power. All the elven princes possessed that ability, of course, as one of their three magical skills. Two of those three skills were bestowed upon them when they became prince: worldwalking and the ability to manipulate the element of their court, like stone or water. And then they also had a third power that varied depending on what they'd been born with.

Not all elves were born with magic, though, and the ones

who were only had one, or in rare cases two, powers. It could range from something as trivial as being able to make a specific kind of flower bloom on the new moon to something as powerful as making people see whatever you wanted. We half-elves were only ever born with one power, if we were lucky, and Felix had somehow been blessed with worldwalking. That was why he was still a valuable member of the Court of Stone despite having a personality that made him less than ideal as a spy.

"Alright, can you come back and pick me up in two hours?" I asked.

"This exact spot?"

"Yes."

Felix nodded and flashed me another grin. "Sure. See you in two hours."

And with that he disappeared, leaving me alone in the secluded forest clearing near the palace in the Court of Trees. Birds chirped in the foliage above and a pleasant hum of nature magic hung over the whole area. I savored the minute of complete peace before striding across the soft moss in the direction of the castle.

Midday sunlight filtered down through the fresh green canopy and made the colorful flowers sparkle. I made sure that my hair was firmly tucked into a bun and straightened my nondescript beige dress while I wove through the thick tree trunks.

Since I was part elven, I was beautiful enough to stand out in a human crowd, there was no denying that. But fortunately for me, being beautiful was more or less a mandatory trait for elves, so if I downplayed my wardrobe and styling, I could make sure that I didn't draw attention to myself. Hence the rather dreary dress I was currently wearing.

The sounds of chatting people close by made me snap my head up. Deeming my appearance as bland as it was about to get, I glided into the shadows of a mighty oak tree and listened to the elves up ahead.

"Come on, you can do it," a male elf said. "Just walk up to her and ask her."

A distressed groan answered him. "What if she says no?"

"It's just a dance. You're not asking her to marry you."

"Fine." A deep sigh echoed between the trees. "But if she says no, you owe me a night of getting wasted."

"Done."

Tucking away that bit of information, I waited until the two elves had scampered off before resuming my walk. I skirted the most populated areas and instead approached my target from the side.

The Court of Trees was everything that the Court of Stone was not. And the other way around too, I supposed. In my court, people lived in an organized city centered around Edric's castle or on the farmlands further out. But here, it was just a mishmash of houses and huts and great wooden mansions scattered in no logical pattern throughout the forest. The only thing that made even remotely sense in this strange court was the castle. Iwdael Vineweaver, the Prince of Trees, at least lived in a sprawling wooden structure in the very center of his territory.

Majestic trees that had been shaped into walls rose before me and provided a formidable barrier that shielded the castle from view. And from unwanted trespassers. The royal grounds were of course also warded against worldwalking, as they were in every court, so that no enemies could just appear inside the castle. Unfortunately for them, that kind of magic did nothing to someone who could physically walk through their walls. A sly smile spread across my lips as I took a step right into the wooden barrier.

The sensation of silk whispering against my skin enveloped me. And then I was out. As soon as I stepped onto the grass inside, I ducked my head and slouched my shoulders while walking with purpose in a randomly selected direction.

One of the limits of my power was that I could only phase through objects if my entire body did it. That meant I couldn't just stick my head in and check it out before stepping through. Instead, I'd had to perfect my ability to quickly blend into crowds and hope that no one was looking directly at the spot I appeared from. Luckily for me, no one noticed the extra elf that joined the flow of people this time either.

Merry chatter and the sounds of singing drifted out from the gigantic structure before me. The castle was made of wood but it hadn't been built with planks. It looked more like an enormous tree trunk with smooth walls that had been twisted into the shape that the prince wanted. Keeping my head down, I followed a group of servants into the strange building.

A bustling kitchen met me as I cleared the first narrow hallway. Cooks were notoriously perceptive people so I didn't want to stay there too long and risk them realizing that I didn't belong. The first chance I got, I picked up a random tray and branched off from the group. Hoping that I remembered the way, I slipped into the corridor leading into the castle proper. When the path split in two, I furrowed my brows but I couldn't stop moving without looking suspicious so I strode towards the one on the left.

I had of course been here before, many times, on other spying missions. But the Court of Trees was such a chaotic place that I always had trouble remembering the layout.

"The Great Hall is on the right," a soft voice said behind me.

Squeezing my eyes shut, I stifled a cringe. "Right. Yes. Sorry, I was just lost in my thoughts there for a bit."

The female elf behind me chuckled. "I get that. With that blasted party coming up, they have everyone in a frenzy."

"I know, right?"

I waited until I heard her dress rustle to mark that she had started walking before I turned around and followed her. With an actual Court of Trees resident as my unwitting guide, finding the Great Hall went without a hitch.

The vast space that served as Prince Iwdael's throne room was filled with courtiers. Still keeping my head down, I moved towards a table by the smooth wooden wall while scanning the crowd from the corner of my eye.

Most elves were clustered into groups. Gorgeous females in dresses that would be severely out of fashion in my court plotted the entrapment of their love interests while the males did the same. I placed my tray on the linen-clad table and started swapping full glasses for empty ones. While I pretended to work, I catalogued each of the elves in the room. All the ones who only had eyes for one person were struck from my mental list. Same went for the confident types who moved like they owned the room.

When my tray was almost full again, I had narrowed it down to a handful of elves. All of them were males who were standing alone. Their posture indicated that they were slightly uncomfortable and that they weren't entirely sure how to behave in this environment. In other words, a perfect mark.

After memorizing each of their faces, I hefted the tray again and started back towards the servants' corridor.

Pretending to be a servant was risky. It only worked for a

very limited amount of time and would only get me so far. If I was to stand any chance of figuring out if the dagger was indeed hidden in the Court of Trees, I would need a reason to be here for extended periods of time. And what better way to do that than on the arm of an elf who would count his blessings if a female showed him the slightest bit of attention. A wicked smile stole across my lips as I disappeared into the twisting hallways. Now, all I had to do was seduce one of my marks. Piece of cake.

CHAPTER 4

*S*oft murmuring hung between the shining stone walls up ahead. I arranged my long red hair around my shoulders and smoothed my black dress before stepping into the grand chamber that served as the throne room in the Court of Stone. Humans and elves filled the vast floor below the dais. They were clustered together in groups and were all waiting patiently for their turn to petition the Prince of Stone. I smiled and nodded at them while weaving my way towards the throne.

Once Felix had worldwalked me back from the Court of Trees, I had changed back into a more fashionable dress before coming here. The fact that I was a spy was not common knowledge. In the eyes of the humans and elves who came to our court, I was only one of many courtiers who were there to provide the prince with something pleasant to look at. They regarded me as nothing more than a glorified piece of arm candy. Which was fine. It made assignments where I had to spy on other courtiers much easier.

"Kenna," a sharp voice said.

Startled out of my reverie, I whipped my head towards the sound. "Patricia?" I blinked in surprise while looking from the brown-haired human to the redheaded one next to her. "Elvin? What are you guys doing here?"

My half-siblings elbowed past the closest group and came to a halt before me. Patricia flicked her brown curls back over her shoulder while Elvin crossed his arms and surveyed me from head to toe.

"We are here to see you," Patricia replied.

"Oh." I raised my eyebrows in surprise and tilted my head to peer behind her. "Are Mother and Father here too?"

"Yes, but it would look bad if it appeared as though the reason we came here was to see you and not the prince, so they sent us to talk to you instead."

"Okay?" I said hesitantly. "Talk to me about what?"

Two pairs of blue eyes stared back at me. My half-siblings had gotten a mix of their parents' coloring. Patricia had inherited the brown hair of their father, Lord Beaufort, and the dark blue eyes of our mother while Elvin, on the other hand, had gotten their father's pale blue eyes and the flaming red hair of our mother. I had also inherited our mother's vibrant hair color but my eyes were of a dark red color, courtesy of my elven father. He had been a War Dancer who had seduced my mother before leaving to fight and then subsequently die in some great battle on another continent. I was the product of that rather scandalous affair.

"We need money," Elvin replied matter-of-factly.

"Money?" Baffled, I flicked my gaze between the two of them. "You're one of the richest human families in this court. How could you possibly need money?"

Patricia pursed her lips while exchanging a glance with Elvin, who nodded. "Our plantations were not producing the way they should so Father invested in something that would solve the problem." She coughed delicately. "It did not go well."

"If we don't get an influx of cash within two weeks, we'll be broke," Elvin clarified. "Which is why we need money."

"Yes." Patricia glanced around before lowering her voice. "We know that you have a lot of money."

Though they didn't know exactly how I acquired the cash, they did indeed know that I was gathering funds to buy my freedom from the Prince of Stone and that I already had a rather impressive amount stashed away.

"And now we really need it so we can clear that debt and not, you know, end up broke," Elvin finished.

I flicked pleading eyes between them. "But I need that money to buy my freedom."

"Yes, we get that. But do you really need to do it right now?" Patricia flicked a hand up and down my body. "You're an elf."

"Half-elf," I corrected softly.

"You will live for centuries," Patricia plowed ahead as if I hadn't said anything. "Is there really such a rush to buy your freedom right at this moment? We only have a few short years compared to your lifespan and we need the money now. You don't want us to live out our lives in poverty, do you?"

"Of course not!"

Guilt twisted in my stomach at the selfish thoughts that swirled in my mind. What she was saying was of course entirely true. As a half-elf, I had also been blessed with the long lifespan of the elves while the rest of my family was completely mortal. So technically, I would have time to build my funds back up from scratch again. Time that my family didn't have. But the thought of having to start over and to wait even longer to buy my freedom still sent dread tumbling down my stomach.

"So you'll help?" Elvin prompted.

By all the gods and spirits, I was such an awful person for not saying yes immediately. But no matter how horrible that made me, I didn't want to give up my chance at freedom just yet, so I resolved to find another way to help them instead.

After blowing out a soft sigh, I gave them an encouraging smile. "I'll think of something."

Patricia opened her mouth but before she could say anything, I winced apologetically and cut her off. "I need to get going. Give Mother and Father my love." And with that, I slipped into the crowd again.

Still trying to shake off the guilt that slithered like cold snakes in my stomach, I resumed my previous mission and made my way towards Prince Edric. I had a plan for infiltrating the Court of Trees but I needed to know as fast as possible if the scheme I had cooked up was already screwed.

The Prince of Stone was sitting straight-backed on the grand marble throne, listening to the petition of an exhausted-looking merchant. I lingered at the edge of the raised dais but said nothing because I knew that he would understand that I needed to speak with him. When the merchant was finished and had backed away from the platform, Edric's gray eyes slid to me. He twitched his fingers.

Keeping my eyes on the ground, I glided up the white steps and curtsied before him.

"What?" he demanded, but kept his voice low so that we wouldn't be overheard.

"I have a plan for infiltrating the Court of Trees," I whispered back. "Have you already responded to their invitation to the dance they're hosting?"

"Not yet. Why?"

"I need you to accept the invitation and bring me with you."

"You *need me to?*"

I flinched. "Of course not. I apologize, my prince. What I meant to say was, could you please accept the invitation and bring me with you? I need to establish a cover for being there before I can begin working on my mark."

With eyes still locked on me, he nodded. "Fine. But you…" He trailed off as running footsteps sounded behind me.

Twisting around, I found an elf in messenger livery half-running towards the throne. Panic bounced around on his face. I glanced back at Edric. When he flicked his hand at me, I withdrew while the prince beckoned for the messenger to approach the throne instead. The entire room seemed to be holding its breath while the frantic-looking elf whispered into Edric's ear.

The Prince of Stone pulled his lips back in a snarl but nodded at the messenger before dismissing him and pushing to his feet. "No more petitions today. Everybody out."

Surprised murmuring drifted across the crowd. Prince Edric held out his arm and drew it in a straight line in front of himself. Stone rumbled and shocked gasps echoed through the throne room as a section of the wall disappeared to create another exit. No one moved. All the petitioners just stared between the hole their prince had created and the great slabs of stone that still stood open and usually served as the doors to the room.

"I said, *out*," Edric snapped.

The crowd lurched into motion and hurried through the hole in the wall that would take them to another part of the castle that led out. I, along with the other spies who had been stationed in the throne room, looked to our prince. When he motioned for us to stay, we took up positions by the wall where we wouldn't be in the way but still be able to assist with whatever was about to happen.

A boom echoed as Edric returned the section of the stone wall to its original position after the last of the petitioners had filed out. Then he sat down on the throne again. I flicked a nervous glance between him and the open double doors. Whatever was about to happen was bad enough that he didn't want his subjects to know about it. My heart pattered in my chest. I drew a deep breath to steady myself.

The dead silence that had settled was broken a few minutes later when the sound of something being dragged across stone, accompanied by footsteps, drifted through the air. I kept my eyes on the open doors as the sound drew closer.

At last, two figures crossed the threshold.

My stomach dropped as the Prince of Shadows strode into the room, dragging Ymas with him.

Mordren Darkbringer, the Prince of Shadows, was as beautiful as he was dangerous. Long black hair cascaded down his back like a shining dark waterfall and his silver eyes glittered like liquid starlight. Lean muscles shifted under a dark suit of impeccable quality as he moved closer to the dais. The room held its breath as the lethal prince stopped a few strides from the throne.

Locking eyes with Edric, he deposited the captured spy on the floor. "I believe this belongs to you."

A thud echoed into the dead silent room as Ymas landed back first on the stone. His eyes were glassy with pain but he scrambled backwards across the floor to get away from his captor. Edric remained seated on his throne but didn't take his eyes off Mordren.

The Prince of Shadows cocked his head. "You would dare to spy on me?" A dangerous glint crept into his silver eyes. "You know what I do to people who spy on me."

Pain shot through me like lightning. My knees buckled and I sucked in a gasp as it intensified, making it feel as though my every nerve was on fire. The impact as I hit the floor jarred my bones but it was nothing compared to the waves of agony that rolled over me. I pressed my palms against the cool stone in an effort to weather it, while all around the room, the rest of the spies were doing the same.

This was one of the reasons why everyone feared Mordren Darkbringer. In addition to shadow manipulation and worldwalking, he possessed the ability to inflict pain without even touching the person. I squeezed my eyes shut and gritted my teeth as another wave pulsed through my body.

"You know that won't work on me," Edric's voice rang out from across the room. "I am the Prince of Stone. I specialize in shielding."

The pain stopped. I gasped in a desperate breath as the last remnants of Mordren's power left me. In my heart, I knew that I wasn't actually hurt or dying, but my mind took an extra couple of seconds to reconfirm that.

"I know," Mordren replied. "But you seem to have forgotten who *I* am as well, so I figured I would remind you of who you are antagonizing. You wouldn't want people to find out what happened on that winter solstice all those years ago, now would you?"

Deafening silence descended on the hall.

This was the second, and most important, reason why the other elven princes took great care to stay on Mordren's good side. He seemed to somehow know all of their dirty little secrets. It was uncanny and it had given rise to the belief that Mordren had managed to cheat fate into giving him an unprecedented four powers, and that the fourth one was some kind of mind reading ability. I fervently hoped that wasn't true considering the rather lengthy string of vicious curses I had directed at him a few moments ago.

"You wouldn't." Edric gripped the armrests of his throne while shaking his head. "You can't."

Mordren's lips curled into a smile. "Beg for my forgiveness, and I'll consider letting it slide."

"I'm sorry."

A midnight laugh drifted from the Prince of Shadows. "You suck at begging." Black hair fluttered in the air as he whirled around and strode back towards the doors.

"Wait!" Edric shot up from his throne and hurried down the steps after him.

Twisting back around, Mordren arched an eyebrow at him.

The muscles in Edric's jaw flickered as he stopped a few strides from the prince. Raising a hand, he snapped his fingers. Most of us were still on our knees after the waves of pain so all the spies in the room simply bowed down and pressed our foreheads against the floor.

"Is this supposed to impress me?" Mordren said.

The Prince of Stone said nothing but I already knew why he had done it. It wasn't for Mordren's sake, but for Edric's. He didn't want us to see him beg.

Clothes rustled faintly. "I apologize for attempting to spy on you." When the silence stretched, he added in a tight voice, "Please."

"That's more like it." Soft footfalls echoed against stone. "If

I ever catch you spying on my court again, I will not be so forgiving."

Only when the footsteps had reached the entrance to the throne room did I dare lift my head enough to glance at the retreating prince. He walked casually, unhurriedly, but his lethal body moved like a predator's. I blew out a soft sigh and prayed to whatever gods or spirits were listening that I would never be cornered by him. Because if I was, I didn't think I would survive that encounter.

CHAPTER 5

A cloud of flowery fragrances assaulted me as soon as I stepped inside the hut. Even with the black mask covering my face, it made my eyes water. It smelled as if someone had smashed a couple hundred perfume bottles of various scents inside this tight space and then left them there to mix. I shook my head, as if that would help clear the sensory onslaught, and switched to breathing through my mouth as much as possible. Even though I had been in here multiple times before, the sheer intensity of all these clashing scents still managed to catch me off guard every time.

Beads clattered as an entire curtain of them was pushed aside to reveal a plump old lady with thick glasses. "Ah, the Black Mask. Back again."

In order to protect my identity, I always wore my disguise when coming here. Straightening my dark jacket, I nodded back at the woman. "Stella. You look well."

"I would say the same, but I can't actually see what you look like." A teasing smile spread across her wrinkled face as she made a show of peering at me. "Will I ever get to see what's beneath that dark mask and hood of yours?"

I flashed her a smile in return, even though she couldn't see it. "Will you ever tell me how a human with no magical powers has managed to become the most well-informed person in the Court of Trees?"

She chuckled. "What can I say? I like gossip." Wood creaked as she plopped down in one of the chairs by the table before motioning for me to do the same. "And I like you." A knowing glint crept into her eyes. "Even though I'm pretty sure that you're not from the Court of Trees. One day I will find out, you know. But for now, what can I do for you?"

A soft laugh slipped my lips as I shook my head while sliding into the chair opposite her. Sticking a hand into one of my numerous jacket pockets, I pulled out a roll of sheets. After smoothening them, I pushed the four drawings towards her. "What can you tell me about these people?"

"Hmm." Stella adjusted her glasses and squinted down at the elves depicted on them. After a few moments of silence, she separated two of the drawings from the others. "These two are second sons of elven nobility who were sent to Iwdael's castle to sort themselves out. This one for drinking and that one for gambling." She tapped the left drawing and then the right one before pushing them aside and sliding out the third one.

"And the other two?"

"As far as I can tell, this one is the son of a lowborn elf who's recently gotten into some money and been sent to the castle to learn the ways of the fancy folk." Stella chuckled as if she found the notion ridiculous. Her hand shot out and yanked the fourth drawing towards her. "And this one…" She drummed her fingers on the table before nodding to herself.

"He was involved in a scandal and is looking to get hitched as soon as possible."

"I see. What are their names?"

After hearing her descriptions, I had already picked my mark but I couldn't let her know that. As she herself had said, she loved to gossip. So when she recounted their names, I nodded after each one but the only one I really paid attention to was the elf from the third drawing. The lowborn who needed to learn how to behave like nobility. Evander Loneleaf. A perfect mark.

"Thank you," I said and slid a hand into one of my pockets again. After pulling out a stack of notes, I placed the money in her waiting palm. "Always a pleasure doing business."

"Likewise." She pushed her glasses back up her nose and shot me a wide grin. "Come back anytime."

Nodding at her, I stood up. "Until next time, then."

The sound of clinking beads followed me as I left Stella's hut and stepped out into the clear evening air again. Drawing a few deep breaths, I tried to clear my lungs of all the perfume I had inhaled these past minutes. An owl hooted in a tree beside me, as if mocking the futile attempt. I shook my head but deemed that he was probably right, so I gave up on restoring my breathing organs to their proper states and stalked deeper into the forest. At least I'd got what I came for. Information. I finally had my mark.

∼

Felix had dropped me off outside the stone castle after worldwalking me back from the Court of Trees. The elven nobles who lived here were getting ready for the evening when I made my way back to my own room. Before I even met back up with Felix, I had pushed back the black mask into the hood of my jacket, but I was still wearing clothes that would be far too suspicious for the courtier I pretended to be. So instead of roaming the halls like a normal person, I used my secret exit and entry point and walked straight through the walls until I reached my room.

A pile of letters had been left on the wooden desk inside. Pulling out the knife strapped to my thigh, I opened the first envelope. Guilt coiled in my gut as I scanned the words written in black ink on the page.

In the days since my family had visited the Court of Stone to tell me that they needed money, I had tried several different methods for solving that problem. I had even gone as far as tentatively broaching the subject with Edric to see if there was something he could do to help them. Needless to say, that was a hard no. Now, I was running out of both time and options. The deadline for this particular problem was the day after King Aldrich's ball which meant that I had two huge problems that needed to be solved in the exact same time span.

Still gripping the letter, I flicked my eyes to the smooth white wall that hid the secret treasure inside. *Maybe I should just give them my money?* The thought was accompanied by an immediate flash of panic. I didn't want to start over! Conflicting emotions fought like wolves inside me as I continued staring between the letter and the stash of blackmail money.

Blowing out a sigh, I shook my head and stuffed the letter into the top drawer. This was going nowhere.

After hiding my jacket and changing into a light dress, I slipped out the door and headed for another one further down the hall. Wood vibrated under my knuckles as I knocked on it. Footsteps sounded inside before the door swung open soundlessly.

"Kenna?" Monette blinked at me before her turquoise eyes darted up and down the empty hall. "What's wrong?"

"Can I come in?"

She widened the gap in the door. "Sure."

Giving her a smile, I strode across the threshold.

Monette's room was the chaos to my order. Mounds of clothes, make-up, hairbrushes, and trinkets covered every piece of furniture in the room. Most of it was in some shade of light blue, or blue-green, that complemented her eyes but even if the color was at least somewhat matching, everything was just too... disorganized. Being in her room always made my stress levels rise. I preferred things to be structured. Logical. Easy to find. Not this absolute mess. I had no idea how someone could live like this.

I remained standing on the floor while Monette pushed aside a pile made of turquoise silk and white lace to make room for me on the bed. Something clinked as it tumbled off the rumpled sheets and landed on the floor, making me cringe.

She plopped down on the bed and motioned for me to do the same. Not wanting to sit in the middle of her mess, I took to pacing the floor instead.

Running my fingers through my hair, I let out a sigh. "Okay, so I have a hypothetical for you."

"A what?"

"A hypothetical..." I shook my head. "Never mind. So, let's just say that you have something. Something that you really need for something. But someone else also needs that for something else. What would you do?"

Monette scrunched up her eyebrows and stared back at me uncomprehendingly. "What?"

Biting my lower lip, I considered my options. I didn't want to tell her too much, but I also really needed her advice, so I decided to start further out and work my way towards the question I really wanted an answer to.

"Do you ever think about buying your freedom?"

"Buying my freedom?" Monette repeated, her brows still furrowed. "Okay, one, where would I get that kind of money? And two, why would I want to?"

"I... well..." I stopped my pacing. After spending another couple of seconds eyeing the spot she had cleared for me on the bed, I stalked forward and flopped down on the mattress. It bounced underneath me as I lay down and sent a powder container rolling into my cheek. I placed it further away on the bed before turning my head to look at Monette again. "Don't you ever just want... more?"

"More?" A disbelieving laugh rolled from her lips as she spread her arms to encompass the room. "We have everything anyone could ever wish for. We live in a castle. We're completely provided for."

"Yes, but we can't leave. He owns us. He has ultimate say in everything in our lives."

Monette picked up a jewel-encrusted bracelet from her bed and rolled it between her fingers. "Has he ever been cruel to you?"

"No." I sat up. "But that's not the point."

"Isn't it?" She turned to face me fully. Exasperation shone in her eyes as she threw out an arm to motion in the direction of the city. "Think of everyone who lives in poverty. Who struggles to just get enough to eat every day. Who lives in horrible conditions. Is that what you want?"

"Well… no."

"Exactly. So what if he owns us? We have a great life! Obeying Edric's orders is a small price to pay for that."

"But I don't want to obey someone else's orders! *I* want to be the one to give the orders." The words were out of my mouth before I could stop them.

Monette's face softened. Leaning over, she placed a hand on my arm and gave it a gentle squeeze. "Look, Kenna, you know I love you and that I'm only trying to look out for you. So please listen to me when I tell you that you have to curb that ambition of yours. It's not going to end well."

"But what if you did have enough money to buy your freedom and start a new life?" I pressed because I hadn't even gotten to the question I wanted to ask yet. "Would you–"

"Kenna." It came out sounding more like a sigh than anything else. "Do we have to talk about this?" Her gaze turned pleading. "It makes me uncomfortable."

I opened my mouth but then closed it again. Blowing out a deep breath, I raked my fingers through my hair. "No, of course not. Sorry." I pushed to my feet. Tins clanked behind me as the mattress shifted with the sudden loss of weight. "I'll just… I'll see you later."

"Just be careful, Kenna."

"Yeah," I replied without looking back as I weaved my way towards the door and slipped back into the corridor.

Light flickered against the pale walls as I made my way back to my room. That had not gone the way I wanted it to. Instead of having arrived at a decision, I was now just more confused. What Monette had said made a lot of sense, there was no questioning that, but I still couldn't stamp out that deep-rooted yearning for freedom in my soul.

When I finally shut the door to my room behind me again,

those conflicting feelings were fighting even harder inside me. I glanced from the letter in the drawer to the wall on my right. Blowing out a breath, I made a decision.

And then I stalked straight towards the hidden compartment behind the wall.

CHAPTER 6

Fabric rustled as the wind tore at my jacket. I quickly checked that my sword and knife were secure before pulling down the black mask over my face. The grand building lay dark and still before me. Sucking in a steadying breath, I sprinted towards it.

This was probably one of the riskiest things I had ever done. At least outside my usual spy work. Whenever I broke into houses and blackmailed people, I only ever did it to humans. And more specifically, to humans who were rich enough to give me a decent sized ransom but not so rich that they belonged to the influential elite. Getting involved with wealthy people only brought more trouble than it was worth, and trying to blackmail elves could easily backfire if they turned out to have magic. But tonight, I was going to have to risk it.

The shining white wall grew larger before me but I couldn't stop in case there were guards watching from somewhere I couldn't see. Slowing only enough not to come crashing through, I ran right through the stone. Soft fabric caressed my skin. And then a wide room appeared before me. I skidded to a halt on the fluffy blue carpet and barely managed to stop my momentum before I slammed right into a table overlain with porcelain plates. While glaring at the inconveniently placed piece of furniture, I let out a soft exhale.

My magic treated everything that lined the walls as part of the actual wall, which meant that I could pass through it even if my entire body normally wouldn't have fit through it. But if there was too large a gap between the wall and the object, normal rules applied. Because of that, I really hated people who decorated their homes with smaller pieces of furniture that they placed *almost* by the wall. Shaking my head, I lifted my hands from the low table and stepped around it.

I had ended up in what appeared to be some kind of storage room for kitchenware. Glittering goblets, plates, and decorated containers filled every shelf and table, and silver cutlery gleamed from a crack in the closest drawer. This had to be worth a fortune. But unfortunately, it was too cumbersome to transport. What I needed was actual money. Or something equally small and valuable. After making sure that my disguise was still firmly in place, I slunk into the corridor beyond.

The elf who lived here was a gem trader. If I could just find his stash of precious stones, I could take that and give it to my family to pay their debts. That way, I wouldn't have to sacrifice my own fortune. But stealing years' worth of ransom money in one night from an elf who might have magic and who definitely belonged to the elite of this city was incredibly risky. My heart slammed against my ribs as I glided down the darkened hall. If I was caught, my life would be forfeit.

Logically, goods as valuable as these would be kept in

some kind of strongroom and those rooms were easier to build on the ground floor than to lug all the material up the stairs. All the doors I had come across so far looked far too simple to house a strongroom. Moving silently, I continued my sweep of the bottom floor.

Wood groaned up ahead. I jerked to a halt and pressed myself flat against the cold stone wall. There was a whole line of bookcases between me and whatever had made that sound, so I couldn't see what it was. With my pulse thrumming in my ears, I leaned out and peered down the hall.

Moonlight fell in from the windows to illuminate the carpeted corridor but the dark shape along the wall was still cloaked in shadow. Trying to steady my racing heart, I stayed close to the wall while sneaking closer to it.

Once I was close enough to see what it was, I stopped dead in my tracks. It was an elf in leather armor. He was sitting on a wooden chair outside what looked like a metal door, and though he looked supremely bored, his eyes were sharp. I shrank back into the darkness.

That had to be the strongroom. But I couldn't very well enter it through the front door, so instead I calculated the distance between us to figure out how large the room was. It was impossible to tell for certain, but I made a rough estimate. I couldn't walk that much further because then I might get spotted by the guard. Hoping that my calculations were right, I edged a bit closer before phasing through the wall behind me.

My heart leaped into my throat. I was standing inside someone's bedroom, and that someone was sleeping in the bed only a couple of strides away. I stifled a gasp. The elf on the bed rolled over on the side but didn't cry out in alarm. I waited another few seconds before I dared breathe again.

When nothing happened, I snuck towards the wall I assumed was connected to the strongroom and I walked through it.

A second gasp almost ripped from my throat and I backpedaled furiously. I had only managed to get a glimpse of the room but what I had seen had been enough. There were guards stationed *inside* the strongroom too.

The bedroom appeared around me again and I prayed fervently to whatever gods or spirits were listening that none of the guards has seen me flash in and out of the wall. Humans prayed to their gods and the elves prayed to their spirits. Since I was both, I prayed to whoever would grant me fortune. Usually none of them ever did, but I still kept up the habit just in case.

Blood roared in my ears as I counted down the seconds. But no alarm came. And the elf on the bed next to me continued sleeping.

While silently cursing my powers for not allowing me to peek into a room before entering it, I walked through the wall on my left and back into the corridor I had been in before.

Stealing the actual gems was a lost cause but there might still be something else to take. Or something with which I could blackmail the merchant. I set course for the staircase on the other side of the hallway.

The second floor was as silent as the one I had just left. Since I wasn't sure where I was going, I randomly walked in and out of rooms until I found one that looked more official than the others. It was also locked, which led me to believe that there had to be something important inside.

A wide study filled with expensive paintings and statues waited for me after I walked through the locked door. By the back wall, there was a gigantic desk made of dark wood. I circled it once before trying the various drawers. All of them were unlocked and contained only ledgers and paperwork connected to the merchant's gem business. Slumping back in the chair, I heaved a disappointed sigh.

I hadn't even bothered looking for a wall safe behind the countless paintings because even if there was one, I wouldn't be able to get into it. Drumming my fingers lightly on the armrest, I glared at the useless drawers. Then I stopped, my fingers still hovering in the air. I squinted at the drawers to my right. The topmost one was bigger on the outside than it had looked on the inside.

Scrambling off the chair, I dropped to my knees in front of the desk while pulling out the drawer. When it was fully extended, I twisted my head to study the underside of it. The bad lighting in the room wasn't exactly helping so I ran my fingers along the wood as well. *There!* A small hole at the front.

Anticipation bounced around inside me as I rummaged through my many pockets. I had to have a hairpin in there somewhere. When my fingers closed around a sharp piece of metal, I smiled and drew it out to expose the plain but functional hair accessory. After bending it slightly, I pushed one end into the hole in the bottom of the drawer.

The false bottom was pushed up with a slight *pop*. I moved aside the stack of papers on top of it before grasping the edge and tilting it up. Straightening, I peered into the dark space.

A small leather-bound book waited for me there. I furrowed my brows at the underwhelming discovery but picked it up and sat back on the ornate chair again. Paper rustled faintly as I flipped through the pages. My frown deepened.

There were two sets of handwriting and it always alternated between every page. I skimmed the contents. It appeared to be... information. I jerked back in the chair as I realized what I was holding. This was a traveling book. A book that had a mirror twin somewhere else and whatever you wrote in this book appeared on the pages of its twin, and the other way around. And written in it was information about the Court of Stone. I glanced at the closed door on the other side of the room. The merchant who lived in this house was a spy for another court.

Both apprehension and excitement swirled around inside me. This could potentially be really bad. But it could also be my salvation. With this, I could blackmail the gem merchant into giving me whatever I wanted. Enough valuables both to pay my family's debts and also to add a substantial sum to my own funds. A wicked grin spread across my lips as I stuffed the book inside one of my magic-infused pockets and strode towards the door.

After another few minutes of searching the darkened house, I finally found the merchant's bedroom. He was sprawled in a large double bed with silk sheets hanging over the edge. His chest rose and fell at a steady rhythm as I approached the right side of his bed. My fingers snaked around the hilt of the knife strapped to my thigh.

Since there were guards in this house, I had to handle this a bit differently than I normally would. If he called out before I could present my leverage, I would either have to fight all of his guards or escape without actually getting to the blackmail part of my scheme.

His hair lay like a pale fan around his head. I drew my knife silently and leaned forward until I could place it above his throat. Once it was in place, I put my other hand against his chest so that he wouldn't jerk up and accidentally slit his own throat.

"Wake up," I said.

Yellow eyes shot open. I could see the scream building in his throat so I angled the knife slightly. The blade caught the moonlight and alerted him to its presence.

"If you scream, I will slit your throat," I said, just in case the weapon above his windpipe hadn't been indication enough. "Do you understand?"

"Yes," he replied.

"Good. You keep a traveling book in your topmost desk drawer. The one on the right. That book is now in my possession. If I give it to the Prince of Stone, your life will end in pain."

Panic crackled behind the merchant's eyes. "What do you want?"

"All of your gems. Every single one."

His face drained of color. "But…"

"It's that, or the prince learns of your treachery."

He swallowed loudly. "Okay."

"Okay?"

"I will get you the gems."

I held his stare even though I knew he couldn't see my eyes clearly from behind the mask that covered my face. Fear shone in his gaze. I relished the sense of control it gave me. "Do it right now. And don't even think about tipping off your guards. If I'm not back in half an hour, my associates have been instructed to present your traveling book to the prince." The lie rolled smoothly off my tongue despite the weight of the book in my pocket.

When he nodded in understanding, I withdrew the knife and stepped back. The merchant rolled off the bed and yanked on a blue silk robe. After smoothing his hair and pushing it back behind his pointed ears, he moved towards the door. I twirled the knife in my hand as a reminder of what would happen if he ratted me out. He flicked a glance at it before hurrying out the door.

I followed him on silent feet because if he did decide to try his luck, I would have a much better chance of escaping if I was on the ground floor. His robes swished around the corner just as I reached the bottom of the stairs. While I waited to see if he would come back with a bag of gems or a company of armed elves, I calculated the fastest route out of the house.

Feet shuffled against the floor. I braced myself while my body got ready to run. But only the irritated merchant rounded the corner. Since he couldn't see my face, I didn't bother hiding the relief that flashed over it.

Stopping before me, he held out a large bag. "This will be the biggest mistake of your life."

"We'll see about that." I took the offered ransom and untied the strings at the top. A mountain of gems in a multitude of colors caught the moonlight and glittered like the literal treasure trove that it was. I grinned. "We will see about that indeed."

"And the book?" he pressed.

"I'm keeping that as collateral." I yanked the strings tight and stuffed the bag into my biggest pocket. "If you ever tell anyone about this, then the book will find its way to the prince."

A muscle flickered in the merchant's jaw but he said nothing.

I jerked my chin towards the staircase. "Go back upstairs."

"You'll regret this," he promised before disappearing back up to the second floor.

As soon as he was out of sight, I darted towards my exit point. Weaving my way through the annoyingly placed furniture, I ran through the walls and deserted rooms until I stepped into the cool night air again. Only once I was a few streets away did I stop.

While leaning my back against a stone wall, I pulled out the bag of gems again. Giddiness bubbled through me as I stuck a hand inside the dark cloth and ran my fingers through the precious stones inside. They clinked merrily.

This was the biggest payday I had ever seen. With this, even after helping my family, I would be able to buy my freedom in no time. If I had known that robbing one of the elven elite was this easy, I would have done it years ago.

Footsteps sounded down the street. I jerked my head up and tore my gaze from the pretty gems before me to study the newcomer. Based on body type, it appeared to be an elven male. He walked with purpose but then stopped abruptly when he saw me.

Dread washed over me. I retied the strings and shoved the bag into my pocket again.

Another second passed while the dark figure and I studied each other.

He cocked his head.

And then two knives shot into his hands.

CHAPTER 7

Panic crackled through me when I realized that I only had a split second to decide whether to run or fight. There was still a chance that my mysterious ambusher didn't know that I carried a king's ransom worth of stolen gems. No. No, there wasn't. He had walked with too much purpose to be a random mugger, which meant that he had been hunting for me specifically.

Knives glinted in the moonlight as he advanced on me. He was taller than me by about half a head and he moved with the lethal grace of someone who knew his way around weapons.

Indecision screamed in my mind.

If I used my power to run through the walls, I might be able to get away. But depending on who my attacker was, that might also give away my identity, which meant that I was screwed even if I managed to escape tonight. His features were hidden beneath dark cloth, making it impossible to see who it was. Uncertainty pounded in my mind.

The window to decide my course of action was closing rapidly.

Run or fight?

Fight.

Steel sang into the crisp fall night as I drew the sword from across my back. The dark figure paused. I could almost feel the surprise and excitement rolling off him. After also pulling out the knife strapped to my thigh, I spun the sword in my hand.

The elf who had sired me might not have been much of a father but he had been a War Dancer, and as such, had decided that any offspring of his should at least know how to handle a sword. He had come by my family's mansion to oversee my training when I was young. That is, until he had left for the grand battle on a faraway continent that had later killed him. Prince Edric had conscripted me into his service soon after that, but I had kept up my training. Now, as I faced down this potentially lethal attacker, I was immensely glad that I had.

The dark-clad elf down the street sunk into an attack position. Blowing out a long breath, I did the same. Winds whistled between the buildings as we stared each other down. Then he darted towards me.

I whirled around and sidestepped his attack but he read my movements. Steel clashed as he slammed his knives right into my defending sword. While both his weapons were temporarily blocked, I swiped at his ribs with my knife. As we disengaged our blades, he jumped back and threw down his own knife to redirect the thrust.

Clanging filled the darkened alley. He feigned a strike to the left so I slammed down my sword on the other side to meet the real attack, only to have my blade sail uselessly through empty air. The move threw me off balance and I stumbled a step forward. My miscalculation got worse when a boot smacked into the back of my knee. I crashed down on the street but managed to roll with the motion. Twisting around, I drew my sword in a low arc.

My attacker leaped into the air before the blade could sever his ankle tendons and I used the second of grace to shoot to my feet. That extra second that he was in the air gave me the advantage I needed. Zigzagging across the stones, I darted forward to get inside his guard.

Pain shattered through me. It was so intense that my attack staggered to a halt. Sucking in a desperate breath, I tried to stop my knees from buckling. Before I could figure out how I had managed to get hit, dark tendrils shot out and wrapped around my limbs. What little air I had left in my lungs was forced out as I slammed back first into the stone wall on my right.

Stars danced in my vision and I was vaguely aware of metallic clattering somewhere close by before I realized that the impact must have knocked the blades from my hands. Blinking, I shook my head to clear it.

Black tendrils were wrapped tightly around my wrists and ankles and kept me pinned to the wall while also preventing me from phasing through it. I stared at them for another second before my scrambled mind finally caught up. The twisting darkness. The flash of pain. By all the gods and all the spirits, I was done for.

"As much fun as that little sparring session was," a midnight voice said, "I do have other places to be tonight."

Dread exploded in my chest like a cloud of poison as the

elf before me removed his disguise, revealing the handsome face of Mordren Darkbringer. A sly smile played over his lips as he sheathed his knives and shook out his long black hair. I yanked against the shadows keeping me trapped against the wall, but they refused to budge. His silver eyes glittered with amusement as he stepped closer.

"Now, let's see who this thieving little blackmailer is." He placed a graceful hand on my black mask and lifted it, pushing it back into the top of my hood. Something sparkled in his eyes as he took in my face. "Oh, I know you. You're one of Edric's spies who pretends to be a courtier." His smile was nothing short of villainous as he trailed a finger along my jaw. "Does your master know that you moonlight as a blackmailer?"

"Of course he does. Who do you think ordered me to root out this traitor to our court?"

"Liar." His finger stopped moving and he grabbed my chin in a tight grip while his smile widened. "If that really was your mission, you would have just taken the traveling book and handed it to Edric. But instead, you blackmailed that poor merchant to keep it secret."

My heart pounded in tune with the rising panic inside me. What he was saying was of course entirely true. And he knew it. I wanted to kick myself. If I had known that the merchant was spying for the damn Prince of Shadows, I would've stayed well clear of all this. But apparently, this was what ambitious spies got when they were a little too greedy.

"This is turning into a most productive night." Mordren released my jaw and took a step back. "But first, let's start by you giving back that bag of gems you so boldly stole. Where is it?"

The odds of him finding it in this custom-tailored jacket were actually pretty slim because it was imbued with magic that made it very difficult to find the pocket you were looking for. Unless you were me, of course. For a moment, I considered denying that I had the bag of gems on me.

When I didn't reply straight away, he dragged his gaze over my body with deliberate slowness. "Unless you would like me to put my hands in every single one of those pockets?"

"No." I heaved a resigned sigh. "Fourth pocket on the right, three pockets down."

"Much obliged."

His graceful fingers undid the fastenings of the indicated pocket before disappearing inside to pull out the bag of gems. I tried to keep the venom from my gaze as I tracked his movements. My chances of surviving this encounter were slim as it was, without adding disrespect to the mix.

The precious stones clinked faintly as he withdrew the pouch and tied it to his belt. Once it had been securely fastened, he cocked his head. Shiny black hair slid over his shoulder as he studied me. Wishing I could at least cross my arms, I pulled against the shadows pinning my arms wide at my sides even though I already knew it was useless.

"I have a proposition for you," he said. "I know that you're trying to find the Dagger of Orias for Edric."

How the hell had he known that?

"I want you to report to me on everything the Court of Stone learns about the dagger," he pressed on. "And if *you* happen to find it, I want you to bring it to me."

That meant he didn't actually have the dagger. Interesting. I met his gaze.

"And if I say no?"

"Then you die tonight."

Fear fluttered in my chest. I didn't want to die. Not now. By all the gods and spirits, I had barely lived! But dying would still be preferable to Edric finding out that I had betrayed him because if that ever happened, I would be in for a fate worse than death. Closing my eyes, I drew a deep breath before meeting Mordren's gaze again.

"No."

His dark eyebrows rose. "No?"

"No."

A short burst of pain pulsed through me, making me flinch. It was gone as quickly as it had appeared.

Smiling, he closed the distance between us again. "Do you have any idea what I could do to you?"

"I do. But the answer is still no."

Mordren's laugh was a midnight wind. "So you do have a spine." He placed a light hand around my throat. "I mean, I could probably snap it in two without much effort. But still. I'm impressed." His eyes gleamed in the silver light as he let his hand drop back to his side again, but he didn't step back. "Unfortunately for you, it won't matter."

I narrowed my eyes at him but said nothing.

"You will spy for me, or I will make sure that Edric finds out about your little blackmailing enterprise." He dragged his fingers through his night-black hair. "Imagine what the unforgiving Prince of Stone would do to you. You would be demoted, kept as a slave forever, and he would probably execute your whole family just to set an example."

Intense terror flashed through me. I couldn't let my family get hurt because of my own selfish desire for freedom. Flicking my gaze around the deserted alley, I tried to think of another way out, but there was none. He held all the cards. All the power. He could end me with one word and he damn well knew it.

Leaning in, he placed his lips next to my ear. "So, spy for me?"

There was nothing else to it. I couldn't refuse him. Defeat weighed heavily on my chest as I sucked in a shuddering breath.

"Yes."

A yelp slipped my lips as the shadows around my left ankle yanked my leg further to the side, widening my stance. The move created an even bigger height difference between us. Tilting my head further back, I found Mordren smirking down at me from only a breath away.

"Yes, what?" he coaxed.

I wanted to slap that smugness right off his sharp cheekbones, but then panic washed over me when I remembered the rumors about him being able to read minds. So instead of retaliating for the infuriating and highly unnecessary power play, I dropped my gaze.

"Yes, my prince."

"That's right." Tracing soft fingers along my jaw, he leaned in again and whispered in my ear. "I own you now."

His hot breath against my skin sent a shiver through my body. I swallowed but stayed silent because we both already knew that he indeed held my fate in the palm of his hand.

"And don't you forget it." The shadows around my limbs disappeared as he withdrew them and stepped back. He flicked a hand towards my jacket. "Keep the traveling book you stole. We'll use that to communicate. And I expect an update as soon as you find out anything new about the dagger's whereabouts."

Not trusting my voice, I simply nodded.

"Good." His triumphant smile was a slash of white. "What a most fortunate turn of events this night took."

A strong fall wind swept through the darkened alley and snatched at our clothes. I righted my hood again while Mordren smoothed back his hair and walked to the middle of the stone street.

Twisting towards me, he winked. "I'll see you soon, my little traitor spy."

And with that, he disappeared.

As soon as the Prince of Shadows had worldwalked back to whatever hell he called home, I heaved a sigh so deep I thought it would never end. Leaning back against the wall, I slid down the cold stone surface until I sat on the street with my knees pulled up to my chest. My blades gleamed in the moonlight where they lay discarded on either side of me.

"Shit," I breathed.

Resting my head against the smooth white wall, I stared up at the glittering stars overhead.

Not only was I a traitor to my own court because I blackmailed Edric's citizens behind his back, but now I would also betray him by spying for another court.

And since Mordren had taken back the bag of gems, I was also no longer able to help my family clear their debt. Time was running out. If I couldn't come up with a solution soon, they would be ruined.

But I couldn't devote all my time to that either, because tomorrow evening I had to attend that dance at the Court of Trees so that I could start seducing Evander Loneleaf in the hopes of finding the Dagger of Orias for Edric. Except if I did find it, I had to somehow figure out a way to give it to Mordren so that he wouldn't spill my secrets and get me and my family killed. But if Edric found that out, I was done for anyway.

My fingers curled around the blades at my sides. One misstep, in any direction, and I was doomed. If this was how my own victims felt, then I almost felt bad for them. Damn. Being blackmailed really sucked.

CHAPTER 8

Cheerful flutes and string music drifted from the hall up ahead. Prince Edric's face looked to have been carved from stone as he led me through the wide corridor and towards the ballroom at the Court of Trees. Even though he knew that I needed it to establish my cover, he hadn't been happy about sacrificing part of his evening for this *frivolous spectacle*, as he put it. But at least he had agreed to come, so I decided to be grateful for that as we crossed the threshold and stepped into an explosion of color.

Everything was structured in the Court of Stone and Edric preferred a muted color scheme of white, gray, and black. There was nothing structured or muted about the Court of Trees. Ribbons in every color fluttered from strings that crisscrossed the ceiling in no discernable pattern. Vines covered in flowers snaked along the walls. Couches, chairs, and tablecloths shone like gems but none of them seemed to be of the same hue. And the partygoers weren't much better.

Everywhere I looked I was met by layered dresses in bright colors. Bows and ribbons and beads decorated the flowing fabric that spun around the female elves as they danced. Everyone was wearing some form of vibrant garment. Except one person. Me.

My night-black dress stood out in stark contrast against the cascade of colors. It fit me perfectly and drew further attention with the help of a plunging neckline and a slit down the long skirt that showed off my legs when I moved. A black leather corset and long gloves in the same material complemented the look. In this, there wasn't a single person who wouldn't notice me. Just the way I wanted it.

"Edric!" a surprised voice called. "I didn't think you would come."

Dropping my gaze, I curtsied as Iwdael Vineweaver, the Prince of Trees, hurried towards us in a swishing of green fabric.

"You kept sending invitations, so I didn't really have much of a choice," Edric replied.

It was hard to tell if he was joking or not, but a hearty laugh erupted from Iwdael's throat, so he appeared to have interpreted it as such.

"You work too hard." The Prince of Trees chuckled again. "A nice little party is good for your health. And I see that you've brought another one this time. What happened to the blond one?"

"I wanted some variety."

"Ah, yes. Variety is also good for your health."

I was used to being treated like an accessory. After all, I wasn't really a person so much as Edric's possession. But I still had to fight the urge to grind my teeth when people talked about me this way. *One day*, I promised myself. One day, I would buy my freedom and then no one would ever address me in this offhanded manner again.

Clothes rustled as Iwdael spun around and threw out an arm to encompass the ballroom. "Please, enjoy yourselves tonight."

"Thank you," Edric replied.

After a nod, the Prince of Trees turned and strode back into the mass of excited revelers. His long brown hair, decorated with green leaves and vines, swung across his back as he moved.

"Come on," Edric muttered at me while stalking forward as well.

Music and laughter filled the air and grew louder with every step as we weaved through the colorful crowd. Many turned to stare at me, or rather at my bold dress, as I passed. I kept an expressionless mask on my face while I let Edric lead me towards a refreshments table along one of the walls.

He picked up a pair of glass flutes filled with sparkling wine and pressed one into my hand. "How long?"

In order to stop an annoyed groan from slipping past my lips, I took a sip of the wine. It had a fresh and fruity flavor that mixed well with the fizziness of the bubbles. "Not too long, I hope. First I have to find my mark and then I just need to make sure that he notices me with you."

Edric grunted in affirmation and downed his drink. While stifling another untimely show of exasperation, I scanned the crowd.

The Prince of Trees had made it back to his wife, Syrene, and was now whispering something in her ear. Considering the way his yellow eyes glittered, and the laughter that bubbled from her in response, it wasn't too hard to guess what was being conveyed. All around them, well-dressed elves lounged on colorful divans. Glass clinked as they toasted and picked at the bowls of fruit. I tore my gaze from the royal couple and let it sweep through the rest of the crowd.

Groups in various stages of inebriation talked and laughed loudly along the edges while couples exited and entered the dancefloor in the middle. Still no sign of my mark. Next to me, Edric heaved a sigh and lifted another glass from the table behind us. I continued studying the elves around me.

There. Along the wall, half hidden by a cluster of thick flower-covered vines, was an elf with short brown hair. He gripped a wooden mug in front of his chest as if it was his only protection against the strange creatures before him, while his dark green eyes flicked back and forth across the room. Evander Loneleaf. The lowborn elf whose father had come into money and sent him here to learn how to behave among nobility. Given the way he hugged the back wall and the slightly overwhelmed expression that shone through his carefully constructed mask, I'd say he still had a lot to learn.

"Okay, I have him," I said. "There by the wall on the left. Now I just need to make sure he sees that I'm with you."

Edric crossed his powerful arms. "How?"

The Prince of Stone certainly wasn't one to waste words. In my mind, I once more lamented my unwilling grifting partner for the night. We couldn't just go and strike up a conversation with Evander because Edric wasn't a skilled enough liar for that. I brought the delicate glass flute to my lips again and took another sip while considering how to best proceed.

Evander's gaze drifted over the dancefloor. I smiled. Of course. What better way to get noticed than that?

"We need to dance," I said.

"Dance?" Edric whirled on me. "You want me to *dance?*"

"Yes. It'll be quick. Just one time and then you can leave."

When his granite eyes hardened, I realized my mistake and flinched. There wasn't a lot of stone inside the castle at the Court of Trees, but if there had been, I was sure I would've felt Edric's power rumble through it as he took a step closer to me.

"Then I *can leave*? You presume to tell me what to do far too much these days, Kenna."

"I'm sorry, my prince." I swallowed. "I didn't mean it like that, I just… I didn't mean it like that. It won't happen again."

He let the silence stretch. Monette was right. My ambition was getting me into a lot of trouble. I actually liked telling others what to do, and since I spent so much time blackmailing people, I had started to grow accustomed to the way I spoke when I was wearing that black mask. It was getting increasingly difficult to remember that I couldn't talk to normal people like that. Let alone the Prince of Stone.

"See to it that it doesn't." He jerked his chin. "One dance. So you'd better make this count."

"Thank you, my prince."

My heart pounded in my chest as he took me by the arm and led me towards the middle of the room. I knew how to dance, of course. All of Edric's spies did since we pretended to be courtiers in order to keep our cover intact. But I was still nervous because there could be no mistakes tonight.

The musicians struck up a fast-paced song right as we stepped onto the dancefloor. Edric placed one hand on my waist and took my hand with the other. I drew in a deep breath. And then we danced.

Vibrant clothes bled into swirls of paint around us as we moved across the floor in tune with the music. The Prince of Stone might hate dancing, but he was very good at it. He led me expertly through the steps while making sure we stayed within Evander's line of sight.

"Is he watching?" I breathed while the music continued building.

Edric flicked a quick glance towards my mark. "Yes."

My pulse thrummed in my ears as we moved faster and the prince's hand tightened on my waist. However, there was nothing romantic about our dance. No longing in his eyes and no intimacy in his touch. With a face like carved stone, he moved as he if was going through a well-rehearsed drill. And I was immensely grateful for it. Not only because I needed to appear available for my plan to work, but also because I didn't think I would have survived my servitude to him if he had expected me to serve him in the bedroom too. Say what you will about a prince who keeps slaves, but at least he drew the line at that.

His hand on my waist disappeared and threw me into a twirl. Black fabric fluttered around me as I spun and spun while the music reached its crescendo. Like waves crashing against rocks, the final notes crested through the ballroom. With one hand still in Edric's, I threw my head back and slammed to a halt right as the song ended and everything fell silent. My chest heaved.

When the music started back up again, I straightened and looked up into Edric's face. He gave me a businesslike nod before leading me back towards the refreshment table with confident steps. I didn't dare glance at my mark while weaving through the crowd but I knew he was watching. *Perfect.* Now, my cover was in place.

The Prince of Stone grabbed a glass of sparkling wine and emptied it in a long gulp before turning to me. "You have what you need?"

"Yes."

"Good. I'll send Felix to collect you later tonight."

"No." I groaned inwardly at my brusque refusal. "I mean, thank you, but please send him in the morning instead. If all goes according to plan, I'll be able to get a lot of work done tonight."

He gave me a curt nod. "Don't get caught."

And with that, he strode away without a second look back. I watched his powerful body until it disappeared out through the doors. Now, it was up to me.

It was time to start seducing my mark.

CHAPTER 9

As soon as Prince Edric was gone, I released a soft breath and picked up a full glass from the table behind me. Letting my shoulders slump slightly, I wandered over to a chair that was right in Evander's line of sight and sat down. I nursed that glass of sparkling wine while staring at the main doors and looking like I was waiting for something. Or someone.

When I judged that an appropriate amount of time had passed, I got up and paced a little. Then I sat down again. Rolling the delicate glass stem between my fingers, I tilted my head and let some worry seep into my red eyes.

From across the room, I could feel Evander's gaze flicking to me. Counting down in my head, I timed the moment and then shifted my eyes to his right when he did. Our eyes met. I started slightly in a show of surprise and then sent him a shy but kind smile. Heat crept into his cheeks but he smiled back.

Biting my lip, I pretended to think carefully about something before I stood up and placed the half-empty glass on the table next to me. While keeping a nervous expression on my face, I approached Evander. He straightened when he realized what I was doing and smoothened his dark green shirt in a rather conspicuous move.

"Did your date disappear too?" I asked playfully by way of greeting.

Evander dragged a hand through his hair. "Oh, uhm, no. No, I don't actually have a date."

Stopping before him, I pressed a hand to my chest. "Oh, I'm so sorry. I didn't mean to–"

"It's fine. Really." He smiled and held out his hand. "I'm Evander Loneleaf."

"Evander," I repeated as if trying it out. Taking his hand, I smiled back. "It's nice to meet you, Evander. I'm Kenna."

"Kenna…?" he said, waiting for my last name, as I knew he would.

I averted my gaze and let an embarrassed expression slide home across my face. "Just Kenna, I'm afraid." Glancing up through my eyelashes, I found the confounded expression I had been hoping for. I cleared my throat as if I didn't want to admit what I was about to say. "I'm a half-elf, you see. So I'm not really entitled to a human last name or an elven one."

"Oh." His cheeks turned crimson. "I… I'm so sorry. I didn't mean to pry. It's just, I saw you dancing with the Prince of Stone earlier so I thought you surely must be a highborn elf." He blinked. "Not that you would have to be highborn just to dance with him, I just meant that… Uhm."

Placing a hand on his arm, I gave it a quick squeeze. "It's quite alright. I assumed that you had come here with a date, so how about we call it even?"

"Deal." He laughed before leaning in and lowering his voice. "Truth be told, I'm not highborn either. My family is what you would call new nobility, so I'm here to learn their ways."

"Really?" I raised my eyebrows as if that was entirely new information to me.

He nodded.

"Wow. I remember how daunting everything was when I first came to the Court of Stone." Leaning in as well, I put on a conspiratorial expression. "How about this, then? You keep me company until Prince Edric returns so I don't look like such a discarded tool, and I'll help teach you everything I know about court life?"

Evander's green eyes lit up. "I would like that very much."

Of course he would. After setting it up the way I had, there was no way he would turn it down. Since I knew that he was feeling out of place here among the elven nobility, I had played the half-elf card to get him to sympathize with me and instinctively trust me without even knowing me because he thought we were the same. It was like shooting fish in a barrel. Or insecure males in a ballroom, I supposed.

We spent the next couple of hours talking at the edge of the room. I helped point out things to look out for when navigating the world of nobility and he told me stories of his previous life in the forest. Though I shared precious little of my own life, I committed all the details of his to memory so that I could use it to manipulate him later.

When I deemed him appropriately warmed up, I started stealing longing glances at the dancefloor. He picked up on it fast. Well, relatively fast, anyway.

His chair scraped against the floor as he stood up and held out his hand to me. "Would you like to dance?"

"I would love to." I let excitement mixed with surprise

descend on my features as I rose and took his offered hand. "How did you know?"

"I could see it in your eyes when you looked at the dancefloor."

Yeah, it only took you like ten minutes to notice it, my inner voice pointed out. However, out loud, I looked up at him with an awed smile on my face and said, "You're so perceptive."

At that, his spine straightened and his smile grew wider. When he continued leading me towards the middle of the room, there was a spring in his step. I resisted the urge to laugh. Like shooting fish in a barrel, indeed.

The merry string instruments and flutes played a cheerful tune when we finally made it to the edge of the dancing crowd. A flash of uncertainty flickered in Evander's eyes for a second but then he placed a tentative hand on my waist. I gave him an encouraging smile. That seemed to wash away the last of his nerves and he led me into the dance with renewed confidence.

Colorful ribbons fluttered above us like butterflies as we glided across the wooden floor. Joyous laughter and pulsing music filled the air. A little to our right, Prince Iwdael was dancing with an extremely handsome male elf. The prince traced elegant fingers across his partner's cheek and through his dark hair. Their eyes glittered as they slipped away to a secluded couch further in. On our other side, Princess Syrene giggled loudly and toasted with her friends over a table filled with fruit and cheese. Closing my eyes for a second, I allowed myself to enjoy the blissful atmosphere.

The Court of Trees was such a carefree place. Being here, surrounded by all these happy people, I had a very difficult time believing that the Dagger of Orias was hidden somewhere in this court. King Aldrich was a good ruler.

Strong. Wise. But also kind. The only reason why one of the five elven princes would want to assassinate him and steal his throne was because they were afraid that he wouldn't choose them as his successor and didn't want to leave things to chance. Based on everything I knew about the Prince of Trees, he didn't seem that desperate to become king. No. My money was on the brutal and antagonistic Court of Fire. Or, despite Mordren Darkbringer claiming otherwise, the scheming Court of Shadows. Those two made much more sense than this one. Maybe I really had scored a win being assigned to this court in search of the dagger.

My ankle twisted and I stumbled into Evander. Sucking in a gasp of surprise, he caught me in his arms and held me tightly so I wouldn't fall. It had been a genuine accident. Well, the stumble had been genuine at least. Since I wasn't skilled enough to be able to dance with my eyes closed, I had intentionally done that to make sure that I stumbled and created this situation.

"Oh, spirits!" I let out an embarrassed laugh as I clung to his arms while righting myself. "I'm so clumsy."

"I've got you." Evander smiled down at me as he guided me upright again.

Keeping eye contact, I let my hands linger on his biceps for a few seconds more than necessary. "Thank you. Good thing I happened to choose a dance partner who is so strong."

With our eyes locked, we rejoined the dance. I made a point of not looking away in the hopes that he wouldn't either because, as with everything I did, I had a reason for doing it.

Staring into someone's eyes for an extended period of time can create actual feelings of love. It's a pretty neat trick. I had used it more than once while conning people for one spy mission or the other, so I was fairly certain that it would help expedite the deepening of the bond between Evander and me as well.

He reached up and pushed a glossy red curl out of my face. "You really are beautiful."

I laughed self-consciously and ran a hand through my hair but didn't break his gaze. "You're too kind."

"No, I truly mean it. The moment I saw you dance with the Prince of Stone I thought to myself, *wow, she's gorgeous*. I'm so grateful for whatever extraordinary luck brought us together tonight."

Luck. Right. It had definitely been luck that had brought us together and not my careful manipulations of his feelings.

"Me too," I said.

When the musicians lapsed into a slow song, Evander pulled me even closer as he steered us through the appropriate steps. I resisted the urge to cackle. This was going to be such an easy mission.

∽

Insects of the night sang into the silver-speckled sky while I sat on a bench in the gardens outside the castle. Evander sat so close next to me that the warmth from his arm leaked into my own.

"I don't think he's coming back," I said.

We were far into the small hours of the night and Prince Edric still hadn't returned. Just as I had instructed. But Evander didn't know that, of course.

"Does he often do this?" he asked. "Leave to deal with something and then forget to bring you back?"

Letting out a soft sigh, I gave him a tired smile. "More often than I would like."

He shook his head in disbelief. "How anyone could forget about you is beyond me."

I gave him a shy smile while glancing up at him through my lashes. A cold night breeze rustled the leaves of the giant trees around the castle and made my hair blow into my face. I smoothed it back and let an apologetic mask fall in place on my features.

"You really don't have to wait with me. It will probably be morning by the time Prince Edric remembers to come and get me."

"Morning?" Evander drummed his fingers against his thigh. "But you can't just sit here until morning. Couldn't we find someone who can worldwalk you back?"

"Do you know anyone?" I dropped my gaze and fiddled with the black skirt of my dress. "I don't really know anyone in the Court of Trees and I don't want to be a bother."

He heaved a deep sigh. "Honestly, I don't know any of them that well either."

"It's okay. I'll just wait here."

Drunken laughter echoed in the distance as the last of the partygoers made their way back to their own homes. I counted down the seconds until Evander reached the conclusion I had paved the way for.

"You could..." He cleared his throat. "I mean, I don't mean to be too forward, but if you want..." Trailing off, he scratched the back of his neck. "Well, you could always wait out the night in my room." He snapped his head up and met my gaze. "I don't mean anything... inappropriate. Just sleeping. Separately."

Squeezing his hand, I shot him a grateful smile. "You're such a gentleman. Thank you, I would appreciate that a lot."

"You would? Fantastic!" He shot to his feet and held out his hand. "I mean, this way, please."

The wooden halls of the castle were deserted when we made our way towards Evander's room. As soon as the prince and princess had retired from the party, the other guests had started trickling back as well. Now, only the sounds of cleaning came from the great ballroom as we passed it. I would have to be mindful of that, but given the amounts of alcohol that everyone had consumed this night, I expected my next mission to proceed more or less unhindered.

A twisting hallway of dark wood deposited us in the east wing of the castle. Several doors lined the hall but Evander set course for one roughly halfway down. After fishing out a small metal key from his pocket, he unlocked the door and held it open for me.

"Please excuse the mess."

Considering what I was used to in Monette's room, Evander didn't have much of a mess to speak of. Though, compared to Monette, I guess no one did. A stack of rumpled clothes lay draped over one of the large green armchairs in one corner and the covers on the wide double bed looked to have been thrown there in a hurry, but other than that, the dark wooden room was relatively neat.

I flicked my gaze across the spacious room, cataloguing everything, while Evander strode towards the armchair. After picking up the whole stack of discarded garments, he stuffed the bundle into the nearest closet. Wood rattled as he slammed the plain doors closed again.

"You can take the bed," he said and motioned at the grand piece of furniture.

"Oh, no, I couldn't possibly." I bit my lip while glancing

around the room. "Maybe we could just... stay up and talk for a while?"

"Of course." He gestured at the comfortable-looking armchairs but I drifted towards a silver tray with four glasses on top.

Tracing my fingers along the rim of a glass, I looked back at Evander. "I'm sorry to ask but do you have anything to drink? Sitting outside made me a bit cold and I would love something strong to help warm me up again."

The double entendre was very much intended and Evander seemed to pick up on it because his cheeks flushed slightly.

Shaking his head as if to clear it, he strode towards a cabinet. "Yes, of course."

While he stuck his head into it to retrieve whatever bottle he was after, I yanked out a small vial that I'd had hidden in my cleavage. Pulling out the stopper, I poured a few drops into one of the glasses. Clinking came from the cabinet. My heart pattered against my ribs as I recorked the vial and shoved it back into its hiding place right before Evander closed the small door and turned to me.

"I think this will do the trick," he said and he strode towards me with a dark green bottle.

I lifted two glasses and held them out to him while he opened the bottle. Liquid of a dark amber color poured out as he tipped it over the first glass. Once he had filled both of them about halfway, he placed the bottle on the set of drawers next to us. I passed him the drink I had spiked while drifting over to the armchairs.

A puff of air escaped the thick cushion as I dropped down on it and stretched out my legs before me. My feet ached after all the dancing in these shoes, but a lady never complained.

Burrowing deeper into the dark green armchair, I took a long drink. It burned pleasantly on the way down. Wood creaked as Evander flopped down in the armchair next to mine and gulped back the amber liquid as well.

"I wish everyone could be as easy to talk to as you." He heaved a deep sigh. "I've been here a few weeks already, but I still haven't made any friends. They all look at me as if I'm a fraud." Swirling the drink in his glass he let out a bitter laugh. "Which I guess is true."

A pang of guilt hit me. Evander was actually a pretty nice guy. If he ever found out that I was only using him for my own mission, he would be devastated.

"You're not a fraud. Nobles in general are just so… full of themselves. They don't like people who exist outside their fixed worldview." I shrugged. "Trust me. I've dealt with lots of them."

"So, how do we make them accept us?"

By becoming powerful enough that they're forced to treat us with respect. But that kind of answer wasn't something I could say out loud, so instead I just tipped my head back against the soft cushion and blew out a breath.

"I don't know."

"Hmm." Evander downed the rest of his drink and set the glass down on the small table between us. "Well, if you ever figure it out, let me know?"

I chuckled. "Of course. And same."

No answer came. I twisted in my seat to look at the elf beside me. Evander was slumped back against the dark green cushions, eyes closed and his arms hanging limply down his sides while his head leaned against the backrest. His chest rose and fell in deep breaths. Being drugged will do that to you.

Raising my glass, I saluted his unconscious form before placing the glass on the table next to his and pushing to my feet. I hadn't drunk a lot because intoxication could impair my ability to phase through walls since I had to actively will my power to work. But my careful manipulation tonight had still required a lot of energy. I shook my head. Exhaustion weighed heavily on me but I shrugged it off because I had a lot of work to do before the sun rose and Evander woke from his involuntary slumber.

Rolling my shoulders, I strode towards the door and walked straight through it, back into the dark corridor outside. I had a castle to scout.

CHAPTER 10

Darkness hung heavy over the castle. Whoever tended the candles expected everyone who traversed the official corridors to be asleep at this hour because all the wall-mounted candelabras were empty. Despite the gloom hiding me from view, I still hugged the twisting wooden walls as I snuck forward.

Blindly searching an entire palace for an object that might not even be here wasn't exactly a recipe for success, which was why I didn't just sneak in here every night and do precisely that without even involving Evander in the first place. Doing that would be like searching for a needle in a very well-guarded haystack. A haystack that might get me killed if I walked into the wrong room. I needed an inside man. But until Evander could narrow it down for me, I at least had to start somewhere.

If the Dagger of Orias was indeed in the Court of Trees, then logically, it should be in Prince Iwdael's possession. The chances that some random noble had found it were slim, and the odds were even worse for ordinary citizens. No. I should be focusing on the royal wing of the castle.

Calling up my mental map of this place, I plotted a route that would take me to my target. Since I couldn't be sure that any potential occupants were sleeping in the rooms I passed, I didn't want to risk taking any shortcuts so I kept to the hallways like a normal person.

Light flickered in the distance. I slowed my pace as I approached the end that emptied out into a wider corridor. Based on the distance I had walked, I calculated that I was nearing the royal wing. Drawing myself up by the wall, I peeked around the corner.

A fluffy green carpet covered the floor of the wide hallway beyond and candles burned brightly inside their glass domes. Apparently, the Prince of Trees needed light in his domain even though he was in another room. Sleeping. One of the perks of being the boss, I supposed.

After listening for any sounds of people for another few minutes, I glided out of the shadows and into the lit corridor. The soft carpet muffled my steps as I snuck deeper into palace.

I had never actually been inside this secure area before, so I wasn't sure how to find the prince's room. The only thing I knew was that this hallway led to the royal wing. My heart thumped in my chest as I neared a bend in the wide corridor. Staying close to the smooth wall, I edged forward until I could get a clear view of what lay beyond.

Four guards blocked the way up ahead. I jerked back. There was no way to approach without them seeing me. Flicking my gaze in every direction, I considered my options. This appeared to be the only path into the royal wing which meant that whoever wanted to get there had to successfully pass the guards. Unless you were me.

Moving carefully, I stole another glance into the hallway. A few doors were visible in the glossy wood on either side. If I walked through the wall here and then continued parallel to the corridor, I should be able to exit on the other side of the guards. In theory. But that depended on what was inside these rooms.

I tipped my head from side to side. There was no knowing when I would get another chance to sneak around the castle while basically everyone was drunk out of their minds. I stared at the domed wooden ceiling as if I could see the night sky far above. There were only a few hours left until sunrise. I had to risk it.

After sending a prayer to any god or spirit who would listen, I drew a soft breath and stepped through the closest wall.

Some kind of linen storage met me on the other side. It was dark and empty but I still kept my eyes sweeping through the room as I weaved through the rows of cloth-covered shelves. A clean yet flowery scent filled the air in here. In order to keep track of how far down the corridor I was, I counted the steps until I reached the opposite wall. By my best estimates, I was about a quarter way down.

The pale white fabric looked soft but since I was still wearing my long black gloves, I couldn't feel it when I placed my hand on one of the shelves that lined the far wall. Fervently hoping that the next room was another storage space as well, I phased through the wall. Silk brushed against my skin. And then I stepped through it and into another dark room.

Relief spread through my chest. I dared a soft sigh as I

swept my gaze around the small space. There was a couple of worn chairs and a round table to my left, and some kind of workstation to the other side. And in the opposite corner–

A scream shattered through the night. I threw myself backwards as a figure sat bolt upright in the bed located in the opposite corner. Glass clinked as they fumbled after something to light the candle on the nightstand but I was already darting back through the wall.

Outside in the corridor, boots pounded against the floor. Panic shot through me as I sprinted across the storage room, dodging shelves and bolts of pale linen as if my life depended on it. Which it did.

Wood rattled as the door to the screaming elf's room was flung open.

"There was someone there!" she called.

I rounded the final sweet-smelling obstacle and practically threw myself through the next wall right as the door to the linen storage was thrown open as well.

"Are you sure?" one of the guards demanded.

"Yes. Well, I think so. It was dark and…"

Footsteps hurried towards the bend in the hallway. My black skirt fluttered behind me as I hurtled forward. Cold dread seeped into my bones when I realized that I would never make it down the hall before the guard rounded the corner. Fear clawed its way up my spine and mixed with the dread. If I was caught, I was dead. I couldn't let them get so much as a glimpse of me because if they suspected that someone had been here, then my cover would be blown.

"These rooms are clear," another guard called. "Check the corridor."

Shit. Making a split-second decision, I abandoned my path and instead sprinted right into the wall on the other side.

Silence enveloped me. I was standing inside what looked like a deserted meeting chamber. There were no alarms being raised on the other side of the wall, or at least not any that I could hear, so I assumed I had disappeared in time. But I had no idea if they could access this room from the corridor too, so I didn't dare stop. Darting forward, I crossed the polished wooden floor and skirted around the gigantic table before throwing myself through the wall on the other side.

My heart hammered against my ribs as I was deposited in a dark hallway. Pressing a hand to my chest, I tried to slow my racing heart while whipping my head from side to side. No one appeared to be following me but that didn't mean I could stay in the same place for too long. Someone might blunder in here any second. I had to move.

There was only one problem.

I had no idea where I was now.

Panic pulsed at the back of my skull as I tried to piece together my mental map. Given where I had been before, and the distance I had run, I made an estimate of where I had ended up while fleeing. Picking what I hoped was the right direction, I turned to the left and headed down the corridor.

The root-covered wall panels snaked to the right in a slight circle. I glared at the twisting corridor while skulking down it. Plain doors dotted the hall but I didn't dare use any of them in case I disturbed another sleeping elf.

Before me, the darkness thickened. I trailed to a halt as I realized why. A dead end.

"Shit," I swore.

Twisting, I checked behind me. I wasn't sure if I was better off turning back or walking through this wall in the hopes that it led somewhere I recognized. After another few seconds, I cracked my neck and strode into the dark wooden wall.

Another empty hallway stared back at me on the other side. Drawing my eyebrows down, I started forward. It led to a four-way crossing further down but none of the paths gave any indication as to where they went. Since I couldn't tell one way or the other, I simply picked the one that ran in the direction I calculated Evander's room to be.

When a surprise roadblock sprang up in the form of yet another dead end, I had to suppress an incredibly strong urge to bang my head against the wall. Why did the Court of Trees have to be so ridiculously disorganized? Was building structured spaces really such a foreign concept to them? While silently cursing this blasted piece of illogical architecture, I ground my teeth and stalked through the wall again.

Tired beyond belief, I almost fell through Evander's door right as the sun stretched its first red rays across the horizon. After stumbling across the floor, I collapsed in the chair next to the still unconscious elf and downed the rest of my leftover drink.

Evander needed to believe that I had slept here next to him so I had to be asleep when he woke up. My head swam with exhaustion after the long day and night of work. Burrowing deeper into the armchair, I pulled my legs up and rested my head against the plush green cushions. Feeling that delicious softness against my cheek, I decided that being asleep when Evander woke up wouldn't be a problem. I closed my eyes and heaved a deep sigh. Not a problem at all.

CHAPTER 11

The sun was too bright. The chattering citizens and the haggling merchants and the rattling wagons were too loud. And the damn Prince of Shadows was entirely too demanding. Murder shone in my red eyes as I stalked through the busy morning market that appeared like clockwork every day here in the Court of Stone.

Elves and humans strolled the streets, inspecting wares and enjoying the brisk fall morning. I had half a mind to elbow past the chirping masses, but since that would draw unwanted attention, I forced myself to slink through them in a more graceful manner as I set course for the coffeehouse I had been so inconveniently summoned to.

When Evander woke up, he had apologized profusely for falling asleep before he could get me settled in the bed. As if it had been his fault and not due to me drugging him. I had waved it off and said that I had slept well in the armchair, even though in truth, I had only gotten about two hours of rest in it. We had parted with a promise to meet again soon, which was of course exactly what my plan had been. And then Felix had shown up and worldwalked me home.

After being quickly debriefed by Prince Edric, I had retired to my room with the intention of sleeping away the better part of the day. But alas, that was not in the cards. The presumptuous Prince of Shadows had contacted me via the traveling book, ordering me to meet him at the White Cat coffeehouse. Which was why I was currently stomping through the streets with a bad headache and a worse attitude.

Savory aromas from fried pork, potatoes and eggs hung like a mist inside the coffeehouse. I pressed a hand over my mouth. Between the alcohol and the lack of sleep, the scent of cooked food made my stomach turn. Bracing myself, I let my hand drop and took another second to acclimatize myself to the smell. The other patrons barely spared me a glance but a young man with a crisp white apron hurried straight towards me.

"You're expected," he announced as he stopped a few strides away.

"Of course I am, otherwise I wouldn't be here," I snapped before remembering that this poor lad wasn't responsible for my current situation. Waving a hand in front of my face, I let out a long exhale. "Sorry. Lead the way."

He shot me a quick smile of understanding before motioning for me to follow him across the white stone floor. We passed neat tables made of pale wood and a well-dressed clientele before we reached a staircase at the back. The young man looked back at me to make sure I was still following before he started up the steps.

The clanking of pots from the kitchen grew fainter as we reached the top. There was only one doorway up here. I narrowed my eyes as my guide moved to the side and pointed through it and into what looked like some kind of VIP area.

"In there." Without waiting for a reply, he scurried back down the stairs as if he was afraid of the person waiting inside. Which he probably was.

I blew out another breath and stalked inside. "Alright, I'm here."

Mordren Darkbringer looked up from the cup of coffee he had just taken a sip from. Crossing my arms, I lingered just inside the doorway while he returned the white porcelain cup to the pale table before him with calculated slowness. It produced a soft thump as he set it down.

He arched a dark eyebrow at me. "Did you forget your manners this morning?"

Forget them? My manners were currently lying incapacitated in the bed I had thought I would be occupying right now. Drawing myself up, I opened my mouth to tell him as much.

His sharp smile was a slash of white, and something incredibly dangerous glittered in his silver eyes. It sent flares of warning through my nerves and snapped me out of my sullen mood as my survival instincts kicked in. So instead of mouthing off to the most feared elven prince in all the courts, I located my previously missing common sense and cleared my throat.

"Yeah, I did forget my manners." I glanced down at the stone floor. "Sorry."

He was silent for a while as if debating whether to punish me for my insolence but then he simply said, "Sit."

Raising my eyes, I found him nodding at the pale chair across from him. I slid into it. Not sure where to look, I flicked my gaze between his well-tailored black shirt and the cup before him on the table. When he didn't say anything straight away, I glanced up at his face. He smiled at me like a predator before his prey and lifted the coffee cup to his lips again. Holding my gaze, he took a slow sip.

"So, tell me about your mission to the Court of Trees yesterday." His eyes bored into mine from across the rim of the delicate cup. "I'll know if you're lying."

Realizing that I'd been fiddling with the skirt of my dress, I locked my fingers and rested them in my lap instead. "What do you want to know?"

He smiled again. "Everything."

This was certainly not the time to test out the rumor that he could read minds, so I did tell him everything. I explained what my plan had been, how I had executed it, and what the result had been. When I was finished, he set his cup down and studied me for a few moments.

"I see." He leaned back and crossed his ankles. "Now, tell me some news from Edric's court that I might not have heard."

I blinked. Wood creaked as I shifted uncomfortably in the chair while opening my mouth and closing it again a couple of times.

Glossy black hair slid over his shoulders and hung like a dark curtain around Mordren's face as he leaned forward again and rested his arms on the table. "Oh, come now. You're already a traitor to your court. The extent of your betrayal won't matter if your master were to ever find out about it." He paused. "But as long as you keep being useful to me, he won't."

The implied threat was loud and clear. The answering flash of annoyance that shot through me made my headache worse so I rubbed my temples to stem the throbbing behind my eyes.

Heaving a sigh, I looked up at him again. "Okay."

Mordren watched me intently while I relayed a handful of different news and pieces of information that I had overheard in various situations during these last few days. If he already knew about them, I didn't know. But seeing as *I* wasn't the one who was rumored to possess the ability to read minds, I figured that he would have to make do with whatever I gave him regardless of whether he had heard it before or not.

"I see," was all he said when I was done.

We continued watching each other in silence for another minute before my already dwindling patience was at an end.

"Was there anything else? My prince," I added with barely hidden irritation.

Keeping his eyes locked on mine, he traced the rim of his cup but didn't reply. Somewhere downstairs, plates clattered and chairs scraped against the floor while murmuring voices drifted in the air. When I was on the verge of drawing my hidden knife if he didn't let me go back and sleep soon, he finally answered.

"No." He nodded at the empty doorway. "You may leave."

I slid out of my seat and turned to go without another word, but I only made it to the top of the stairs before a sudden thought struck me. Twisting back around, I met Mordren's gaze.

"What about that guy who showed me up here?" I hiked a thumb over my shoulder and in the direction of the stairs. "Won't he tell people that he saw us together?"

A smirk played across Mordren's handsome features. "You don't need to worry about him."

"Ah." I blew out something between a huff and a chuckle. "Threatened or bribed?"

His eyes glittered and a dangerous smile spread over his lips. "Why not both?"

"Right. Of course." Clearing my throat, I gave him a nod in farewell.

"I'll see you soon, Kenna."

He somehow made the words sound like both a promise and a threat. Before he could do anything further to tip the scales in either direction, I turned and disappeared down the stairs.

Brisk fall winds filled my lungs as I left the White Cat behind and stepped onto the busy street. Drawing my cloak tighter around my shoulders, I started the trek back up to the castle. I knew I was just being paranoid but I swore I could feel those silver eyes on my back the whole way across town. With a shake of my head, I picked up the pace. That damn Prince of Shadows was going to be the death of me.

CHAPTER 12

Frantic knocking cut through the silence in my room. I looked up from the letter I'd been reading. It had been delivered earlier, but after my meeting with Mordren yesterday, I had spent the rest of the day sleeping and trying to turn myself back into a somewhat presentable person, so I hadn't opened it until this morning. Now, that decision made guilt seep into my veins. I still hadn't figured out a solution to my family's debt problem, which had made my mother send another letter.

Wood vibrated as a series of sharp knocks sounded again. After stuffing the letter into a drawer, I hurried towards the door.

"What's going on?" I asked while opening the dark slab of wood.

Monette's face met me on the other side but she didn't reply. At the sight of her unnaturally pale face, my next sentence faltered.

Instead, I repeated more forcefully, *"What's going on?"*

"I don't know." Her turquoise eyes darted around the white stone corridor. "But something's happened. Prince Edric is furious." She sucked in an unsteady breath as her eyes finally found mine. "And the Void is here."

Ice tumbled down my stomach. Keeping my voice steady took great effort when dread spread through my body like cold poison. "Okay. Has he called a meeting?"

"Yeah."

"When?"

"In fifteen minutes."

"Should we…?"

"Yes."

Nodding, I closed the door behind me and locked it before falling into step beside Monette. We walked towards the spies' meeting chamber in silence.

To the outside world, I presented a neutral mask. On the inside, however, a miniature Kenna was running around screaming with her arms flapping in the air. There was a strong possibility that I was walking to my death. But if Edric had somehow found out about my deal with Mordren and this was indeed to be my end, then I would go to it denying my betrayal to the last breath in order to spare my family.

My heart slammed against my ribs as Monette and I crossed the threshold into the marble chamber. I picked a spot along the bookshelves so that I could use its sturdy frame as support. Monette took up position close by as well.

More spies arrived as the minutes ticked by. The news seemed to have traveled fast because worry hung like a wet blanket over the silent room.

Power rumbled in the corridor. I sucked in a breath to compose myself just as the Prince of Stone strode into the chamber with another elf a few steps behind. With his short brown hair and gray eyes, he was about as bland as one could get and he had one of those faces that most people forgot as soon as he was gone. We all knew that he was incredibly dangerous, but he didn't look it. Which was probably what made him such a good spy.

Edric Mountaincleaver drew himself up before his throne while the Void took up position on his right. All the other spies in the room bowed low. But this time, the Prince of Stone didn't lower himself onto the throne.

He simply flicked his hand, motioning for us to rise, and said in a voice like grating rocks, "We have a traitor in our court."

Searing terror burned through me but I forced an appropriate amount of shock onto my face. All around me, the other spies looked equally surprised.

Edric swept hard eyes across the room. "Information that has only been circulated inside the castle was recently shared with someone from another court."

Another burst of panic shot through me. *Had I somehow slipped up with the information I gave Mordren? But with what?*

"They acted on that information last night," the Prince of Stone continued. "We almost caught them red-handed but they managed to get away before their identities could be established. That means we still don't know who the traitor is, and which court they work for."

A small sigh of relief was building in my chest but I forced it down.

"We cannot allow a mole to operate inside our court, which is why I have pulled the Void from his other assignments. He will be leading the traitor hunt and you will all do whatever he tells you to do." A muscle flickered in Edric's jaw, the only outward sign of the true depths of his fury. "The traitor *must* be found. Am I making myself clear?"

"Yes, my prince," we answered in unison.

"Don't fail me in this." Stone rumbled throughout the room as Edric whirled around and stalked back out the still open doors.

A nervous ripple went through the group of spies but no one dared say anything. Once the last remnants of Edric's power had disappeared along with his footsteps, we all shifted our gaze to the unassuming elf who was still standing next to the throne.

The Void crossed his arms and leveled eyes dripping with disdain on us. "I hear you've managed to screw up rather spectacularly while I've been away. Not only have you gotten caught in the Court of Shadows and embarrassed our prince, you have also let a traitor go unnoticed in our own court."

"Respectfully," Ymas said in a voice that was anything but respectful, "infiltrating the Court of Shadows is almost impossible. Everyone knows that. So getting caught doing that isn't exactly uncommon."

Taking a casual step off the short platform, the Void sauntered up to the black-haired elf and stopped within striking distance. Ymas, who was a lot taller than the Void, crossed powerful arms over his chest but worry flickered in his eyes. Despite being of medium height and build, the Void commanded an enormous amount of respect. For one, he was one of the few elves who possessed worldwalking in combination with another skill. But most importantly, none of us actually knew what that second skill was. All we knew was that he was the best spy the Court of Stone had ever seen, but his power was a closely guarded secret. And that made him incredibly dangerous.

Cocking his head, the Void looked up at the towering elf before him. "Incompetence is not an excuse for failure."

Ymas clenched his jaw, and the veins in his muscled arms bulged as if he was physically restraining himself from punching the arrogant spy in the mouth. The comment had really struck a nerve, that much was clear. Challenge glittered in the Void's eyes as he arched an eyebrow at the pissed-off male, daring him to do something about it.

The whole room held its breath. A struggle was taking place in the tall spy's eyes for another few seconds before he reached a conclusion. Averting his gaze, Ymas dipped his chin. The Void blew out a satisfied snort.

"Now that the useless excuses are out of the way," he said as he brushed past Ymas, "here's how this is going to work. The traitor is most likely one of the nobles or courtiers, since they are the only ones who had access to the leaked information. I'll be assigning you different missions to root them out. However… it could also be one of you."

"That's ridiculous," Ymas blurted out.

The Void swept hard gray eyes around the room, and I could've sworn his gaze lingered slightly on me, while a cruel smile curved his lips. "Is it?"

"Yes. Why would any of us sell out our own court? It doesn't make any sense."

"If this is the extent of your intelligence, then I'm beginning to understand why you got caught so easily in the Court of Shadows." Shaking his head, the Void turned his back on the now furious-looking elf. "Yes, it is possible that the traitor is one of you. Which is why, in addition to looking into the nobles and courtiers, I will also be scrutinizing *you*."

Cold dread washed over me. With every word that came out of his mouth, the walls seemed to close in further around me. Not only was I blackmailing people in order to get money for myself, I was now also trying to find a more or less illegal way to clear my family's debt, *and* I was spying for Mordren Darkbringer. There were a lot of skeletons in my closet. And if the Void looked too closely at me, there was a strong possibility that he would find at least one of them.

"Any questions?" he demanded, as if anyone would actually dare ask any questions after all this. "Good. Then go do your job."

He jerked his chin in a dismissive gesture. For a moment, everyone appeared too stunned to move, but then the spell broke and the crowd of spies shuffled out the door. Monette and I exchanged a glance.

"Do you really think the traitor is one of us?" She looped her arm through mine and steered us towards the hallway. "Would anyone here actually betray Prince Edric?"

"No." I cast a brief glance over my shoulder to make sure that the Void was out of earshot. He was, but I still lowered my voice. "I think this is just his way of scaring us into following his orders. He knows that none of us did it, but if we think he does, he knows that we'll do whatever he says. It's a power play. That's all."

"You think?"

"I know," I said with the kind of confidence that only came from years of lying.

Worried murmurs bounced around the pale stone corridor as we followed the other spies back to our living quarters, but Monette seemed satisfied with my explanation because she visibly relaxed. Her grip on me loosened and her stiff walk transformed into her customary swishing of hips. I kept my face neutral as we neared our rooms. In my chest, however, my heart was thumping wildly.

My already precarious situation had just become even more lethal. I only hoped that the Void wouldn't pay me too much attention. And that I didn't slip up. Again. Because if I did, it would be game over. But first, I had another manipulation to get ready for. It was time for my first interrogation date with Evander Loneleaf.

CHAPTER 13

"Hey, we match!" Evander blurted out as if that was a coincidence.

A small smile spread across my lips as I smoothed the skirt of my dark green dress while closing the distance between us. At the dance, he had told me that his favorite color was green. Since I knew that he would want to make a good impression, I had surmised that he would probably be wearing a shirt in that color on our first social outing. Hence my own matching outfit.

"Yes, we do." I laughed. "Great minds think alike, I guess."

Birds chirped their cheerful tunes in the trees around the castle. When I stopped in front of Evander on the lawn just outside the towering walls, my shoes sank into the thick damp grass. Drawing a lungful of foggy morning air, I banished the last of my worries concerning Mordren, my family, my freedom, and the Void. At least for the moment.

"You look beautiful," Evander said.

"Thank you." I winked at him. "You're not so bad yourself."

A blush crept up his cheeks. For a few seconds, we only

watched each other. Then he seemed to remember himself and shook his head vigorously.

"Oh, uhm." He cleared his throat and motioned towards the woods on my right in jerky movements. "I've arranged for a picnic."

I stifled a groan. If I was going to learn anything useful, I needed to be inside the palace grounds.

"That sounds lovely." Taking his arm, I gave him an innocent smile. "And perhaps we could take a walk through the castle gardens first? To work up an appetite."

The red staining his cheeks deepened at my casual touch. "Y-yes, of course. I would love that."

Satisfaction sparkled in my chest as I turned us around and steered us back inside the walls. However, I couldn't appear too eager, so when we passed through the open gate, I slowed and let him pick the path. After a moment of hesitation, he led us towards the colorful hedge formations on our left.

Even though we were far into fall, the deep green bushes were covered in flowers of every hue. I knew that it was due to someone's magic here in the Court of Trees but it still surprised me. There wasn't too much vegetation in the Court of Stone, at least not in the city proper, but what was there actually reflected the season. Here, nature was whatever the inhabitants willed it to be. Apparently, that was blooming summer. It was pretty, though.

"Everything is so different here," I said, adding a dreamy note to my voice. "It's so flowing and colorful. In my court, it's all straight lines and stone."

"I can only imagine. I've never been outside the Court of Trees." Evander scratched the back of his neck. "I hadn't even been outside my section before coming here."

Most other courts were made up of a city that served as the capital and housed the castle, and then other small towns that dotted the rest of the area. The Court of Trees, however, didn't subscribe to that kind of normal organization. Instead, the forest was divided into sections. There was no logic behind the division but it was the only form of structuring that this chaotic court deigned to adhere to.

"Really?" I raised my eyebrows in genuine surprise. "It must have been very strange for you, coming here, then."

Evander drew his fingers through a thick bush covered in pale blue flowers. "It was. There are so many strange customs here."

I saw an opportunity to steer the conversation into some light interrogation and turned to give him a sympathetic smile. "I know what you mean. I felt the same thing when I first arrived at the castle in the Court of Stone. What were some of the strangest customs you learned?"

Leaves rustled gently into the silence while Evander considered. I freed the edge of my dress that had gotten caught in some brambles when we rounded a corner in the hedge formation. Somewhere on the other side of the tall greenery, soft voices chatted merrily.

"Well, I suppose it was more the lack of restrictions." He squinted at the path ahead. "Almost nothing here is off limits. At least for people who live in the castle."

"What do you mean?"

"I thought there would be strict rules on where you were allowed to go inside the castle, but there are really only a few parts of it that are off limits."

Anticipation fluttered in my stomach but I managed to keep my tone casual as I said, "Oh? That is strange. Most parts of the castle in my court are off limits." I let a mischievous smile flash over my lips. "I've always wanted to see what's there. I used to make up my own answers to it. Like, I'd decide which room was secretly filled with treasure, which one held deadly traps and so on."

Evander laughed in a way that made his green eyes sparkle. "That sounds kind of fun."

"It is!" I giggled and then made my voice playfully conspiratorial. "Do you want to do it for your court too?"

"Sure." He tapped his chin with his free hand as we neared the end of the path. "Let's see. What should we fill the royal wing with?"

"How about… hidden treasure?"

"Hmm."

"No?" I pretended to think carefully before whirling back to face him. "Oh! What about samples from every single flower and plant in the forest?"

Tipping his head back, he laughed again. "Let's go with that. Alright, then what should we fill the…" He trailed off.

Come on, I urged in my head. I needed him to tell me which areas were off limits so that I could come back and search those specifically. If the dagger was here, it had to be hidden in one of those places.

However, before I could get the conversation back on track, we rounded the final bend and came face to face with the reason for his abrupt silence. The Prince of Trees and a male elf with blond hair and a dull face, or at least dull compared to the company the prince usually kept, approached at a leisurely pace. Evander and I stepped to the side of the path so that they could pass.

"Your Highness," we mumbled in unison while Evander bowed and I curtsied.

Iwdael Vineweaver gave us a nod in acknowledgement

before strolling past us. The other elf kept his gaze on the road ahead.

As soon as they were out of earshot, Evander blew out a long sigh and then chuckled. "That was close."

"Yeah, it was." I was just about to steer us back to the previous topic but before I could, Evander charged on.

"Should we head back?" He waved a hand in the general direction of the gates. "To the picnic, I mean."

Since there was no way to pick up the thread of conversation now, at least not without arousing suspicion, I accepted my temporary failure and shot him a beaming smile. "That sounds great."

His eyes sparkled as he tightened his arm around mine. "Then follow me."

I inclined my head as he led us towards the picnic spot he had picked.

There was still time. This was only our second meeting and I had already made some progress. If I could just get him to trust me and open up to me a little more, then I could broach the topic of the forbidden areas again. Maybe even get him to take me there.

Schemes swirled in my mind as we made our way into the forest. This was going to work. It had to. I straightened my spine as we disappeared under the thick canopy. No. It would work. It definitely would.

CHAPTER 14

The forest lay empty and quiet around me. Crossing my arms, I leaned one shoulder against a thick tree trunk while waiting for Felix to arrive.

The picnic with Evander hadn't yielded a lot of useful information but it had been... nice. I knew that he was just a mark, like all the others, but he wasn't half bad company. He had even taken the trouble to put together a meal that consisted of a multitude of different dishes since he didn't know what I liked. People weren't usually that thoughtful. At least not to me.

Tapping my foot against the damp grass, I tried to will Felix into existence. I might have had a good time with Evander but I still didn't want him to accompany me to the pickup location. I had spun some convincing lie about not wanting to start rumors in my court, but in truth, I just didn't want him to see Felix and somehow start putting things together. Waiting in a deserted glen for said half-elf to show up was grating on my patience, though.

A figure appeared in the corner of my eye. I turned around

but the greeting died on my tongue when I realized who it was.

Mordren Darkbringer stalked across the grass. Bloody murder shone in his eyes as they locked on me.

With alarm bells tolling in my head, I straightened from the tree and reached for my dagger. Only to realize that it wasn't there. I'd had to leave it behind this morning since bringing a knife to a date might be a bit awkward. Though now that the Prince of Shadows was advancing on me with fury burning in his eyes, I sincerely regretted that decision.

Holding up my hands in an appeasing gesture, I took a step towards him. "Look, whatever you think I–"

Shadows shot out from around him. I threw myself backwards and willed my body to phase through the tree I had been leaning against. The move made his attack fall short and bought me another few seconds to do... what? Whipping my head around the empty glen, I tried to formulate some kind of plan but I didn't have a lot to work with. I had no weapons, no allies, and nowhere to run. Not to mention that I was facing down an elven prince who could send me to my knees in pain without so much as lifting a finger.

Black shadows crept along the soft moss as Mordren rounded the thick tree trunk. I backed away but didn't make it far before the dark tendrils around him shot straight at me again. Only, this time there was no tree to block their advance. Their cold smooth forms wrapped around my body, trapping me in place.

The Prince of Shadows closed the distance between us. "You betrayed me."

"What? No!"

"Don't try to deny it. It's unbecoming. And pathetic."

"I didn't betray you. I..." Apprehension washed over me

and I trailed off as I suddenly realized what he was talking about. The leaked information that had almost gotten someone caught when they had acted on it. "Oh. Look, it's not what it–"

"It's not what it looks like? Because it looks like you set me up." His shadows snaked higher up my legs and arms. "The information you gave me was a trap. I barely got out before the cavalry arrived."

My heart thumped in my chest as a dark tendril branched off from the others and slithered across my collarbone before encircling my throat. Mordren watched its progress from a stride away.

"I didn't know." I swallowed as the cold silken shadow completed its arc around my neck. "I swear."

"You swear? How am I supposed to believe anything you say?"

"Because I'm telling the truth! I just told you stuff I'd overheard. I didn't know it was a trap."

Leaves rustled above us as a strong fall wind swept through the canopy. Mordren shifted his weight, making a twig snap under his polished black shoes. I tried not to think about the fact that my neck might be making that same sound in a minute or two.

"Then prove your loyalty now." Mordren's silver eyes gleamed. "Give me the names of the other spies in your court."

Ice spread through my veins. This was the only truly valuable information I had about the Court of Stone. Prince Edric compartmentalized everything of importance for exactly these kinds of situations, but the one thing he couldn't prevent us from knowing was of course who else spied for him. We all lived together in the castle, after all. But if I gave them up, they would all be in danger.

"No."

A lethal smile spread across his lips. "You refuse?"

The noose around my throat tightened until I had to struggle to get my next words out. "You can believe whatever the hell you want but I didn't set you up. And I'm not giving you the names."

A flash of pain seared through me. I sucked in a gasp as my vision went white for a second before the wave of agony receded again.

Mordren leaned down until I could feel his breath against my lips. "I will make you beg for the privilege of giving me those names."

I glared up at him but said nothing. His wicked smile widened. Pain exploded through me again but this time it deepened with every second until another gasp was forced out of me. The shadow around my throat tightened in response to it.

"Last chance before this gets really ugly." Mordren held my gaze as the pain intensified. "The names."

"No," I croaked.

I collapsed to the ground. Stars danced before my eyes and it took me a moment to realize that the pain wasn't getting worse. It was gone. And so were Mordren's shadows. Pressing my palms against the damp grass, I stared at the pair of black shoes before me while trying to piece together what was going on.

"There's that spine again." Mordren chuckled. "I really am impressed."

Since I didn't trust my legs just yet, I remained on my knees while the final echoes of his power left me. After another few seconds, I at least mustered the strength to tilt my head up and meet his eyes. When I did, I found amusement playing over his features.

"I believe you. You didn't set me up," he announced. "And now I know that you won't betray *me* either, if someone else were to try and threaten you like I just did. Because if you ever did betray me, I would share your secret and those you care about would pay the price. And if this little experiment is any proof, you will go to great lengths to make sure that doesn't happen." His dark eyebrows creased slightly in surprise. "You really care about people. How interesting."

Experiment? I was about to inform him exactly what I thought he could do with that experiment but then thought better of it and instead settled for a scowl. Heaving a deep sigh, I pushed to my feet.

"Couldn't you have just read my mind to find out what you wanted instead?" I muttered.

A smile flashed over his lips. "What would be the fun in that?"

I opened my mouth to say something I would most likely have regretted, but before I could get anything out, Mordren was gone. For a moment, I just remained standing there, glaring at the slight imprints his shoes had left in the moss. Rubbing my temples, I blew out an exasperated breath.

"Kenna?"

Startled, I whipped my head towards the sound. Felix was standing between two tree trunks a few strides away. Suspicion crept into my mind. Mordren had worldwalked away right before Felix got here, as if he had known exactly when he would arrive.

"Are you alright?" the redheaded half-elf pressed.

After brushing some leaves off my dress, I plastered a

smile on my face and approached him. "Yeah, of course. Why wouldn't I be?"

"You look a bit... flustered."

"I didn't get as much from my mark as I had planned." It was true enough. "I just expected to be further along by now."

Felix gave me a sympathetic smile. "You've only met him twice."

"Yeah, but you saw Prince Edric this morning. His patience is short as it is."

"True." He put his arm around my back and drew me close before glancing over at me. "Ready?"

Steeling my stomach, I nodded. The world warped around me and my body felt as though it was folding in on itself. When my surroundings turned corporeal again, I was standing in front of tall walls made of white stone. Felix released me and took a step to the side while straightening his white shirt. I gave him a nod before we both started out towards the castle.

We had only made it through the wide gate before I could sense that something was wrong. Felix kept throwing nervous glances at me from the corner of his eye when he thought I wasn't looking and he opened and closed his mouth repeatedly without actually saying anything.

"What?" I asked at last and turned to peer at him.

"Well, two things," he began as we crossed the white stone courtyard. "The Void is in a very... dictatorial mood today."

I rolled my eyes. "When is he not?"

Felix fell silent as a cluster of elven nobility strolled towards us from the other direction. They stayed their course so the two of us moved aside to let them pass instead. They barely spared us a glance as they chatted while continuing towards the main gate and the bustling city that lay beyond.

When they were gone, I turned back to Felix while we started towards the castle again. "And the second?"

He was quiet for a moment before replying, "Your family is here."

That wasn't usually very noteworthy since they belonged to the class of human nobles and thus were welcome to visit the palace if they had business there. I frowned at the half-elf beside me.

"So?"

"They seem a bit... agitated." He gave me a helpless shrug. "And they have demanded to speak with you."

"Demanded?"

"Yeah."

Tipping my head back, I raked my fingers through my hair while staring up at the decorated stone spires high above. I knew why my family was on edge, of course. But them drawing attention to it in this way didn't benefit any of us.

"They're waiting for you in the throne room," Felix supplied while combing back his hair with his fingers.

"Alright, I'll handle it." My brows furrowed and I looked him up and down as he straightened his shirt a second time. "Are you alright?"

"What? Yes. Of course." He shook his head in quick jerky motions that messed up his hair, which made him immediately smooth it down again. "Of course I am."

"Uh-huh."

Our feet echoed against the shining white walls as we reached the top of the stairs and moved through the passage leading into the throne room. Carved statues of all the elves who had held the title Prince of Stone lined the walls. I let my gaze glide over their imposing features while I waited for an appropriate amount of time to pass. When we were almost at the gigantic doors separating the walkway from the throne room, I estimated that the pause had been long enough for Felix to miss the connection.

"What's your next assignment?" I asked innocently as if it had nothing to do with my previous question.

His brown eyes lit up. "I'm taking Monette to the Court of Water."

"Ah okay, cool."

I had guessed as much. Monette was like one of those really bright lights that all insects were drawn to. Or in this case, all suitors were drawn to. She was gorgeous, charming, and never had a shortage of people vying for her attention. Sometimes I envied her.

"Oh, there she is," Felix blurted out as we crossed into the high-ceilinged hall filled with human and elven nobility.

Monette was waiting a short distance inside the wide doorway. She was wearing a white dress that hugged her figure, and precious gems sparkled in her hair and around her neck. They were of the exact same turquoise color as her eyes. The slight upward curving of her lips as she surveyed the crowd told me that she was well aware that the nobles were stealing subtle glances at her, and that she relished the fact.

"I-I should go," Felix stammered.

"Tell her that she looks great and that the necklace brings out her eyes," I said and gave him a soft push in her direction.

He looked back at me, bewilderment written all over his face. "What?"

"Tell her."

Before he could say anything else, I slipped towards the other side of the room where two humans had already spotted me. Adeline and Elmer Beaufort, my mother and my adoptive father, strode towards me but I changed course and led us towards a more secluded corner, away from all the other people. When we were finally out of earshot, they stopped and faced me.

My mother's voice was frantic as she said, "Where have you been? We've been waiting for hours."

"I was away on an errand. For the prince," I added while fiddling with the sleeve of my dress.

"Have you forgotten our situation?" Lord Beaufort demanded.

"No, of course not."

"Then why haven't we heard back from you?"

I opened my mouth and then closed it again. Forcing myself to stop fiddling with my dress, I glanced between the two humans in front of me. Lord and Lady Beaufort were definitely a matching set. Both of them were clad in shades of blue that went well with their eyes, and sapphire jewelry complemented their outfits. I wondered idly how much money they could raise towards their debts if they sold those, but the thought was wiped from my mind by the expression on their faces.

Worry and frustration creased my mother's brows as she ran a hand over her hair, which was the exact same shade of red as my own, while my father crossed his arms. Disappointment shone clearly on his angular face.

"I'm still working on a solution," I said finally in response to his previous question.

"What solution?" he retorted. "Do you have the money or not?"

How was I supposed to explain to them that I did have the money but I didn't want to give it to them?

"It's complicated." I shot a quick look at the rest of the

throne room. No one was paying any attention to us. "Who is it that you owe money to?"

My mother crossed her slender arms over her chest. "Why does that matter?"

"It might help me figure out a solution. So, who do you owe all that money to?"

Lord and Lady Beaufort exchanged a look and then Elmer drew himself up to his full height. "A gang boss here in the city."

"Which one?"

"The big one. With a beard."

My heart sank. There was only one gang leader who was both known for lending money and fit that description. Collum. Also nicknamed the Skullcrusher. This would probably end well.

I was just about to ask them for more information when a fast-moving figure caught my attention. The Void stalked through the crowd with his sights set on me. *Shit.*

"Alright, I'll take care of it," I said hastily to my parents.

They started stammering protests but I was already walking away. I had barely made it to the edge of the crowd when the Void stepped out in front of me.

He jerked his chin towards the wall where my parents were still standing. "Socializing on the job, are we?"

"For your information, I've already been out on a job." Drawing myself up, I crossed my arms. "So what I do with my free afternoon is none of your business."

"Wrong. It is my business and you don't have a free afternoon." He tipped his head to indicate the nobles behind him. "We have a traitor to catch and you're going to work this crowd. Right now."

"I already have plans." Namely, to go see a certain Skullcrusher about a certain debt.

"No, you don't. Because you do whatever I tell you to do." He held my gaze, daring me to challenge him.

I was suddenly very glad that I hadn't brought my knife when I left this morning. Because if I had, it would have ended up somewhere in his chest cavity at this point. Narrowing my eyes at him, I considered how good it would feel to run him through with a blade for another few seconds before I forced my gaze down.

"Fine," I bit out.

He scoffed and then jerked his chin again while a smirk settled on his face. "Get to work."

Not stomping as I walked away took tremendous effort. I took a few deep breaths through my nose in order to calm myself as I slipped through the groups of gathered elves and humans.

It was such a ridiculous waste of my time since I already knew who the traitor was. Me. But I couldn't very well tell anyone that, so now I was stuck sneaking through the throne room and eavesdropping on conversations with the mission of finding the nonexistent noble who had betrayed us. What I should be doing was seeking out Collum.

Resolving to do that after I had satisfied the Void's dictatorial needs, I started my covert sweep of the grand stone hall. This was going to be a long day.

CHAPTER 15

Cold winds ripped at my clothes as I stalked down the street wearing my black jacket, pants, and boots. The sword strapped across my back was a comforting weight that kept my anger in check. For now.

I had a very strong urge to kick in the door I had been striding towards, but managed to fight it off and instead walked right through it. The hallway beyond was dark. I took the stairs two at a time and then veered left into what looked to be the factory manager's office. Once there, I faced the outer wall and pulled down the black mask in front of my face.

And then I sprinted right towards it.

While phasing through the wall, I pushed off from the floor with all my strength. Black fabric fluttered in the night as I flew across the gap between the buildings and straight towards the solid wall on the other side. But instead of getting splattered against it like an insect, I passed through that one as well and crashed into the room on the other side.

Rolling to my feet, I yanked the sword from my back and

swung it in the direction of the man in the chair. Collum shot up from his seat but only gaped at me in absolute shock. I used the extra second to close the distance between us and position the sharpened blade at the base of his throat. Adrenaline pumped through my veins and a wicked smile spread across my lips.

There had definitely been easier ways to go about this. But maybe I'd been looking for a fight. Between being completely at Mordren's mercy, seeing my family's disappointment in me when I couldn't solve their problems, and being ordered around by the Void, I was desperate for a situation where I was in control. I needed to hold the power. To be the one who made others do what I wanted. And holding a sword to a gang leader's throat most certainly gave me that sweet satisfaction. So yes, I had definitely been looking for a fight.

"I can push this through your windpipe before you can scream," I announced when Collum opened his mouth.

He closed it again. I flicked my gaze around the neat room. The desk he'd been sitting behind was covered in papers but everything else was in its proper place. Books and ledgers filled the bookcases and two leather armchairs waited on either side of a small circular table. All his loan contracts were probably in those ledgers but there were simply too many of them to search on my own.

"You lent money to Lord and Lady Beaufort," I said.

"Who?"

I pressed the sword harder against his throat. The human before me raised his chin to make sure that I didn't damage his thick dark brown beard but the confused look stayed on his face.

"Don't lie," I snapped. "I know that the Beauforts owe you money. Now go get their contract."

His pale gray eyes were steady as he held my gaze. "I've never lent money to someone called Beaufort."

Uncertainty fluttered in my stomach. He looked and sounded sincere, but he had to be lying. Based on what my parents had told me, it couldn't be anyone else.

"Where are your contracts for names beginning with B?"

Collum turned slowly and nodded at a row of ledgers to his left. Keeping the blade at his throat, I steered him towards it.

"Show me," I said.

Raucous laughter echoed from somewhere downstairs while the muscled gang leader pulled out a thick leather-bound book and offered it to me. I wrapped a gloved hand around it before moving us back towards his desk so that I could flip through it while still holding on to the sword. With one eye on Collum, I turned the pages until I got to all the last names starting with *Be*. Nothing. I must have missed it. Turning slightly, I squinted at the page.

As soon as I took my eyes off him, Collum made his move. My arm snapped to the side as he shoved the sword away from his throat and launched himself at me. I jerked back and whipped my blade up again but he was already inside my guard. Air rushed out of my lungs as he tackled me and I crashed down on the floor with him on top of me.

Before he could pin me completely, I threw a knee into his side and rolled out from under him when the move made him shift his weight. Shooting to my feet, I rammed the sword back in its scabbard and sprinted towards the outer wall so that I could jump back through the gap between the buildings.

A meaty hand wrapped around my ankle. I let out a yelp as it yanked my leg back and threw me off balance. My body hit the carpeted floor with a dull thud. Kicking blindly with my free leg, I tried to break his grip.

Something crunched as my boot connected with his face and he let out a roar. I tried to roll over on my side but before I could, Collum yanked me towards him. The buttons on my jacket dug into my stomach as I was hauled across the floor.

In the corridor outside, stomping feet and raised voices drew closer. If his crew got here before I could slip away, I was doomed.

The iron grip around my ankle disappeared. Placing my palms against the floor, I got ready to jump up and sprint away but I barely managed to push myself up before a boot landed on my back. I let out a snarl as Collum used his superior weight to shove me back onto the ground.

Wood crashed against stone as the door was flung open. I tried to count the number of boots as Collum's men flooded the room but before I could, I was hauled up by the back of my jacket.

My breath was yet again knocked out of me as I slammed back first into the wall on the opposite side of my escape route. A host of burly men formed a circle around me. But that wasn't my biggest problem. It was the angry gang leader who was pinning me to the wall with his hand around my throat.

Fury danced in Collum's pale eyes as he wiped blood from his nose. "Now, let's get that mask off your face. I wanna see the idiot who thought she could try and threaten me."

Panic washed over me as he raised his other hand. I couldn't let them see my face. My finger curled around the handle of the knife still strapped to my thigh. With a quick prayer to any god or spirit who would listen, I ripped it free and rammed it into Collum's leg.

A bellow of shock and pain tore from his throat and his hands went to the wound as I yanked the blade free. As soon as his grip on me had disappeared, I called on my magic and stepped backwards, right through the wall.

The corridor outside was jarringly quiet and empty compared to the study but I knew it would only last for another second or so. Since I didn't know what was on the other side of the building, I sprinted for the stairs. Right as I reached the topmost step, the men in the study figured out that I was no long inside the room. The door burst open with another crash of wood on stone and angry gang members poured out.

I didn't dare look back as I thundered down the stairs. Cheerful voices and boisterous laughter still drifted from the room at the bottom so I hoped I'd be able to sneak away before they noticed me.

"Stop her!" Collum bellowed from upstairs. "The girl in the black jacket, don't let her leave!"

Jumping the last few steps, I landed at the back of what looked like a crowded tavern. Only, no one was drinking and laughing anymore. On their leader's orders, every single human in the room had shot to their feet and drawn some kind of weapon. A sea of swords, daggers, axes, and maces now separated me from the door on the other side. Behind me, boots thudded on the steps.

I whirled around and darted towards the back wall. Shouts of surprise rose and metal clanged as the tavern scrambled to catch me. They didn't make it.

Cool night air enveloped me as I passed through the stone wall and skidded into the dark alley on the other side.

"Hey!" a man's voice called. "Where the hell did you come from? Who are you?"

Snapping my head up, I found a human man who looked like he had been guarding the back of Collum's headquarters. I opened my mouth to feed him some kind of lie but he had already drawn his sword.

Steel sang into the moonlit night as I unsheathed mine as well. "I was just leaving. Just let me pass and we won't have a problem."

"You're inside my perimeter. We already have a problem."

Well, it had been worth a shot.

I lunged at him.

He sidestepped my attack and drew his sword in a wide arc. Twisting, I threw mine up to meet it. The impact vibrated through my arm but I managed to push his blade away while drawing my knife. With a calculated shove, I disengaged our swords and spun in a half circle to get inside his guard.

Shock flashed across his features as I buried my knife in his shoulder. His sword clattered to the stones as he lost his grip and staggered backwards at the impact.

From the other side of the building, shouts echoed into the air. The people inside the tavern were making their way here. Letting out a vicious string of curses, I yanked the knife back out of the stunned man. It slid free with a wet squishy sound.

As soon as it was out, I turned and ran as fast as I could. I might be skilled with a sword but I couldn't fight off an entire gang. If they caught up to me, it would not end well.

Still gripping the sword and the bloody knife, I hurtled through the streets. Stampeding feet thumped behind me. I sucked in desperate breaths as I sprinted towards the less shady areas of town.

Since I wasn't sure what awaited me on the other side, I didn't want to run through any houses. It might buy me a few seconds but it might also land me in even worse trouble if one of the buildings belonged to other hostile people. I knew a lot about my city, but I didn't know everything.

The road I was following branched in two up ahead. Both of them led out of the slums and into merchant territory, so as long as it was empty, I would be fine. Hoping that I picked one that was, I aimed for the left one.

A sharp whistle sounded.

"This one's empty. That one's not."

I jerked my head up to find two cloaked figures standing atop the roof of the building between the two roads. Backlit by the moon, they were only dark silhouettes.

"Empty," the voice repeated and pointed at the road on my right before motioning at the left street. "Not."

Indecision flashed through me. I had set my sights on the street to the left but according to these two, the other road would be empty. And there was no way of knowing if they were telling the truth. The two paths drew closer. I had to make a decision.

After shoving my sword back into its sheath, I raised a hand to my brow in salute and sprinted down the street on my right.

My hurried footsteps echoed between the stone buildings but that was the only sound. The street was indeed empty. Sending silent thanks to the strangers on the roof, I raced towards the castle in the distance with my knife still in hand.

This night had turned into a disaster. Mostly because I had been too pissed off about the day's events to plan this better and had instead gone in there wanting a fight. But also because my parents had actually lied to me.

My own stupidity aside, this mission had been doomed from the start because Collum wasn't the person that my family owed money to. Why had they lied about that?

I turned the thought over and over in my head as I made my way towards the castle. Before entering the grounds, I pushed the mask back up into my hood, wiped the bloody knife, and stuck it back in its holster.

Still preoccupied with my parents' odd dishonesty, I wandered through the walls of the castle until I reached the hidden part of my room. After placing my weapons on their racks, I shrugged out of the black jacket and hung it on the hook next to them.

While stretching my tired limbs, I walked through the final wall and into my room.

I jerked to a halt.

Lounging in the chair by the desk, staring straight at me, was the Void.

CHAPTER 16

"Where have you been?"

I blinked at the arrogant spy seated in my chair. What the hell was the Void doing in here?

He cocked his head. "I said, where have you been?"

Shaking off the shock and panic, I crossed my arms and instead donned an annoyed scowl. When in doubt, attack was the best defense.

"I think the better question is, what are you doing here?" I jerked my chin in the direction of the door. "This is *my* room. You have no right to just barge in here without my permission."

"Your room?" He huffed a condescending laugh and crossed his ankles in a lazy manner. "You're a spy in this court."

"So are you."

"Yes, but the difference is that I *work* for Prince Edric. He pays me for my skillset. You on the other hand..." A smirk curled his lips as he flicked his gaze up and down my body. "He *owns* you. Any privacy you have, anything you have at all, is only because he allows it."

The truth in his words burned like acid in my stomach. This wasn't my room. Not really. Nothing in here belonged to me. The only items that I truly owned were hidden away in the secret compartment behind me. My jacket, my sword, and my knife. The sword had been a gift from my biological father and was the only thing I had smuggled in here with me when I left my family's mansion. The knife I had bought with ransom money. Same with the jacket. The well-tailored black garment with its multitude of shifting pockets had been incredibly expensive since it was imbued with magic, but I had bought it anyway so that I could expand my blackmailing operation. And those three things were my sole possessions. Everything else had been provided by Prince Edric.

"And until this traitor is caught, you're not allowed to have any privacy," the Void finished. "So I will ask again, where have you been?"

I let my arms drop and plastered a defeated look on my face while I blew out a sigh. "In the city. I'm not really getting anywhere with the Court of Trees so I had to meet a contact to see if I could get something I can use to speed things up."

"And did it go well?"

"Yeah, it did." I shrugged. "But he didn't really have anything for me. Well, at least nothing new. He only told me that Evander, the guy I'm seducing, is new to the scene and often acts awkward in social gatherings." Flicking my gaze upwards, I shook my head. "As if I didn't already know that."

"Uh-huh."

Wood scraped against stone as the Void rose, pushing the chair backwards across the floor. For a moment, he just remained standing there. I fought the urge to fidget beneath the weight of those gray eyes but managed to keep a disinterested mask on my face.

Then, he chuckled. "Liar."

"Excuse me?"

"You're a good one too. It's a shame something else gave you away." A cocky smile stretched his lips as he flicked a hand in my direction. "There's blood on your neck."

On instinct, my hand shot up and I drew two fingers along my neck. They did indeed come back with small red smudges. My heart thumped in my chest and I opened my mouth to spin some kind of tale but the Void was already striding towards the door.

"I'll report this to Prince Edric and advise him to keep a tail on you at all times." He threw a glance at me over his shoulder. "You just jumped to the top of my suspect list."

"Wait!"

Almost at the door, the Void stopped and turned with calculated slowness. He arched an eyebrow expectantly but didn't say anything. I wanted to scream. There were just too many secrets and they were starting to get in the way of one another. I mean, yes, I *was* the traitor that the Void was looking for but that wasn't why there was blood on my neck. That was because of my family's secret debt. And the way I handled that tricky situation was connected to my own blackmailing. Which was yet another secret. I couldn't keep doing this. If I was to survive juggling all of this, I would have to give him something.

I locked eyes with the Void. "What do you want?"

"What do I want?" He started back towards me again. "Funny you should ask."

The Void and I were the same height, and he wasn't particularly muscular either. In fact, I was pretty sure I would win if we ever got into a fight, and especially if I could get my hands on a weapon. So he wasn't physically intimidating. Not really. But I still found myself retreating as he advanced on me. When I realized that, however, I forced myself to a stop and stand my ground a couple of strides from the wall.

"What I want is for you…" His gray eyes glinted dangerously as he stopped only a breath away, forcing me to take another half step back. "…to tell me the truth."

"Alright. Fine." I met his demanding stare. "My family has racked up a lot of debt. Enough that they might lose everything. I was down in the shady parts of town, meeting a gang leader and trying to find a way to get my family out of that debt, but it didn't go all that well. Hence the blood. That's what I was doing. It has nothing to do with this traitor situation."

"Which gang leader?"

"Collum." I motioned in the general direction of the city. "You can ask anyone in that area if there was an intruder and a fight at his headquarters tonight."

"I plan to."

I tried to keep the pleading tone out of my voice as I asked, "Will you still tell Prince Edric to have me tailed?"

"Why do you care?" His stare turned challenging. "If you're not the traitor then it shouldn't matter."

"Because you were right. I don't have a lot of privacy and I really don't want to lose what little I still have." I dropped my gaze and allowed true desperation to seep into my tone. "Please."

For a moment, he was silent. My pulse thrummed in my ears as I waited for his judgement. What I had told him had been the truth. I hated the thought of my freedom and privacy being limited even further. The fact that I actually *was* a traitor, in more ways than one, was the ginormous second reason, of course, but I hoped that fact could hide behind the first reason a little longer.

"*If* your story checks out, I'll consider it." Before I could press him for an actual answer, he turned around and sauntered towards the door. "I'd do my best to stay in my good graces from now on, if I were you."

The door shut behind him with a soft click. I remained staring at the slab of wood while clenching and unclenching my right hand. If I'd been holding something right then, I would've thrown it at the door.

That rude arrogant bastard. He was far too dangerous to have running around. Drumming my fingers against my thigh, I considered whether there was a way to get rid of him. Perhaps I could leak his identity to Mordren? The Void often worked the Court of Shadows and we all knew how the Darkbringer prince handled captured spies. If I were to *accidentally* share that information with him, then he could handle the Void for me.

Jerking back, I blinked and shook my head. Had I really considered selling out one of my fellow spies just to make my double life as a traitor easier? Gods and spirits, how awful was I? Tipping my head back, I raked my fingers through my hair and blew out a deep sigh. I couldn't set him up. But I couldn't let him figure out that I was the traitor either, so I would have to play it even smarter from now on.

I pulled the shirt over my head as I made my way towards the bed. Tomorrow afternoon, I was meeting up with Evander in the Court of Trees again but I had something else to do before that as well.

The shirt flapped in distress as I pitched it towards the armchair by the wall before getting to work on my pants. I would have to clean up that mess in the morning. Right now, I needed sleep because tomorrow I would be doing something that filled me with more dread than being cornered by the Void. I was going to confront my parents about their lies. Rolling into bed, I pulled the cover over me. This was going to be rough.

CHAPTER 17

His warm powerful body moved underneath me. I pulled on the reins as we left the wide road behind and started down the smaller one on the right. The large black stallion I had borrowed from the stables let out a disappointed snort that our thundering gallop was over, but slowed to a trot. Leaning down, I patted him on the neck as our destination rose before us.

The mansion was a symbol of power. Built entirely of white stone, the rectangular structure gleamed like a jewel among the surrounding farms. An allée of trees ran from the main road to the front of the house and manicured gardens spread out around it. I watched the bright fall sun play across the canopy above before turning back to the building ahead. The Beaufort mansion. My former home.

Sadness drifted through me at the sight of it. I still remembered the day that Prince Edric's people came and took me. They hadn't been violent or anything, but the fact that they had come to conscript me into Prince Edric's service had come as a complete shock to me. And that small pathetic part inside my heart wished that my family had fought harder for me. Or fought at all, really. Far from all half-elves were slaves. Hell, slavery didn't even exist in all courts. And there were plenty of people like me, both in my court and the other courts, who lived normal lives. My particular magical skill was most likely what had drawn Prince Edric's attention, I knew that, and one did not refuse an elven prince. But still. The naïve child in me couldn't help wishing that my family had somehow found a way to stop him anyway.

"Miss Kenna!"

Coming to a complete stop before the white stairs leading up to the front door, I turned in the saddle to find a young man with brown hair hurrying out of the stables. A wide smile decorated his face.

"Hello, Anders," I said. The sadness in my chest disappeared as a smile spread across my own lips.

I had always liked the excited stable hand. He was nineteen, just like me, and before I was forced into Prince Edric's service, we had more or less grown up together. His family tended the horses and gardens here at the mansion so he had always been around when I lived here. There was something so carefree about him that it always made me smile, and he had always treated me as if I was actually a member of the Beaufort family, which was something I truly appreciated.

"It's so good to see you!" Anders brushed hay off his loose shirt as he ran towards me. "It's been a while."

Swinging a leg over the side of my horse, I jumped down and landed on the ground right as Anders reached us. "I know, it really has. It's good to see you too."

He took the stallion's reins and ran a calloused hand over

its neck before turning to peer at me again. "Just visiting or is it business?"

"Business, I'm afraid. I have to get going soon again."

"Totally get it. I won't keep you then." He flashed me a grin and began leading the horse away. "I'll just spend some time with this beauty until you're ready to leave."

"Thanks, Anders."

It was indeed business that had brought me to see my parents this morning. For a moment, I just stared up at the front door while cold dread seeped into my stomach. I was not looking forward to this conversation. Blowing out a deep breath, I ran my fingers through my long red curls to smoothen them after the ride, and then ascended the stairs.

A grand door made of pale wood rose before me, but since this was technically my home too, I didn't bother knocking and instead just strode inside. The white stone foyer beyond was empty. I swept my gaze across the shining surfaces in an attempt to figure out where my parents could be at this hour. Before I could come to a conclusion, an older man with graying temples appeared from a room on my right.

"Kenna," he said.

"Jorgen." I motioned vaguely at the building around us. "Do you know where my parents are?"

Jorgen, who had been a butler here for as long as I could remember, cleared his throat and rested his hands behind his back. "Lord and Lady Beaufort are indisposed at the moment."

"Indisposed?"

"They are still sleeping."

Surprised, I frowned at him. *Sleeping? At this hour?* Though, I supposed that sleeping in was something rich people with no actual job titles could afford.

Jorgen motioned at the room on his left. "You can wait in the receiving room if you like."

I knew that he was probably just doing it out of formality but every word out of the aging butler's mouth made me feel like I was a guest instead of an actual member of the family. It made that small pathetic part of my heart crack a little.

"Sure," I said and followed Jorgen towards the neat room my parents used when receiving strangers who came to visit unexpectedly.

Plopping down on the blue velvet couch, I settled in to wait for the noble lord and lady to deign to rise out of bed. While tracing patterns in the arm of the sofa, I rehearsed what I was going to say. With every minute I waited, the dread built further in my chest.

When I finally heard soft footsteps descending the stairs and moving towards me, my heart was thumping in my chest. Wood creaked as the door swung open. I pushed to my feet right as Elmer and Adeline Beaufort entered the room.

"Ah, Kenna," Elmer said. "I assume you have come to deliver the money."

"No." Irritation slashed through my anxiety and I drew myself up to my full height. "I've come for answers."

Lord Beaufort came to a halt on the dark blue carpet and blinked at me. "Excuse me?"

"I went to Collum last night in order to clear your debt."

My mother cringed because she knew where this was going.

"Yeah, exactly." I gave them a hard stare. "He was mighty confused because he's never lent you any money. Why did you lie to me?"

"Lie?" Elmer harrumphed. "We–"

"No," I interrupted. "I don't want any excuses. Here is

what's going to happen. You are going to tell me why you lied to me and who it is that you really owe all this money to. Right now."

"Don't you dare take that tone with me." He took a step towards me while his face flashed red in outrage. "I am a lord and you–"

"Elmer," my mother said and placed a hand on her husband's arm. When he grunted in agreement, she turned back to me. "Of course we will tell you. After all, we need your help." She motioned for us to sit down. "But, Kenna dear, please think about how you address others. You need to learn how to be polite and ask or request when you want something. Giving orders is unseemly. Especially for... someone like you."

Fiery rage flared up inside me at her words but was quickly smothered by the cold and oily feeling of shame. Maybe I *had* pushed a bit too hard? They might be my parents but they were also elite members of society whom very few people had the right to order around. Especially someone like... well, someone like me.

A small cloud of dust swirled into the air as Lord Elmer dropped onto the couch opposite me. Adeline seated herself on his left and smoothened her blue dress over her legs. Expelling a weary breath, I sat down as well.

"Who do you really owe the money to?" I asked.

My parents exchanged a glance.

"One of the other human lords," Elmer finally replied.

Keeping my face carefully neutral, I flicked my gaze between the two of them. "Which one?"

For a moment, no one said anything. I waited patiently while Elmer seemed to fight some kind of internal struggle. Next to him, my mother placed a graceful hand on his knee and gave it an encouraging squeeze. After drawing in a breath, he opened his mouth to finally reply.

Raised voices came from outside the door. The three of us shot to our feet as Jorgen's distraught voice cut through the house, followed by stomping boots. We had barely gotten to our feet when the door to the receiving room banged open. Delicate glass figurines clinked in distress as they toppled over when the door slammed into the shelf behind it.

"Morning." Lord Arquette strolled into the room, accompanied by two men who looked like they had more muscle than brain. "Elmer. Adeline." When his blue eyes landed on me, a cruel smile curled his lips. "And Kenna." He dragged his gaze up and down my body. "What a surprise to see you here. At this time of day, I thought you'd still be warming Prince Edric's sheets."

Taking a step forward, I was about to spit something equally vicious back in his face but Lord Beaufort cut me a scathing look in warning before I could.

"Lord Arquette," he said instead. "What brings you here?"

Behind the uninvited lord and his two bodyguards, Jorgen stood looking flustered by the open door. Elmer motioned for him to withdraw. The aging butler looked furious at having been unable to stop Lord Arquette from just barging in, but he bowed to Elmer and closed the door to the receiving room.

"You know why I'm here," Lord Arquette said. "You're running out of time. I want my money."

"You will get your money," Elmer growled. "We still have a few days."

"Yes. No stress, though." He wandered through the room, inspecting the different shelves before drawing a finger down the gleaming white wall next to him. "If you can't come up with the money, I'll just have to settle for the house." His hungry eyes lingered on me for a moment before sliding back to Elmer. "Unless you have something else that you want to sell?"

"How dare you come into my home and threaten me in this way?"

"If you didn't want me to threaten you, you should have thought about that before you lost a king's ransom to me while gambling."

It took great effort not to turn and openly gape at my adoptive father. They were in debt and about to lose their home because he had *gambled* the money away? By all the gods and spirits, how could he have been so reckless?

"You will get your money." Lord Beaufort cleared his throat and placed a protective arm around his wife's shoulders while flicking nervous eyes between Arquette and the two muscled men who still remained by the door. "Now, please leave."

"You have five days, Elmer." He waved a hand to encompass the room. "If you do not have the money when I return on the fifth day, all this will be mine."

Lord Beaufort said nothing as Arquette sauntered out of the room with his bodyguards behind him. The door swung shut with a soft click. As soon as the footsteps had receded on the other side, I whirled around to face my parents.

"Patricia and Elvin said you lost it in some farming investment gone bad." I stabbed a hand in Elmer's direction. "But you gambled it away! That's why you lied about owing Collum money." Pressing my fingers to my temple, I shook my head. "How could you jeopardize our house like this?"

"First of all, it's not our house. It's *my* house," he snapped. "And I have warned you once already not to take that tone with me. Now, are you going to help or not?"

"Kenna dear," my mother added in a pleading voice. "We know that you have money to spare. Can you not find it in your heart to help your family? Surely you do not want us to end up on the street, do you?"

"Of course not, Mother." I stared at the now closed door where Lord Arquette had disappeared while the desperate yearning for freedom battled the rising guilt in my chest.

"So you will give us the money?"

Every selfish survival instinct inside me was screaming 'no!' but they were swiftly being drowned out by Patricia's voice telling me that I didn't need to buy my freedom right now. After all, what was a few more years of slavery in the face of my elven lifespan? If I didn't help my family right now, they would be ruined.

"Yes." I heaved a deep sigh. "Yes, I will give you the money. I'll make sure it's all here in five days when Lord Arquette comes back."

"Good." Elmer gave me a curt nod.

Shaking off the heavy feeling that was settling in my stomach, I just expelled another sigh and walked out.

Anders could probably read whatever was on my face when I descended the smooth white steps outside the front door because he only handed me back the reins and wished me well. After a mumbled response, I climbed into the saddle and took off without a second look back.

Too many emotions were fighting like beasts inside me so I spurred the black stallion into a gallop and lost myself in the wind ripping through my hair. Yellow, orange, and red flashed past in the corner of my vision as I hurtled through the fall-colored landscape. The thundering hooves and the powerful muscles shifting underneath me helped chase away the cold feeling that had been burrowing into my chest like slimy worms.

When I finally reached the grand city at the heart of the Court of Stone, schemes were swirling in my mind instead. If I had to give my money away, I was going to get my freedom another way. And I had just the plan.

Slowing to a walk, I made my way through the bustling streets and towards the white castle.

It was a simple yet daring plan. I was going to blackmail my way to freedom. One last time. It was going to be the riskiest scheme I had ever pulled off because I would need to fool not one, not two, but three elven princes, as well as a certain lowborn elf in the Court of Trees. Not to mention every single spy in my own court, including the Void.

I would stick to my original assignment to find the Dagger of Orias, but I wasn't going to give it to Prince Edric. Or Mordren Darkbringer. No, I was going to get the dagger for myself. And then I was going to use it to get my freedom in a way no one would ever even expect.

A wicked smile drifted over my lips as I crested the final hill to the palace.

I was going to blackmail the King of Elves.

CHAPTER 18

Merry chatter hung in the air. Everywhere I looked, I found excited elves strolling across the moss-covered forest floor and bright-faced vendors calling out encouragements. Wood and metal clinked at the game booths, and the heavenly scent of well-seasoned meat and vegetables drifted from frying pans. Laughter rang out from the families gathered at the tables scattered throughout the forest. Tilting my head up, I turned in a slow circle and watched the colorful decorations tied between the trees. I knew I was here on a job, but the fall fête at the Court of Trees was certainly something to behold.

"It really is pretty, isn't it?"

Tipping my head back down, I found Evander watching me. After the meeting with my family this morning, my head wasn't really in the game but I forced my mind back to the task at hand anyway and plastered a smile on my face.

"Yeah, it really is. Did you used to come here with your family before... well, before you came to live at the castle?"

A wistful smile drifted over his lips. "We sure did. I think everyone in the Court of Trees comes here. Maybe not for the full week, but at least for one day." He chuckled. "Besides, we common people need somewhere to celebrate too, while all the fancy folk are at the king's equinox ball."

The reminder sent a spike of panic through me. If I hadn't located the Dagger of Orias before that ball, there was a big chance that whoever had it would use it to kill King Aldrich at the event. And that would mean I couldn't blackmail him with the dagger to get my freedom. Not to mention that our entire world would most likely also descend into civil war. But that somehow felt a bit less important. Regardless, I had to find the dagger. A dark voice whispered at the back of my mind that the dagger might not even be in the Court of Trees, and if it wasn't, all my scheming would have been for nothing anyway. I smothered it and turned to Evander instead.

"True." I looped my arm through his while we walked, and glanced up at him with a secretive smile. "But this year, we will both be at the ball."

"That we will." A soft blush colored his cheeks at my casual touch but he drew me closer. "And now I suddenly find myself looking forward to a ball. Who would've thought?"

I giggled and pushed a lock of hair back behind my ear. "Me too."

A brisk fall wind swirled through the trees, making the leaves flutter in the afternoon sun and bringing with it the smell of damp soil and fresh grass. I drew my dark green cloak tighter around my shoulders.

"Here." Evander steered us to a small table on our right. "This should help us keep warm."

The scratched wooden table was filled to the brim with small ceramic mugs. A large iron pot hung over a low-burning fire next to it and each time the silver-haired elf behind it stirred the pot, it released an aroma of spices.

"Two, please," Evander said to the smiling female.

After filling two mugs with the dark red liquid, she handed them to us. "There you go, dears."

"Thank you." He paid her before taking my free arm again and steering us back into the slow-moving crowd. Turning to me, he grinned and lifted the small mug.

I clinked mine against his before lifting it to my lips.

The mulled wine tasted rich and fruity and left a pleasant warmth in my chest. I took a few more sips before deciding to start my covert interrogation again. Only, Evander beat me to it.

"What's your family like?" he asked with a genuinely open and curious expression on his face. "Do you ever go to things like this with them?"

"Oh, uhm…" I brought the cup to my lips again in order to buy some time to think.

These were the kinds of topics I preferred to stay away from. Whenever Evander and I spent time together, we talked a lot but I never really shared anything. Unless it would benefit me.

"No, not really," I said as I lowered the mug of mulled wine again. "There isn't really a lot of stuff like this to go to in the Court of Stone."

That was a blatant lie. We had celebrations too, of course. I had just never attended any as a normal person. Only as a spy.

"Which is why I really love being here with you now," I added and stepped a little closer.

"Then we should definitely make the most of it!" Evander pulled me towards a booth with a small table and a wide board with round circles a short distance from it. "Have you ever played darts?"

"Is that the game where you throw the little arrows at the…" I frowned and waved a hand at the painted red and green circles.

"Yep." Grinning from ear to ear, he picked up a cluster of darts and handed them to me. "Give it a try."

Luckily, I was pretty bad at shooting and throwing things so I already knew that I would suck at this. Showing that I was skilled at something had never worked out well for me when I was trying to seduce someone. People liked feeling good about themselves, so making them feel inferior by beating them in something was never a good strategy. Which was why I was glad I didn't have to fake being bad.

The first dart whizzed through the air and hit the edge of the wooden board before falling to the ground. I laughed and threw the other darts. They hit terrible spots too but at least a few of them actually stuck to the board.

I drew a hand through my hair and let out an embarrassed giggle. "Oh spirits, I'm so bad at this. Can't you show me how it's supposed to be done?"

"Of course. It's easy once you get the hang of it."

While he threw his darts at the board, I finished the rest of my mulled wine and let out an impressed *oh* and *ah* at the appropriate moments. His green eyes glittered in the sun as he turned to me with a wide smile after successfully hurling tiny arrows at a wooden board.

"See, it's all in the wrist." After handing over our mugs to a passing dish collector, he picked up another dart and handed it to me. "I'll show you."

Placing his hands on my shoulders, he guided me into the right position. Then he took my wrist and lifted it up to show

how to throw the dart. His breath tickled my neck as he explained the technique. I deliberately leaned back into his warm body, making him stutter through his next explanation.

When I finally threw the dart and it actually landed inside the outer ring, he beamed like the sun itself. I laughed and swatted him on the arm while he led me towards another booth. This one was filled with fried venison and vegetables. After purchasing two plates and two cups of wine, we sat down opposite each other at a well-used wooden table.

"This is my favorite food at the fête," Evander said and motioned at the plates. "I eat it every year and it somehow always tastes better than the year before." Lifting the cup, he grinned at me. "The wine is pretty good too."

I raised my own. "Well, cheers then."

"Cheers."

The wine *was* good. And so was the food. The fruity flavor of the wine paired perfectly with the berries they had used to season the venison. I smiled as I dug in. Evander did the same.

Since he was now feeling good about himself, both after showing off his skills at darts and after some food and wine in his stomach, I tried once more to get the conversation back on track. At least the track I wanted.

"So, anything interesting happen since we saw each other last?" I asked while sipping innocently from my wine cup.

"Well, I did almost get arrested last night."

I choked on my wine. Slapping a hand in front of my mouth, I tried to avoid spitting it all over the table as incredulous laughter bubbled up my throat. Evander chuckled and scratched the back of his head while I forced myself to swallow the mouthful of wine.

"You what?" I croaked once the wine-spraying hazard had been dealt with.

"You know how there are like tons of passageways and stuff in the castle? I was just wandering the halls last night because, well, I didn't really have anything better to do. So then I ended up in the ballroom and there was this door I'd never seen before, so I walked through it." He lifted his shoulders in an embarrassed shrug. "Next thing I know, there are guards with swords yelling at me."

My scheming mind lit up but I simply laughed and asked, "How did you explain your way out of that?"

"I told them what I told you, but they almost didn't believe it because the door was so close to the royal area." He speared a fried mushroom with his fork and waved it in the air while mimicking the voice of a fancy noble. "Shame on you. Your peasant feet almost trod the sacred ground of nobility. Oh, the horror!"

A laugh erupted from my chest. He blinked in surprise at the boisterous sound. And so did I. Every smile, every giggle, every touch, and every word this afternoon had been a calculated move. None of it real. Only a carefully planned manipulation in order to get him to like me and trust me. But *that* had been my real laugh. This elf from somewhere on the outskirts of the Court of Trees had somehow managed to bring out the real me for a second.

"I can't believe you almost got arrested for walking," I pressed out between bursts of laughter.

Evander popped the mushroom in his mouth and raised a finger in the air. "Ah, but the keyword in that sentence is *almost.*"

Another bout of real laugher bubbled from my throat. While still grinning, I shook my head and took another swig of wine. Seducing Evander was a job, I knew that, but sitting there with him under the sunlit canopy of leaves, laughing about silly things, I realized that I actually liked spending time with him. He made me feel comfortable. Like I belonged. It made something warm and fuzzy sparkle in my chest.

As we finished up our meal and moved on to a different part of the fall fête, I tried to ignore the nagging feeling of guilt that was creeping in from all sides.

I might like spending time with Evander.

But I would still have to betray him.

CHAPTER 19

*L*ast time I had seen this grand hall, it had been filled with music, color, and people. Now, the ballroom at Iwdael's Court of Trees lay silent and dark. Moving quietly, I snuck towards the luxurious area that the royals usually occupied. Evander had said that there was supposed to be a hidden door somewhere here, and if he had almost gotten arrested walking through it, then it had to lead to some kind of secret room. Hopefully, one that contained the Dagger of Orias.

After spending the entire afternoon yesterday with Evander, I had gone back to the Court of Stone to plan this break-in. It had taken most of the night and the day today, but it had been worth it because I had gotten inside the palace and into the ballroom without a hitch. I had told the others that it was another stunt to gather intel, so that I could get Felix to worldwalk me here and then back again in a few hours without them knowing that I might have found the dagger. Because otherwise, I wouldn't be able to use it to blackmail the King of Elves.

The usually so colorful furniture looked gray in the poor light but it was no less impressive. Divans, couches, and tables in intricate designs filled the floor at the front of the room. I weaved through them and approached the wall behind. Starting in one end, I walked the length of the wall while running a gloved hand along the uneven surface of the wood.

As I neared the middle of the section, I could make out dark cracks in the wall up ahead. I stopped once I reached them. It was indeed the marks of a door cut into the wood. No wonder Evander had stumbled onto it. It wasn't exactly hidden. Which begged the question, how in the world had I missed this earlier?

After scowling at the slab of wood for another couple of seconds without coming up with an adequate explanation, I checked that my black mask was securely fastened over my face and stepped through the door.

A long corridor shrouded in darkness met me. I remained standing just inside the door for a while in order to get my bearings. Once my eyes had become accustomed to the thicker blackness inside the passageway, I started down it on silent feet. Since I had no idea what awaited me in here, I hadn't been able to form a plan for this part. Instead, I was forced to simply play it by ear.

The hallway changed up ahead. I slowed down even more as I reached the top of a flight of stairs. Peering down, I tried to see what awaited me at the bottom but the shadows were even thicker there. *Shit*. I didn't like basements. They severely limited my ability to walk through walls, because if there was no empty space on the other side, my powers wouldn't work.

I glanced back at the dark corridor behind me. There was nothing else for it. I had to go downstairs if I was ever going to find out if the dagger was here. Steeling my slamming heart, I blew out a long breath and descended the stairs.

Everything smelled cold, wet, and musky. Like damp soil and decaying leaves. But nothing jumped out to attack me. Yet. I stayed close to the wall as I slunk down the final steps and into the space beyond. Another hallway. This one was much shorter though, and it ended in a massive wooden door. I stopped before it.

Hoping against hope that there was another room on the side of the corridor, I turned to the right and walked straight into the wall. A dull thud rang out as my body connected with the solid wall of packed earth. I rubbed a sore spot on my shoulder as I silently cursed the inconvenient wall and turned back to the door ahead. No other way but through. After brushing a hand over the hilt of my sword and knife, I stepped through the door.

Bright light blinded me. I threw myself backwards again as clamor rose around me, but before I could phase back through the door, something yanked me forward by the front of my jacket. On reflex, I dove slightly to the side in order to break the path my attacker had picked for me.

My hands went straight to my weapons as I rolled to my feet in a ring of dark figures. Blinking furiously, I tried to get my vision to adjust back to the brighter conditions. When it finally cleared, I found myself surrounded by an entire squad of guards in the brown leather armor favored by the Court of Trees.

"You're trespassing," one of them snapped. "Identify yourself."

Gripping my weapons tighter, I turned in a slow circle to keep them all in view while also searching for the dagger. And a way out.

"Identify yourself," the blond elf ordered again.

My eyes glided over tables filled with mugs and discarded dice and playing cards. This wasn't some secret treasure room. It was the breakroom for the palace guards. No wonder Evander had almost been arrested barging in here in the middle of the night. And now I was about to be too. Fantastic.

"Is she alone?" the guard asked his men before jerking his head in the direction of the door. "Go check the corridor."

No. That was my only way out. If they got there before I did, there was no chance in hell I would be able to escape. Throwing caution to the wind, I made a decision. And lunged at the elf closest to the door.

He threw his sword up to block the strike but my surprise attack had caught him off guard and he barely managed to parry as I shoved him a step to the side. Steel whooshed through the air behind me. I slammed up my knife over my head while drawing my sword in a wide arch. The sword coming at me from behind crashed into my raised knife and absorbed the impact while my swiping blade kept the other attackers at bay.

Twisting around, I redirected the sword blocking my knife and whirled around to face the elf attached to it. He jumped back just before my blade could find its mark.

The move bought me a precious second of respite that I used to dive towards the door.

Pain crackled through me as my roll was interrupted by a boot to the side of my ribs. The force sent me skidding across the floor. Brown leather boots hurried towards me as I came to an abrupt halt against the wall. Sucking in a breath, I suppressed the urge to press a hand to my ribs and instead swung my sword with every smidgen of strength I had.

Startled yelps rang out as the advancing guards were

forced to jump in order to avoid getting their ankles severed. Only rising into a crouch in order to save time, I used the second of grace to launch myself at the door.

A curtain of sheets whispered against my skin as I passed through it but the pleasant feeling was soon replaced by pain. I had leaped through at an angle, which had me slamming into the packed dirt wall outside the door. I shook my head to clear the dancing black spots from my vision and then took off in a sprint right as the door was ripped open behind me.

Taking the steps three at a time, I raced up the stairs while shouts of pursuit echoed behind me. I rammed my weapons back in their holsters just as the wooden door appeared before me. Not even slowing a fraction, I dashed right through it and into the empty ballroom.

And then, everything was silent again. The guards still hadn't made it through the door but as soon as they did, they would see me and the hunt would be on again. Pushing my legs to go as fast as possible, I flew through the maze of furniture and sprinted towards the closest wall. Wood banged behind me as the door to the secret corridor was thrown open but I was already through the wall before it had even finished vibrating.

Cool night air enveloped me. I continued running while trying to figure out the best course of action. Felix wouldn't be back to pick me up for another couple of hours. There were probably rogue worldwalkers for hire in the Court of Trees too, just like in my court, but the problem was that I didn't know any in this court. Which left only one option. I was going to have to hide until Felix showed up.

With my heart slamming in my chest, I darted through the hedge formation in the royal gardens. Leaves flapped in annoyance as I barged ahead.

There was still a chance that the guards hadn't seen which wall I ran through. And even if they had, they would have to go around and exit through a door like normal people, which gave me a head start.

The tall palace walls rose in the distance. Praying to whatever gods or spirits were listening, I hoped that no one was stationed at this exact spot as I set course for a section of the wall and ran through it.

A dense forest appeared before me. No guards. I whipped my head from side to side before taking off towards the nearest cluster of buildings. Pressing myself into the wooden wall, I edged upwards and peered into the window of the closest one. It was dark but I thought I could make out crates stacked along the back wall.

Hiding too close to the castle was dangerous, but so was hurtling blindly through the forest hoping that I wouldn't run into anyone. I cast a glance over my shoulder. No alarms sounded into the night. Yet. But it was only a matter of time and it was always better to already have a hiding place when that happened than to be chased through the woods like a rabbit. After peering into the darkened building one more time to make sure that it really was empty, I slipped through the wall.

The air inside was stale and dusty, but at least it was free of traps. I snuck a bit further into the room before sinking down on the floor. Tipping my head back against a crate, I pushed the mask back into my hood and heaved a few deep breaths.

"Did you get it?"

I shot to my feet with both blades in my hands. A dark-haired elf advanced on me with lethal grace. My mouth dropped open.

"Mordren," I blurted out.

The Prince of Shadows raised his eyebrows. "Oh, it's *Mordren* now, is it? A bit casual, don't you think? What happened to *my prince*?"

"What are you doing here?" I said, completely ignoring his jabs.

"I said, did you get it?"

"Get what?"

"The dagger, of course."

Mordren was quickly closing the distance between us and even though I was the one with the weapons, I found myself retreating. I was almost at the wall when I realized that I didn't know if I would be better off phasing through it and taking my chances with the guards out there or staying here with the Prince of Shadows. However, before I could make a decision, dark tendrils shot towards me.

"No leaving yet," Mordren said as his shadows wrapped around my arms and pinned them to the wall above my head. "First, you have to answer my question. Did you get the Dagger of Orias?"

"Does it look like I got it?" I tried to gesture at my frazzled looks but only managed to wave my weapons back and forth against the wall. "I was investigating what I thought was a secret treasure room but that turned out to be a breakroom for the palace guards."

"Is that so?" He pushed down my hood and then plucked the knife from my left hand. After spinning it in his hand, he trailed the point down along my arm, across my collarbone, and then over my chest before finally positioning the tip right over my heart. Holding the blade steady, he locked eyes with me. "Is that really so?"

I drew shallow breaths to avoid impaling myself. "Yes."

For a moment, Mordren Darkbringer held my gaze as if he could see straight into my very soul. Then he huffed a short laugh and removed the blade. "How unfortunate." His shadows released my wrists and slithered back to their master, who handed the knife back to me but jerked his chin towards the two blades. "Put those away. Before I make you."

I glared at him but did as he said. "How did you even know I was breaking in tonight?"

"I know everything."

"Right," I snorted.

Turning slowly, he arched a dark eyebrow at me in challenge. I cleared my throat and glanced away but didn't apologize. He took a step forward, making me retreat on instinct. When a satisfied smirk spread across his lips, I knew that the power play had been intentional.

"So, what's the plan?" Mordren waved a hand at the crate-filled building around us while a mocking laugh slipped his lips. "You're just going to hide out here all night?"

Crossing my arms, I raised my chin but said nothing. When I didn't reply, the smile on his mouth grew and his silver eyes glittered in amusement.

"That *is* your plan. And here I thought you were actually good at your job." He took another step towards me. "Haven't you even arranged for someone to worldwalk you home?"

"Of course I have," I snapped. "But they won't be here for another two hours."

"I see." Mordren lifted one shoulder in a nonchalant shrug. "I could take you home."

Suspicion crept into my mind and I narrowed my eyes at him. "That right?"

"Hmm."

"Is there a cost?"

A chuckle drifted through the air. "Smart girl."

Taking another step forward, he closed the final distance between us. My back was already against the wall, so unless I phased through it, there was no more space left to retreat to. The Prince of Shadows placed a hand on the wood next to my head and leaned down until his lips brushed my ear.

"With me, there usually is." His warm breath danced over my skin as he huffed another laugh. "If *you* had been the one to ask *me*, then I would have made you… do something for me in return." He drew back and instead locked eyes with me. "But since I just," a smile curled his lips, "*happened* to be in the vicinity, and since I'm feeling generous tonight, I'll let you have this one for free. Just this once."

I was pretty sure I was supposed to say thank you. At least, that's what someone who possessed a shred of common sense would do when the freaking Prince of Shadows offered to bail you out for free. But I couldn't quite bring myself to do it.

"Then I accept," I simply said instead.

Mordren's smirk grew as he took a step back and curled a finger at me, forcing me to come to him. I swallowed the rude reply on my tongue and stalked up to him. When he only looked at me expectantly, I blew out a breath and put my arms around him.

His lean muscles shifted against my body as he twisted and looped an arm around my back as well. Heat flared into my cheeks but before I could change my mind, the world spun around me and I felt as though I was folding in on myself.

Then the cramped cabin in the woods was replaced by a city of white stone. I drew a deep breath to steady my stomach and reorient myself. A soft chuckle ruffled my hair. It took another second for me to realize that I still had my arms around the Prince of Shadows. I jerked back.

"Here we are," he said, and motioned at the tall white walls that surrounded the castle.

I flicked my gaze in that direction before glancing back at him. "Thank you."

"Huh, so you did find your manners in the end." Reaching out, he placed light fingers under my chin and leaned closer. "Make sure they're there from the start the next time we meet."

Before I could take back the 'thank you' and curse him instead, he released me and worldwalked away. Muttering profanities under my breath, I stalked towards the front gates of Prince Edric's castle.

The guards cast curious glances at my weapons but let me in without question. Since it was so late in the night, no one else stopped me on my way to the spy wing. After slipping a quick note under Felix's door that I was already back, I staggered into my room.

But I had barely returned my sword, knife, and jacket to the hidden compartment before a knock sounded at my door. For a moment, I considered pretending to already be asleep but then the knock came again. Dragging a hand through my messy hair, I walked back to face whoever was on the other side.

"Kenna, you're awake," Monette said as soon as I opened the door.

"Yeah, I just got back from my mission." I frowned at her. "What's wrong?"

"Nothing, it's just…" She breezed past me and turned a couple of times in my room before continuing. "I've been doing really well in the Court of Water and I've managed to search almost the whole castle, but there's one place I can't get into." A hopeful smile graced her lips as she looked up at me through her lashes. "But you could."

"Okay?" I stared at her until she elaborated.

"So, well, I guess I was wondering if you could go and check it out?"

"Right now?"

"Yeah."

Exhaustion washed over me like a tidal wave. I was tired. Tired after my late nights trying to figure out how to clear my family's debt, after being blackmailed by the Prince of Shadows, after the meeting with my family yesterday, after dealing with the guilt of using Evander as my key to the castle, and after the near disaster tonight. I rubbed a hand over my sore ribs that still ached from the fight. All I wanted was to sleep for a few hours.

"Look, Monette," I began. "I would love to help you but it's been a really long day. A long week, actually. And I really need to sleep."

"Okay. I understand." Her bottom lip quivered slightly as she nodded. "I just thought that since we were friends, I could come to you for help but... It's fine. I get it."

Blond hair fluttered behind her as she strode back towards the door. Guilt burrowed into my chest.

"Wait." I heaved a sigh so deep I thought it would never end. "Alright. I'll do it."

Her turquoise eyes lit up. "You will? I knew I could count on you."

I cast one last longing look at the bed I had spent far too little time in lately but then tied my hair back and followed Monette out the door.

This was going to be a long night.

Again.

CHAPTER 20

"You have disappointed me." Stone rumbled around us as Prince Edric slammed his fist down on the arm of his throne. "The fall equinox is tomorrow and you still haven't managed to locate the Dagger of Orias."

I had to very subtly keep a hand on the stone bookcase next to me in order to avoid toppling over. Helping Monette had taken most of the night and I had only managed to cram in two hours of sleep before the Prince of Stone had summoned us all to another spy meeting.

"The only one who has managed to produce some kind of result is Monette," Edric continued and swung a hand in the direction of the blond half-elf. "Yesterday, she finished sweeping the entire palace in the Court of Water and has successfully been able to rule out Prince Rayan."

Monette beamed like a satisfied cat at the praise while the rest of us were trying to keep the dread at bay.

"What the hell have the rest of you been doing?" Prince Edric demanded, his face darkening and his granite eyes flashing as he shot to his feet. Powerful muscles shifted under his white shirt as he stabbed a hand in my direction. "Especially you. Not only have you produced no results whatsoever, you also caused a scene in the Court of Trees last night!"

"I–" I began but he cut me off.

"You were *lucky* they didn't figure out it was you! Do you have any idea the kind of strain it would put on our relationship if Iwdael found out that I had been spying on him?"

I wanted to scream that *I* was the one who had cleared an entire wing in the Court of Water last night. The one who had confirmed that Prince Rayan didn't have the dagger. That I *had* produced results. But I didn't. Instead, I dropped my gaze.

"I'm sorry, my prince," I said. "It won't happen again."

"No, it won't."

Stone cracked and shifted throughout the room. My survival instincts were screaming at me to disappear through the wall but I ignored them and remained in my position by the bookshelf. Only when the noise had stopped did I dare look back up at the prince. His gray eyes were still hard but the fury was gone from his face.

"We have one last shot at this," Edric said. "Tomorrow. At the ball. If whoever has the dagger plans to assassinate King Aldrich, then they will do it at the equinox ball. After that, they would have to wait another few months for his next public appearance, and if I was sitting on the Dagger of Orias and planned to kill the King of Elves, I would want to get to it before I was found out and executed."

"Why can't you just tell King Aldrich about the dagger?" Felix blurted out. "You know, so that he can look out for it?"

"Because the king is a kind and trusting soul." Admiration

mixed with sadness drifted across Edric's face. "He would never believe that any of us would try to kill him. So if I were to tell him about this, he would just think that I was trying to paint the other princes in a bad light."

And that would worsen Prince Edric's chances of being selected as the next King of Elves, I finished in my mind.

Felix's copper-colored brows were still furrowed and he looked like he was about to continue the line of inquiry, but the Prince of Stone pressed on before he could.

"As I was saying…" He stared at Felix until the half-elf shut his mouth again. "Tomorrow is our last chance of finding the dagger. Whoever has it will be carrying it on them, which means that you need to find excuses to stealthily search our suspects."

"You want us to frisk an elven prince?" Tena, the brown-haired half-elf who had been working the Court of Fire, openly gaped at Edric while incredulity colored her face.

"Yes. And not *an* elven prince. All of them."

"Spirits," she swore softly and shook her head. "Well, dibs on not getting the Prince of Fire."

Monette scoffed in reply. "You–"

"Enough!" Prince Edric snapped. The books on the shelves vibrated as he sent his power pulsing through the room. "Enough with the squabbling and the interruptions and the questions."

Dead silence descended on the room of spies as we all involuntarily shrank back.

"You *will* find a way to search the three remaining princes for the dagger." Edric heaved a sigh and nodded at Tena. "But you do have a point. You can't go after the prince whose court you've been infiltrating. It will look far too suspicious." His gaze flicked through the room. "Tena, you get Trees. Kenna,

Shadows. Monette, Fire. And, Ymas, I want you to check Prince Rayan. Just in case Monette missed something."

I sagged against the white bookcase. The cold stone against my shoulder helped anchor me as I fought against the wave of exhaustion and hopelessness that threatened to drown me.

Prince Edric was disappointed in me. I was no closer to finding the dagger or obtaining my freedom. All my money would be gone in a few days' time. I was starting to feel bad about seducing Evander because I was beginning to actually like him. Everything I did, I failed at. And now I was going to have to figure out a way to *frisk Mordren Darkbringer.*

Resting my temple against the cool stone surface, I stared unseeing at the marble wall ahead.

This was never going to work.

CHAPTER 21

The scenery took my breath away. Tilting my head back, I gaped at the view before me. We were standing high up on the slopes of a gigantic mountain, but the peak looked like it had been shaved off. In its place rose an awe-inspiring castle made of shining white stone. Twisting spires and archways reached towards the heavens and stained glass glinted in the bright moonlight. Soft white clouds swirled around the whole mountaintop.

"Wow," I breathed.

"Yeah," Felix said, equally stunned, before tearing his gaze from King Aldrich's sparkling palace and shaking his head. "I have to get going." He cast a longing glance at Monette before stepping back. "Have fun."

Before I could reply, he had already disappeared into thin air.

The only way to get to Aldrich Spiritsinger's castle was to worldwalk to the somewhat flat plateau that encircled the top of the mountain and then walk the final stretch up to the gates. That meant that everyone who possessed the worldwalking skill had their work cut out for them tonight, ferrying partygoers to the ball.

I ran through several plans and scenarios in my head while waiting for everyone in Prince Edric's entourage to arrive. Since I was pretty sure that Mordren didn't actually have the Dagger of Orias, I only needed to do the barest amount of work there in order to satisfy Edric and then I could get started on finding the dagger for real. My spirits rose as everyone gathered and we finally started the walk up to the gates. This might actually work.

Once the guards had checked our papers, we were ushered into the palace. Music drifted from a pair of open doors at the end of the hall. The ordinary courtiers in our group were chattering and practically bouncing with nervous excitement while the handful of spies swept scrutinizing eyes across every surface. Prince Edric gave us a pointed look and a nod before striding through the wide doorway and into the ballroom. The rest of us waited another second to allow the prince to make an entrance before following him into the high-ceilinged hall.

It took great effort not to gawk.

The ballroom was bedecked in white stone, silver, and crystal. Clear gems sparkled in the dancing candlelight from hundreds of candelabras and the enormous chandelier in the vaulted ceiling glittered like ice in a bright winter sun. Tables covered in crisp white cloth held crystal goblets filled with different colored liquids, and silver plates were piled high with a multitude of food.

"Kenna," Monette whispered and gave my shoulder a soft push.

Realizing that I had stopped in the middle of the entrance,

I gave my head a quick shake and moved further into the room.

An orchestra was playing on a stage by the far wall and the dancefloor was already filled with well-dressed elves. I let my gaze glide over them while I made my way towards the nearest table and picked up a glass of sparkling wine.

Satisfaction coursed through me when I realized that I fit in rather well with this crowd. I was wearing a black dress with a skirt that fell like waves from my waist and a bodice that was covered in gold-studded black gems. There was no plunging neckline but it did leave my shoulders and arms bare. A fact I accented with golden jewelry and a hairstyle that pinned my long red curls up behind me before letting them flow down my back. I looked rich and powerful. Like I actually belonged in this place.

"Kenna? Is that you?"

Startled, I turned so quickly I almost spilled my drink. "Evander."

"Wow, I almost didn't recognize you." His eyes trailed up and down my body. "You look gorgeous."

A surprised chuckle slipped my lips. "Uhm, thanks... I think?"

"Oh, no, wait... I didn't mean that the way it came out." He scratched the back of his neck while a deep red color settled on his cheeks. "You always look beautiful. You just look extra beautiful tonight."

I smiled. "Thank you. You look great too, Evander."

He did. His short brown hair had been swept back and he was wearing a well-cut suit in black and dark green that matched his eyes.

"Thanks." He picked up a champagne flute and drained it in one go before turning back to me with a nervous laugh. "I feel a bit out of place here with all..." Waving the empty glass in front of himself, he motioned at the glittering dancefloor. "Well, this."

"At least we can feel out of place together, then." I gave him a secretive smile and placed both of our empty glasses on the table behind us before taking his arm. "Let's take a stroll through the room and see what fun we might encounter in this foreign territory."

Evander laughed. "Let's."

There was no sign of Iwdael or Mordren yet, so I needed to inventory what I had to work with and how I might use it to search for the dagger.

Up ahead, a group of already intoxicated male elves were giving each other subtle shoves and words of encouragement. It looked like they were gathering the courage to ask a cluster of females on the other side to dance. Their targets chatted among themselves, completely oblivious, at a table filled with plates of fruit.

"I bet you one drink that they won't have the courage to ask them," Evander said and nodded at the males.

Surprise pulled me out of my scheming and I looked up at him before flicking my gaze between the two groups ahead. "You know what, I'll take that bet. In fact, I'll bet you one drink that they'll go and ask them but that they'll get turned down."

Evander raised his eyebrows as we trailed to a halt. "Deal."

Elegant tunes from strings and piano mingled with joyous laughter all around us while we waited for the elven males to make their move. At last, the one at the front bounced up and down on his toes, gave his head a quick shake, and then strode towards the talking females. His friends exchanged a glance and then hurried after. When the encounter ended with apologetic smiles and embarrassed looks, Evander turned to stare at me.

"How did you know?" he asked.

I know how to read a room because I manipulate people for a living.

"Lucky guess," I said instead. Another glance across the ballroom informed me that all the elven princes had finally arrived. "Come on, we should–"

Silver trumpets rang out across the gleaming hall. As one, the whole party turned towards the grand double doors as a figure appeared in the space between them.

Aldrich Spiritsinger, the King of Elves, strode across the threshold with confident steps. His long white hair was held back from his face by a circlet of silver and his pale robes were trimmed with thread of the same color. Even from this distance, I could see the twinkle in his brown eyes as he smiled at the gathered crowd.

With the music now silent, the rustling of clothes and clinking of jewelry was audible throughout the ballroom as everyone in it bowed or curtsied for their king.

"Welcome to this year's fall equinox ball," King Aldrich called, his voice reverberating through the cavernous hall. "May the spirits guide our way."

"May the spirits guide our way," we all echoed.

He clapped his hands. "That's enough formality. Maestro, music please." Waving his hands in the air, he broke into a wide grin. "And do please join me on the dancefloor."

Scattered laughter answered the king's antics but all the elven princes and a lot of the nobles moved towards the shining dancefloor in the middle. An idea flashed into my mind.

Taking Evander by the hand, I pulled him towards the

section where the princes were lining up. "Come on, let's dance."

My unwitting companion blinked at me in surprise but before he could protest, I had already positioned us in the spot I wanted. Normally, you danced with your partner, but in formal dances like these, there were rules and predetermined steps. And the best part of all was something that would solve a lot of my problems tonight. Namely, that these formal dances involved switching partners.

The orchestra struck up a slow tune. I placed one hand in Evander's and the other on his shoulder. He glanced around nervously but moved us into the dance.

"This is making me feel even more out of place," he whispered as we took paced steps in the appropriate pattern.

"Same," I lied. "But I want to be able to tell my future children and grandchildren that I have danced on the same dancefloor as the King of Elves."

Evander's brows shot up, but then he grinned. "That is indeed a tale to tell."

As the first part of the song ended, he lifted his arm and spun me around. I twirled across the floor, my black skirts flowing around me, before ending up in the arms of Iwdael Vineweaver.

"My prince," I said and bowed my head while the Prince of Trees steered us into the next part on the dance.

"I saw you at my party the other week," he said. "You danced with Edric."

There was no question in there but I nodded anyway. When he spun me out and then pulled me back in again, I pressed a bit too close to him and drew my hand along his suit jacket on the way back to his shoulder. No dagger. Yet.

Iwdael locked eyes with me. "However did you get that stiff, uptight workaholic to dance at a party?"

A choked laugh ripped from my throat at the unexpected bluntness of his words. I hadn't planned it but I decided to use my involuntary outburst to my advantage and stumbled slightly into the prince's other side. While straightening again, I ran soft fingers over his other side. No dagger there either.

"Sorry," I said, and the embarrassment on my face was only half faked. "I... uhm. Your question caught me off guard."

"I can tell." His yellow eyes glittered mischievously as he raised his eyebrows at me. "Well, how did you get him to dance?"

Having regained my composure, I threw him a knowing smile. "I'm a person of many talents."

"I can tell that too." He grinned at me before tipping his head in the direction of a large round table. "Maybe you could work your magic on my wife as well?"

I glanced at Princess Syrene while her husband spun me in another circle. She was sitting with her friends, talking and laughing just like she had at the previous party.

"Princess Syrene doesn't like to dance?" I asked as Iwdael pulled me back again.

"No," he replied while I did one final and very subtle check to confirm that he indeed didn't have the dagger on him. "But she's happy with her friends, so I don't want to push her." The somber expression on his face disappeared and he winked at me. "But if you have some special magic, maybe just sprinkle it her way?"

Smiling, I gave him a nod even though it was very obviously a joke. "I'll see what I can do."

The music shifted again and the Prince of Trees spun me away and into another pair of arms. I glanced up to find

Mordren Darkbringer smirking at me. Taking my hand and waist in a firm grip, he moved us into the dance once more.

"Kenna," he said slowly, as if rolling my name over his tongue. "What a lovely surprise."

I bowed my head. "My prince."

"I see you remembered your manners today."

Looking back up, I met his amused gaze with a challenging stare of my own. "Well, we are in public, so..."

A midnight laugh drifted from his lips. The music swelled in a dramatic arch and our steps quickened to match it. His silver eyes never left mine as he guided us through it.

I let out a soft gasp as he drew me close and then leaned me back, tipping me towards the floor.

After the second of stunned surprise, I used our proximity and intimate position to run a hand over his body. Lean muscles met my fingertips through the fabric of his black shirt. They hardened as he pulled me back up again and I couldn't help but wonder what he would look like without a shirt. When a half smirk curled his lips, I caught myself and remembered the rumors about his mind reading ability. A furious blush flared into my cheeks.

"You find me attractive," Mordren stated.

I huffed. "Everyone finds you attractive so that's hardly noteworthy."

His hand trailed down to the small of my back as he drew me closer, pressing his honed body into mine. Leaning down, he placed his lips next to my ear. "Is that so?"

A shudder passed through me as his breath caressed my skin. I was having a hard time formulating complete sentences with his lips this close to my throat so I pulled back. Mordren's eyes glinted as he grinned at me, well aware of the effect he'd had on me. I blew out a breath and narrowed my eyes at him.

The Prince of Shadows was arrogant, entitled, and a bully. But he was damn attractive. Even though I hated him, I had to admit that. He was also incredibly dangerous. I kept that thought at the front of my mind as we finished our dance.

Since I already knew that he didn't have the dagger, I kept my hands to myself until Mordren spun me into another pair of arms.

Two down. Two to go.

CHAPTER 22

Worry gnawed at my chest. None of the elven princes had been carrying the Dagger of Orias, or any kind of weapon, for that matter. I cast a glance at the bright moon shining in through the tall stained-glass windows. Time was running out. If I didn't find the dagger soon, it might be too late.

"Kenna? Are you listening?"

I blinked. "Yes, sorry. What were you saying?"

A worried frown settled on Evander's face. "You seem distracted. Is something wrong?"

"No, of course not. I just…" I trailed off as my eyes scanned the crowd.

All evening, I had been tracking King Aldrich through the crowd to see who might be trying to get close. The merry king had chatted and laughed with several groups while making his way through the ballroom without issue. But now, the King of Elves was gone. Since this was *his* castle, it didn't surprise me that Aldrich was capable of suddenly disappearing to some other part of it without anyone noticing, but it made my job of making sure he didn't get assassinated a whole lot harder.

"I just need to find a bathroom," I finished while pushing to my feet.

"Oh, okay. Should I…?"

"No, no, it's fine." I gave his arm a quick squeeze before breezing past.

Setting course for the exit that King Aldrich had been closest to the last time I saw him, I walked as fast as I could without drawing attention. A set of glass doors had been thrown open along one wall. That had to be where the king went. I slipped through the increasingly intoxicated crowd until I reached the doors. Peering out, I found that they led to a balcony set into the side of the castle.

Moonlight bathed the white stone in silvery light and turned the potted plants the color of molten iron instead of green. I gathered up my black skirt in one hand and snuck out.

The king was standing by the railing on the far side of the balcony. His back was to the doors so he didn't see me as I slunk through the shadows and took up position behind a tall plant with thick leaves. Though to be fair, when one had been blessed with impenetrable stone skin, I supposed there was no need to be overly concerned with keeping an eye out for assassins.

For a moment, I just watched him from my hiding place.

His white hair shone like a river in the darkness but he stood perfectly still. With his hands behind his back, he stared out at the mountains around us. Wisps of cloud drifted lazily over the dark blue heavens and blotted out the stars for a few seconds before their glittering forms were back again.

At that moment, I wished I could have seen the king's face.

I wondered if there was awe, sadness, excitement, or something else entirely on it. What had someone as old as King Aldrich experienced in his life? What sorrows did he carry? What joys? Could someone with impenetrable stone skin even feel pain? Fear? Worry? As he stood there staring into the night, away from the rest of his party, I couldn't help wondering what had made him come out here all alone.

I was jerked out of my musings as something dark moved on the other side of the balcony. Vines crept along the wall opposite me. They formed a dense cluster and were moving silently but straight towards the king. My heart leaped into my throat.

It was going down right now.

Shock and panic flashed through me.

The cluster of vines moved towards the king at a steady pace while blood rushed in my ears.

Someone was about to kill the King of Elves right now.

And I had to stop them.

But without tipping my hand.

Plans flashed through my mind while my body screamed at me to move. If I just called out and warned the king, then I would lose my chance to get the dagger for myself and then use it to blackmail him. But if I didn't warn him, he was going to die right now. But if I wanted the dagger, I couldn't let the assassin know that I knew that they had the dagger.

The unknown murderer was closing the distance fast.

My pulse thrummed in my ears.

Think!

"Whoa!" I called and stumbled out of my hiding place. "You're not the guy I danced with."

The vines snapped back to reveal the person who had commanded them. It took all my considerable training not to gasp in shock. Standing at an angle where the king couldn't see yet, was the person who had tried to kill the King of Elves.

Princess Syrene.

Moonlight glinted off a wavy dagger etched with markings that seemed to glow from within, exactly like legend said they would, before the princess jerked it out of sight. The Dagger of Orias. In a matter of moments, the weapon that could kill a king was well-hidden behind Syrene's violet skirts, but Aldrich wasn't looking at her anyway. He had whirled around and was staring at me.

Shock was still rattling around in my skull but I forced myself to remain in character. Pretending to be drunk, I stumbled another couple of steps and swayed on my feet before throwing out an arm and clumsily grabbing the railing.

"We're meeting out here to hook up." Giggling, I placed an uncoordinated finger against my lips and made a shushing sound. "But don't tell anyone."

King Aldrich's frown cleared and he let out a pleasant chuckle. "I won't. I promise."

"Thanks." I giggled again and then made a show of squinting hard. "Hey, aren't you the king?"

"Yes." The skin around his eyes crinkled as he smiled conspiratorially. "But don't tell anyone."

Matching his smile, I put a finger to my lips again.

"Syrene?" came a voice from the glass doors. A second later, Prince Iwdael popped out. "Oh, there you are."

True panic flashed over her face, but from this angle, only I could see it. Discounting me as an incredibly drunk and lovesick girl, Princess Syrene focused on keeping out of sight from the other two as she twisted and rammed the dagger back in her bodice.

I kept the loopy expression on my face but frowned

internally. *So, Prince Iwdael didn't know about the dagger. Why would the princess try to kill the king on her own?*

"I'm here," she said with forced lightness. "I just needed some air and then this drunk girl stumbled out."

Turning my back on them, I braced my arms on the cool stone railing for a second before giving them a wave with the back of my hand. "I'm just a bit... drunk." I slurred the words and let out another nonsensical giggle. "I just need some air."

"Let's leave her to it," King Aldrich said before lowering his voice so that the alleged drunk wouldn't be able to hear. "Boy troubles."

"Ah," Prince Iwdael said. "Come, my dear. Let's head back to the party."

Feet shuffled against stone until the three of them had left the balcony. As soon as they were gone, I slumped down and rested my forehead on my arms. Bafflement echoed inside my stunned mind.

Princess Syrene was the one who had the dagger, and she had just tried to kill the king. Why? Why would she try to kill the king?

Letting the cold stone anchor me, I drew a bracing breath.

But no wonder I hadn't been able to locate the dagger. I had been so convinced that it would be the prince who had it. This changed everything. I needed to start looking into places where the princess could hide things from her husband.

Drawing another deep breath, I steadied myself and turned back towards the glass doors.

But first, I had to make sure that she didn't try to assassinate the king a second time tonight.

∽

"Okay, what about that one?"

Squinting against the poor light provided by the low-burning candles, I studied the indicated elf. She was leaning against the short fence surrounding one of the seating areas, twirling a lock of silver hair around her finger and looking incredibly bored.

"She's the daughter of a wealthy jewel merchant," I said. "Her parents want her to marry well, which is why she is here, but… what she really wants is to run away with the stable master's son and become a professional horse racer."

Evander burst out laughing. "Yep, I can definitely see it."

"Alright, your turn." I swept my gaze across the thinning crowd before tilting my goblet towards a male elf in a rather spectacular purple suit. "What about him?"

"Hmm…" He tapped a finger to his lips, pondering.

The fall equinox ball was drawing to a close. I had spent the majority of it keeping track of Syrene while using Evander as my cover for moving around the room. And as far as covers went, Evander wasn't half bad. I had ended up having a lot of fun along the way. More than I had expected. It even got to the point where I was laughing so hard or lost myself in his easy manner that I forgot I was working a few times.

But most of the night, I had been on high alert. Only once King Aldrich had bade his guests goodnight and left the party, had I finally allowed myself to relax. I still kept track of the princess, though. Just in case. But she was once again seated with her friends at a table full of empty wine glasses.

Since chaos would ensue if every court tried to gather and worldwalk out all at once, a departure schedule had been set up. The Court of Water had already left the mountain, and now while we waited to see which court was next up on the list, Evander and I made up backstories about random people in the ballroom.

"He is a–"

Evander's story was cut off by a short blare of trumpets. The room turned towards the main doors as an attendant in impeccable silver robes raised his voice.

"The Court of Trees," he called. "Please proceed to the platform below the gates to begin your departure."

"Well, I guess that's me." Evander shrugged and pushed to his feet.

Placing my half full goblet on the table, I got to my feet as well. Murmuring and shuffling feet filled the high-ceilinged hall as all the members of the Court of Trees made their way towards the exit. Evander and I remained standing silently staring at each other for another moment. Then he cleared his throat.

"I... uhm." Glancing down briefly, he rubbed the back of his neck. "I had a lot of fun tonight."

Resisting the urge to fidget with my dress, I took a half step closer instead. "So did I."

His dark green eyes flicked up to meet my gaze. He opened his mouth to say something but then closed it again, only to lean towards me and then jerk back. Shaking his head, he expelled a short breath and then took a step forward and brushed a quick kiss on my cheek.

"Thank you," he breathed, his lips lingering slightly on my skin.

It made a warm sparkling feeling spread through my chest, but before I could reply, he was already striding away. I watched him go until he had been swallowed up by the mass of people at the door.

Grabbing a fresh glass of wine, I downed it all in one go in an effort to drown the fuzzy feeling in my chest. This was ridiculous. I was a spy and he was a mark. End of story.

After slamming the empty goblet back on the table, I stalked towards the other side of the room. The orchestra was still playing on the stage in the corner, but it was just soft background music. Not something that was meant to be danced to. That meant the dancefloor in the middle was empty and all the remaining partygoers were now clustered around the tables and seating arrangements. Staying close to the wall, I weaved through groups in various stages of intoxication and towards the still open doors to the balcony.

Cool night air filled my lungs as I stepped outside and drew a deep breath. The air up here tasted crisp and cold, like snow. Not wanting to miss the call for my court, I debated whether to be satisfied with that one breath and head back in or to stay a little longer. I cast a longing gaze at the white stone railing on the other side but then turned to walk back inside.

A hiss ripped from my lips as something wrapped around my wrist and jerked me to the side. I stumbled a few steps and had to brace myself on the wall to keep from falling. When I looked up, I found silver eyes staring down at me.

"Kenna."

"Mordren," I ground out, refusing to use his title.

Lifting my hand, I glared between his face and the shadow still encircling my wrist until he withdrew it. A sly smile spread over his lips as he took a step closer, forcing me to press myself against the wall, and rested both palms against the stone on either side of my head.

"No manners this time." He leaned a little closer. "You're

awfully bold for someone who is alone on a balcony with an elven prince."

"And you're awfully overconfident in your own abilities for someone whose opponent," I rapped my knuckles against the white stone pressing against my back, "can walk through walls."

A dark laugh drifted into the air between us. Mordren moved one of his hands from the wall and placed it around my throat. His fingers were cold against my heated skin.

"What about now?" His eyes glittered as they bored into mine. "Can you escape through the wall now?"

I couldn't. As long as I was attached to something that couldn't move through the wall with me, then I couldn't phase through it either. It was one of the limitations of my power. But he didn't need to know that.

Grabbing a fistful of his shirt, I pulled him towards me until he was so close that our lips almost brushed. "Try me and find out."

His breath danced against my mouth. Staring into those glittering silver eyes and that lethal smile, with his muscled body pressed against mine and his hand around my throat, I wanted him to do it. For some insane reason, I wanted to see what his lips tasted like. What it felt like when his hands roamed my body. To feel the heat of his skin against my own. It would be so easy. Just one pull on his shirt and his mouth would be on mine.

Reality slammed back into me and shattered the vision like a glass window. I wasn't sure if I really had a death wish or if I had considered actually kissing the Prince of Shadows just so that I could get the confusing and inconvenient feelings about Evander out of my head. Regardless of which, the thought sobered me up enough that I let go of Mordren's shirt and gently pushed him back.

"What do you want, my prince?" My voice came out sounding wearier than I had intended.

Mordren took his hand from my throat and let his other arm drop down from the wall as he retreated a step. "Have you managed to locate the dagger yet?"

"No." Tipping my head back, I rested it against the cold stone wall and heaved a tired sigh. "But the ball is over and the king isn't dead, so at least now I have more time to figure it out."

"If you find it, or hear anything about it, you will come to me first."

"Or risk torture, death, the annihilation of my family." I huffed a humorless laugh. "Yeah, I know." Narrowing my eyes, I studied his face. "Why do you even want the dagger? So that you can kill King Aldrich yourself? Aren't you already favored to take the throne?"

"What I do with the dagger once it's mine is none of your concern."

Before I could reply, a trumpet blast sounded from inside the ballroom. It was followed by the same attendant calling, "The Court of Stone, please proceed to the platform below the gates to begin your departure."

"And that's my cue." I pushed off from the wall and started towards the door. Without looking at him, I lifted a hand in Mordren's direction and gave him a little wave. "Good talk."

To my surprise, the Prince of Shadows said nothing as I slipped back into the ballroom. Warmth and noise assaulted me as soon as I stepped across the threshold but I didn't dare stop to get my bearings because my heart was pounding in my chest. I had just successfully lied to Mordren Darkbringer.

And I had to get far away before he could see the lie written on my face.

Fortunately for me, the return to the Court of Stone proceeded without incident. My feet were sore and my heart was tired as we reached the spy wing of the castle, but the night wasn't over yet. Prince Edric directed us all towards our meeting chamber and shut the door, but at least he didn't sit down on his throne, which meant that it would be a short debriefing.

Since there were only a handful of us in there, the room felt far too large for this. The small group of spies who had attended the ball clustered together in the middle while Edric remained standing with his back against the closed doors.

"We got lucky tonight," he said. "Do you understand that? We got lucky that no one tried to kill the king." His granite eyes slid to me. "Kenna, I saw you dancing with all the princes. I assume you patted them down?"

"Yeah, I did." I lifted my shoulders in an apologetic shrug. "None of them had the dagger."

"I managed a very thorough search of the Prince of Fire," Monette added, her cheeks still flushed after the dancing and alcohol and… whatever she had done with the prince that had resulted in an intimate pat down. "I can confirm that he didn't have the dagger."

Ymas and Tena nodded their agreement as well. Edric pinched the bridge of his nose and blew out a deep sigh. For a few moments, he said nothing. Then he dragged a hand through his long blond hair and looked back up at us, meeting each of our gazes in turn.

"Did you find any lead, any clue, *anything*, that might be able to tell us who has the dagger?"

"No, my prince," I said.

The others replied the same thing when his eyes turned to them.

"The dagger is still out there and we have until the king's next public appearance to find it." Stone ground against stone as Edric flicked his wrist and the heavy doors swung open again. "Get some sleep. You can have tomorrow off but after that, we're back to work on finding the dagger."

As one, we bowed low while the prince turned on his heel and strode back into the corridor.

I briefly considered lying down right there on the floor to sleep, but thankfully, Monette slipped her arm through mine and started us both towards the door.

"What happened with the Prince of Fire?" I asked, glancing over at her as we crossed the threshold into the corridor.

"I don't want to talk about it."

There was an edge to her voice so I didn't press the matter. Instead, we continued down the hall and towards our rooms in silence.

"I noticed that you spent a lot of time with one guy in particular," Monette said at last, breaking the heavy silence that had settled.

"Yeah, he's a mark. My ticket into the Court of Trees."

She nudged an elbow in my ribs as we neared our rooms. "He's handsome."

"Is he?"

While clicking her tongue, she gave me a theatrical eye roll. "You know he is."

Candlelight danced over the smooth white walls while Monette waited for me to say something, but I didn't want to talk about Evander. Didn't want to admit that I was actually starting to like him. That I had almost kissed the ruthless and ridiculously dangerous Prince of Shadows just to get Evander out of my head. Because if I said all that out loud, it would become real.

When it became clear that I wasn't going to reply, Monette released a dramatic sigh. "You're such a bore, Kenna. Here I was, hoping for some juicy details and you refuse to spill." She let go of my arm as we neared my door. "You're lucky I'm tired tonight. Next time, you won't get off so easily." Grinning, she blew me a kiss before sauntering down the hall to her room.

With a smile, I shook my head at her and then disappeared into the safety of my own room. Closing my eyes, I slumped back against the door as soon as I had closed it and heaved a deep sigh.

"Did you have a productive evening?"

"Gah!" I jumped to the side like a startled crab and reached for my knife. My fingers brushed against my empty thigh at the same time as my eyes found the source of the unexpected voice.

The Void raised his eyebrows expectantly where he was draped against the wall right inside the door. "Well?"

"What the hell are you doing in here? If you want to know what happened tonight, why don't you go ask Prince Edric? I literally just came from a debriefing with him so if you had just waited one damn minute, he would probably have told you that none of us found the dagger."

His gray eyes hardened as he detached himself from the wall and straightened. "Let's get one thing straight. I don't answer to you. You answer to me. Your story about Collum might have checked out but that doesn't mean you're off the hook. Last time we talked, I advised you to make an effort to stay in my good graces. Don't make me remind you again."

The implied threat hung in the air between us. For a few

seconds, we just remained standing there, staring at each other while I once more considered how much of a death wish I really had. But then I dropped my gaze.

"Understood."

"Good." He brushed imaginary dirt off his dark gray shirt. "And?"

"And no, I didn't have a productive evening. We still don't know who has the dagger."

"How Prince Edric can stand this kind of incompetence baffles me. He should've put me on the job. I would've found both the traitor and the dagger by now if he had brought me in from the beginning."

I barely managed to prevent myself from pointing out that his little traitor hunt really hadn't yielded any results either. Seeing as I was the traitor, I would know. But saying that would just make him take his anger out on me, so I simply swallowed the insult instead.

"Don't disappoint him again." The Void yanked open the door and stalked out while throwing over his shoulder, "I'll be watching you."

As soon as the door had swung shut behind him, I picked up the nearest pillow and hurled it at the spot he had just vacated. It bounced off the white stone and plopped down on the floor below with a faint rustling sound. Suddenly feeling bad for my poor pillow which had done nothing to deserve being flung across the room, I picked it up and dusted it off before returning it to the bed. After kicking off my shoes, I dropped down on the mattress as well. I raked my fingers through my hair while the events of the night caught up with me.

I had actually found the Dagger of Orias.

And then I had lied about it to three separate people.

Three incredibly dangerous and powerful people who could end me with a snap of their fingers. A crazed laugh bubbled from my throat. I had successfully fooled all of them.

Now, all I could do was hope that I could keep the lies going.

CHAPTER 23

"What are you wearing?" Lord Elmer scowled down at me. "And why are you armed?"

"Better to have weapons and not need them than need them and not have them," I replied, stepping out of the way while Anders lifted the large trunk I had brought and hauled it from the wagon towards the front door.

"You're certainly your father's daughter."

Twisting away, I pretended to adjust something on the horse's harness so that he wouldn't see the hurt that flashed over my face. I knew that Lord Beaufort wasn't my real father but I still liked to pretend sometimes.

Once I had wiped the expression off my face, I turned back and followed Anders up the white steps to the mansion.

Prince Edric had given us the day off, which was very timely since today was the day Lord Arquette would be back to collect his debt. Sneaking an entire trunk's worth of high value paper bills out of the castle and into the wagon I had borrowed had taken most of the morning, but I had made it to the Beaufort estate with time to spare.

"What are you wearing?" another voice demanded as I crossed the threshold into the shining foyer.

Looking up, I found Patricia descending the stairs in a frilly blue dress. I glanced down at the tight-fitting black pants and jacket I wore before giving her a shrug in reply. The sword across my back shifted slightly with the movement.

"Is that the money?" Her eyes tracked the trunk Anders was carrying as she hopped down the final step.

"Of course it is," Elvin said behind her. "What else would it be?"

My two half-siblings trailed me as we followed Anders and Elmer into the receiving room. The young stable hand set the trunk full of money down on the dark blue carpet before bowing to his lord and retreating. Before he disappeared out the door again, he threw me a quick smile. I returned it.

"Now, let's see what we have," Lord Elmer said. Twitching his fingers, he motioned at me to hand him the key.

I ignored his outstretched hand and walked up to the trunk myself instead. Crouching down before it, I unlocked it and flipped the heavy wooden lid open. After sticking the key back in my pocket, I took a step back.

Elvin let out a low whistle. "That's a lot of money."

His father furrowed his brows as he stared down at the stacks upon stacks of notes. "Yes, it is."

"How did you even manage to get this much money?" Patricia asked with a suspicious look on her face.

I shrugged. "Work." Stepping forward again, I closed the lid and locked the trunk once more while explaining, "Until Lord Arquette has agreed that the debt is cleared, we're not taking any chances."

"What, you think one of us would steal it?" Elvin scoffed.

"Of course not. I just think–"

The front door banged open. Drawing my weapons, I leaped over the chest and darted back into the foyer just in time to see four people pour across the threshold with swords raised. The shock of realizing that all of them were elves had me hesitating, but as soon as Patricia's terrified cry cut through the house, I snapped back into fight mode and positioned myself in the hall where I blocked the way to the receiving room.

"Get back!" I ordered my family while I spun the sword in my hand.

Feet slapping against stone behind me informed me that they took my advice and ran towards the back of the house. The four elves before me didn't even spare them a glance. Their eyes were solely focused on me.

Confusion flitted through me. If they had been here to rob us on behalf of Lord Arquette, they would have been human. Not elven. And they appeared to have no interest in the rest of my family, which meant that they were here for me. But who the hell were they?

Before I could figure it out, the closest elf lunged at me.

I jumped back. Steel cut through the air and missed me by scant margins. Not taking my eyes off the attackers, I backed further into the house. Falling into formation, the four of them followed. The hallway was too narrow for them to attack all at once, which was of course the point, so I stopped retreating before we reached the wide room beyond.

The elves exchanged a glance. And then the first one attacked again.

Throwing up my sword, I met his blade while taking a step to the side. Metal ground against metal as I shoved his weapon aside and jabbed at his ribs with my knife. He moved with the motion and slammed his fist into my side. A gasp burst from my lips as it connected and my attack faltered as I stumbled into the wall.

A pale blue ceramic vase wobbled precariously as I used the closest side table for support. Steel glinted in the corner of my eye as my opponent went for the kill.

Just like I wanted.

Once I saw him leap towards me, I took a step backwards. Right through the wall.

Calm silence enveloped me as I appeared in the family library but I didn't stop to appreciate it. I took two steps to the side and then threw myself back through the wall while ramming my sword to the left.

A surprised gasp rang out. Wide eyes stared at me in shock and pain as I withdrew the blade. It made a wet sliding sound as it left my attacker's chest.

"No!" the elf behind him screamed.

Momentarily trapped between the dying male on my left and the attacking one on the right, I barely managed to redirect his thrust in time. His blade slid down my knife and nicked my thigh. I sucked in a sharp breath between my teeth and swung my sword in a wide arc. It grazed his stomach but wasn't enough to stop him.

With red eyes blazing, he grabbed my forearm and threw me back down the corridor so that I was between him and the third elf. Holding my blades out in both directions, I flicked my gaze between the two opponents now boxing me in.

Their eyes met. And then they both lunged at the same time.

I shot forward and phased through the wall in front of me. Skidding to a halt on the dark blue carpet in the receiving room, I whirled around and calculated the trajectory. Then I sprinted through the wall at the edge of the room.

"Watch out!"

The warning came too late. I buried my sword in the second elf's back and then yanked it out. While his body was still crumpling to the floor, I had already leaped through the wall to the library again.

Taking three quick strides, I estimated the distance to the next attacker and then phased through the library wall. Another quiet room met me as I sprinted down the polished stone floor before throwing myself through the solid wall and into the corridor again.

A panicked cry tore from the fourth elf's throat. He had been standing close to the front door and probably thought that he would be safe with three other people between him and me. Oh how wrong he was.

These elves had put themselves at a severe disadvantage when they decided to attack me here. This was my home ground. I had grown up here. I knew every room in this house like the back of my hand. Which was why I knew that if I sprinted through the library and then the storage closet by the stairs, I would end up right in front of the poor unfortunate elf standing there.

His cry was cut off abruptly as I rammed my knife into his throat. With a vicious smile on my lips, I yanked it out and whirled towards the final remaining attacker.

He flinched as he met my gaze. Standing in the middle of the hallway with his dead companions around him, he flicked his eyes between me and the still open front door behind me. Then he blew out a long breath and raised his sword. I darted through the wall.

As soon as I was in the receiving room, I threw myself back out.

My attacker had shifted to the side so that he could see both sides of the corridor. I flashed him another malicious grin before sprinting into the opposite wall. Estimating the distance in my head, I ran along the library wall until I reached the spot where I had calculated he would be. And then I jumped through.

He had turned so that his back was towards the other wall instead but it didn't matter. I crashed right into him. Steel clattered against stone as his blade went flying while I shoved him into the opposite wall. Whipping up my own sword, I pressed it to his throat.

"Who sent you?" I snarled in his face.

His eyes flicked up and down between my eyes and my blade but he kept quiet.

"This can either be fast." Narrowing my eyes, I pushed the sword harder against his throat. "Or really painful."

He opened his mouth but then closed it again. Irritation flared through me.

I rammed my knife into his shoulder. "I said, who sent you!"

A scream shattered through the gleaming mansion as I twisted the blade. And I liked it. I liked seeing the fear in his eyes and knowing that I was the one in control. Guilt shot through me at the thought, but I twisted the blade again because I still needed information. His voice cracked.

"The princess," he blurted out. "Princess Syrene."

Shit. I stopped turning the knife but leaned forward.

"Why?" I already knew why, of course, but I wanted to know how many other people did.

"I don't know." Desperation poured into his eyes as he

glanced down at the knife in his shoulder. "I swear I don't know. She just gave us a drawing of you and paid us to kill you when you were outside the castle. One of our contacts saw you on the road and tipped us off so we rushed over here. Spirits, if we'd known you were a magic user…"

I thanked those same spirits while he trailed off and shook his head. If the princess had known that I could use magic, she would've sent magic users as well. She probably still believed that I was just a drunk courtier who had been in the wrong place at the wrong time and seen something she shouldn't have. Thank the gods and spirits for that. If she had sent four magic-wielding assassins, I would be the one lying dead on the floor right now.

Shoving the thought out of my mind, I flexed my fingers around the hilt of the knife. "Are there any more of you?"

"No."

While gripping the hilt firmly again, I arched an eyebrow at him expectantly.

"There's no one else. That I know of," he added. "I swear. No one."

"Good." I slit his throat.

Wet gurgling sounded into the too quiet hallway as he collapsed to the floor. I cast a glance around me. My hands and clothes were slick with blood. As were my weapons. And four corpses littered the floor of the hallway while ever expanding crimson puddles stained the shining white floor. Tipping my head back, I drew a deep breath but even the air was filled with the coppery tang of blood.

"What are you?"

I whirled around to find Lord Elmer standing in the doorway further down the corridor. The horrified expression on his face was mirrored on both Patricia and Elvin's features.

However, before I could say anything, a shriek tore through the mansion as my mother leaped down the final steps and ran across the hallway.

She clutched her dark blue dress so tightly that her knuckles turned white. Holding her skirts up to protect it from the blood-slick floor, she hurried towards my half-siblings. I took a step back to give her space as she flashed past me.

"Are you hurt?" she demanded. Letting go of her dress, she grabbed Patricia and Elvin by the shoulders and drew them into a crushing hug. "Tell me you're not hurt."

"We're not hurt, Mother," Patricia said while patting her back.

After another second of embracing, my mother pulled back and whirled around to face me. As she ran her dark blue eyes up and down my body, I suddenly became acutely aware of the fact that I was standing in a sea of corpses with two blood-dripping blades in my hands.

"How could you?" Anger pushed out the worry on her face and her voice rose to a shriek again. "How could you bring this kind of violence to my home? To my children, for gods' sake!"

Pain that had nothing to do with the fight shot through my chest. *My children*. As if I wasn't one of them.

I glanced away. "I'm sorry."

"What are we supposed to do now?" Patricia interrupted. "Lord Arquette will be here any minute. If he sees this, he'll tell Prince Edric and then we'll be done for."

If my hands hadn't been covered in blood or holding weapons, I would've raked them through my hair in exasperation. Did the problems never stop piling up?

"Here's what we're going to do: you are going to take the

trunk of money outside," I cut off before anyone else could open their mouth, and threw the key to Lord Elmer. "They don't need to come into the house to get the money. Put it below the stairs and then close the front door behind you. You are going to wait for Lord Arquette outside, while I deal with this."

Elmer glared at me. "You do not give me orders in my own house."

"Today, I do." I stabbed a bloodstained sword in the direction of the receiving room. "Now go pick up the trunk and go wait outside."

My adoptive father fumed at the words but did as I said. He and Elvin went to collect the wooden trunk while my mother draped a protective arm around Patricia's shoulder and led her towards the front door. Her eyes burned with accusation when she looked over at me as she passed, but she said nothing.

Once the front door was firmly shut behind them, I wiped my hands and then my blades before sticking them back in their holsters. While yanking out a small leather book from my jacket, I stalked into the living room beyond the hallway.

There was only one person who would both have the means to dispose of these bodies and the inclination to do so. Or at least, so I hoped.

After scrawling a quick note in the outmost corner of one page, I stuck the book back into one of my pockets. And then I waited. Fortunately, I didn't have to wait long.

"What a bloody mess."

"I know," I replied.

Mordren Darkbringer sauntered across the floor and plopped down on the couch before me. Swinging his legs up on the table, he crossed his ankles and leaned back against the pale blue cushions. He jerked his chin towards the bodies in the hallway.

"You did this?"

"Yeah."

"Huh."

I couldn't tell if he was surprised or impressed or didn't really care at all. Glancing away, I cleared my throat.

"I need your help."

He huffed a laugh. "Yes, you do."

"There's a human lord coming to collect a debt." I nodded towards the front door. "And I need to be out there when he does to make sure that the debt is cleared. But I also need to make these bodies and this blood disappear before anyone sees it and Prince Edric finds out."

Mordren studied his nails. "You don't say."

"Do you have people that can make this go away?"

"Yes."

"Will you?"

The Prince of Shadows met my gaze again before shifting it to the bloodstained hallway. "Who were they? Why did they attack you?"

"Because I blackmailed the wrong person." I shot him a disgruntled look. "Again."

Wood creaked as he leaned forward on the sofa, bracing his elbows on his knees, while narrowing his eyes at me. "What is it with you and all this blackmailing? Why do you need the money?"

"I already told you." Jerking my chin, I motioned at the closed front door. "To clear my family's debt."

He waved a hand to indicate the expensive living room we were currently occupying. "They couldn't clear that themselves?"

Dodging his question, I blew out a sigh. "Look, will you help me or not?"

A challenging smile spread across his lips. "If I do this for you, what will you give me?"

"If you want the dagger, you will do this for me." Raising my chin, I crossed my arms. "Because if Prince Edric finds out about this, about my blackmailing, that will be the end of my spy career. Which means, no dagger."

Mordren held my gaze. Even though he was sitting down and I was standing several strides away, I felt the urge to shrink back as those silver eyes judged me. Then a short chuckle broke the tension.

"Fine." He lifted one shoulder in a nonchalant shrug. "I'll settle for some light groveling."

Grinding my teeth, I glared at him. *I'm going to kill you one day.*

He smirked. "Good luck. You'll find that I'm not that easy to kill."

Panic washed over me. The thought had flashed through my mind before I could stop it. "I'm sorry. I didn't mean–"

"I was just going to make you say please," he interrupted and cast a pointed glance at the floor by his feet. "But now I want you on your knees too."

Somewhere outside the mansion, horses neighed and a wagon rattled. Lord Arquette was here. I didn't have time for the Prince of Shadows and his damn power plays.

"No," I snapped, my patience having run dry four dead bodies ago. "Do you want the dagger or not? If you do, you will take care of this for me."

Silence descended on the room. When Mordren only continued staring me down, I was afraid that I had taken it too far. Pushed too hard. The sound of a wagon door slamming shut echoed from outside.

"Please," I added softly.

Wood groaned as he pushed himself off the delicate piece of furniture and prowled towards me. Instinctively, I retreated a step. Something dangerous glinted in his eyes as he stopped in front of me and placed two fingers under my chin, tilting it up.

"Alright, I'll take care of it. But you'd better find that dagger now, or I will have done all this for nothing."

"I know." I held his gaze. "Thank you."

"Uh-huh."

I glanced towards the door. "I have to go."

Dropping his hand, he jerked his chin in dismissal.

While running my palms across my face and neck to make sure that there was no blood left there, I hurried through the corridor. There was blood on my clothes but they were black, so hopefully no one would be able to tell.

Raised voices met me as I yanked open the front door and stalked down the white steps outside.

"What do you mean it's not enough?" Lord Elmer demanded. "This here is exactly the amount I owed you."

Lord Arquette was standing in front of the open trunk with the same two muscled bodyguards on either side of him. A mocking smile curled his lips. "Yes, this is what you originally owed. But you have forgotten to take the interest into account."

"Interest? What interest?"

"Every day that you have not paid me back has added interest to the sum you owed."

A strong fall wind swept through the landscape, making

the trees along the road quiver. I let the briskness cool my temper as I strode up to the bickering party below the stairs.

"Surely we can work something out," I said. "What additional amount are we talking about?"

Arquette arched an eyebrow at me before turning back to Elmer. "Does the prince's whore speak for you?"

"Of course not," he snapped and shot me a withering look.

While cursing myself for forgetting that I wasn't supposed to give orders or handle negotiations, I bowed my head and took up position next to my siblings.

Running a hand through his brown hair, Lord Arquette considered the stacks of paper before him. "This will buy you a few more weeks, but I want the full amount."

"And what is the full amount?" Elmer asked.

Hopelessness washed over me while Arquette pulled out a ledger and began writing. The money in that trunk was basically everything I had. I had only kept enough for bribes and other necessary expenses that might be required for me to survive the next few weeks. But the bulk of it was in that wooden chest.

"Here." He ripped off a page and handed it to Lord Beaufort. "Three weeks. Then I'll be back."

Before anyone could argue, he spun on his heel and disappeared back into his lacquered wooden coach. The two bodyguards stared us down for another few seconds before flipping the lid of the trunk closed and lifting it to the back of the wagon. It rocked slightly as they climbed aboard as well. With a snap of the reins, it lurched forward.

A pang of sadness hit me as I watched my hard-earned money disappear between the rows of trees.

Without a word, Elmer shoved the piece of paper into my

hand. My stomach dropped as I glanced down at the sum that was still owed.

It had taken years to acquire the fortune that was now being carted away on the back of Lord Arquette's carved coach. But now he wanted more. Tilting my head up, I sighed into the overcast sky above.

There was no way I would be able to give it to him.

CHAPTER 24

Maps covered every surface of the desk. Pushing one aside, I frowned at the one underneath it. It didn't look the way I remembered it. The main sections were still in the same place but the corridors that connected everything looked slightly different. I heaved a deep sigh. Damn Court of Trees. It wouldn't surprise me at all if they routinely changed the passageways that ran throughout the castle. Tapping my pen against the desk, I continued trying to figure out where the dagger might be kept.

It had been a week since the four elves had tried to kill me in my family's mansion. Since Princess Syrene knew who I was and knew that I was aware of her attempted assassination of King Aldrich, I couldn't risk returning to the Court of Trees. Until I had figured out where the dagger was and went there to steal it, that is. Unfortunately, not being able to scout it out in person slowed down my scheming rather considerably. Blowing out another sigh, I slumped down and rested my forehead against the map-covered desk.

The door banged open. I shot to my feet, my fingers going straight for weapons I wasn't actually carrying.

"Did I not tell you that incompetence would not be tolerated?" the Void growled as he stalked into my room.

And did I not tell you that you don't get to just barge in here, I thought but wisely enough decided not to say. Instead, I crossed my arms. "What are you talking about?"

"Your mark is here."

I blinked at him. "What?"

"Yeah." He stopped a stride away and locked hard eyes on me. "That ignorant little commoner you've been manipulating, he's here. In the throne room. Asking for you."

"Don't call him an ignorant commoner," I snapped before I could stop it.

The Void raised his eyebrows. Realizing that I had just defended a mark, someone I shouldn't be caring about, I cleared my throat and scrambled for something else to say.

"What does he want?"

"What are you, deaf? I already told you. He's asking for you." The Void jerked his chin towards the door. "Now go deal with this before it can turn into a situation."

"Alright." I started towards my closet. "I'll be up in a minute."

"You'd better be."

The door slammed shut somewhere behind me, signaling that the rude spy had left. I ran my gaze over the rows of dresses while formulating excuses for why I hadn't been to see him or even contacted him for an entire week. If he was going to believe me, I would need something that was pretty close to the truth.

After shimmying into a cream-colored dress, I grabbed my dark green cloak and hurried towards the throne room.

The grand hall was filled with courtiers, as usual, but Prince Edric was thankfully nowhere to be seen. I weaved through the gleaming crowd while scanning for Evander before I finally found him standing about as close to the exit as one could possibly get. His handsome face was full of uncertainty. The sight tugged at my heartstrings but I told myself that the look on his face was because of the unfamiliar setting and not because he thought I had dumped him without even bothering to explain. Forcing a bright smile onto my lips, I made my way towards him.

"Evander," I called as I drew closer.

He turned in my direction and his face lit up as soon as he saw me. "Kenna."

"I'm so sorry I haven't been in touch. Something came up and I…" Trailing off, I glanced around the room. "Could we… could we go somewhere else? Somewhere more private?"

Worry blew across his face but he held out his arm to me. "Of course."

Taking it, I steered us back out through the double doors and towards the main gate. The statues of the former princes stared down at us as we moved silently between them. Since the explanation I had decided on was very close to the truth, I wanted to be out of earshot of any eavesdropping courtiers before sharing it.

"How have you been?" I asked, a bit awkwardly, when the silence was becoming uncomfortable.

Evander glanced down at me. "Worried about you. Are you okay?"

"I'm sorry." Keeping my eyes on the doors ahead, I tried to ignore the waves of guilt rolling over me at the anxiousness in his voice. "Yes, I'm okay. I'll explain everything as soon as we're outside."

He was just about to reply when a blond figure breezed through the door. Monette blinked in surprise as she stopped before us.

"Kenna." She flicked her gaze up and down my body. "You look like you just rolled out of bed." A smile bloomed on her lips as she stole a glance at Evander. "*Did you* just roll out of bed?"

My companion made a choking noise while heat seared his cheeks.

I rolled my eyes at Monette. "No, I didn't."

"Huh." She lifted her delicate shoulders in a shrug before casting a quick look at the courtyard she had just left. "Well, I guess there's no point in brushing your hair when it's this windy outside." One side of her mouth quirked upwards as she turned back to us while twining a smooth lock of glossy hair around her finger. "Or if you plan to make it messy again doing other… activities."

When the red color on Evander's cheeks deepened, I shot a warning look at Monette. She probably thought she was helping, but I had a feeling that poor Evander was going to suffer a heart attack if she kept this topic up.

"We should go," I announced, pulling my companion with me towards the door.

Monette winked at us. "Have fun."

Cold winds snatched at our clothes when we stepped across the threshold and descended the white stairs outside. It was only afternoon but the dark clouds above painted the whole courtyard in a dusky gloom. Drawing my cloak tighter around me, I led us towards the gardens on our left.

"Sorry about my friend." I turned to grimace at Evander. "She can be a bit… overenthusiastic."

"I noticed." He let out a chuckle and shook his head before

a serious expression settled on his face. "But for what it's worth, you don't look like you just rolled out of bed at all. You look beautiful."

The sincerity in his voice made me blush. I met his earnest eyes briefly before glancing away. "Thank you. Most people don't think so after seeing me next to her."

"Most people are idiots."

A surprised laugh tore from my throat. Another *real* laugh. Evander beamed down at me, satisfied that the comment had cheered me up, right as we entered the garden.

Though, someone from the Court of Trees would never classify this as a garden. The ground was covered in white stone, and statues made of the same material dotted this section of the palace area. In the middle was a large pond complete with a fountain that sent water trickling down it. The only things that remotely helped justify the name *garden* were the thick green bushes that had been planted in white marble pots throughout the space. We weaved through them as I led us towards one of the benches that encircled the pond.

Detaching myself from Evander's arm, I smoothened my cloak and dress behind me before sitting down. The clothes provided a layer of protection against the cold stone but I still shuddered when another gust of wind whirled through the gloomy garden. Evander caught the gesture and scooted closer to me until we sat so close beside each other that our arms and legs were touching. I savored the warmth spreading from his body to mine.

"Okay, here it goes." I drew a deep breath. "The reason why I haven't seen you or contacted you this last week is because I've been trying to find a way to clear my family's debt. My father has been gambling and owed someone a lot of money. I actually had a rather considerable fortune of my own, but I needed time to transfer all of that to them so they could clear some of their debt. And on top of that, that friend you just met, she needed help with some other stuff too and I couldn't say no because, well, she's my friend and of course I wanted to help her. So, yeah, it's just been a very stressful week and honestly, I was a bit embarrassed too, so I didn't want to tell you."

The words were true enough. Helping my family and helping Monette with her mission in the Court of Water had taken a lot of time I didn't really have, but it hadn't happened *this* week. I had of course spent time plotting how to get my family out of that final debt this week as well, but not nearly as much as I had in the weeks before. But Evander didn't need to know that.

"Oh."

"Yeah," I sighed.

While I'd been talking, I had kept my eyes fixed on the gurgling water rushing towards the pond, but now I turned back towards Evander. His dark green eyes were full of concern. And... affection. Holding my gaze, he took my hand and squeezed gently.

"You did the right thing. Spending all of that time helping your family and your friends. It was the right thing to do." A wistful smile drifted across his lips as he leaned forward to hook a loose strand of hair back behind my ear. His fingers brushed my cheek and lingered there for a moment before completing their task. "That's what I love about you. You're so selfless and kind."

Strange feelings surged through my body. At first, tiny drops of disappointment peppered my chest, but they were quickly pushed aside as sparkles danced over my skin in response to his touch and the adoration in his dark green eyes.

"That's what you love about me?" I echoed, my voice coming out more breathless than I had expected.

"Yes." His hand lingered on my skin, just beneath my ear, for a moment before he let it fall to his lap again. "I've never met anyone like you. You're beautiful and graceful, and yet you're not as self-absorbed as most of the noble ladies in court can be. You make me feel comfortable and at ease."

I swallowed against the guilt trying to claw its way up my throat. Here he was, pouring his heart out, when all I had done was use him for my own ends. The truth was that I felt comfortable and at ease around him too. He didn't expect anything of me. Didn't expect me to smile while he showed me off like some kind of accessory. Didn't expect me to sleep with him. Didn't expect me to do anything for him, and most certainly not things that I didn't want to do. And for me, people like that were rare.

"I like spending time with you too," I said softly. "You're a kind person, Evander."

"Then maybe..." He trailed off as fat drops splashed against the ground around us.

Craning my neck, I looked up at the dark clouds covering the heavens. Raindrops hit my face and ran down my cheeks.

"Oh no." I pulled him up by the hand while rain splashed down around us with increasing speed. "Hurry, we need to get–"

The skies opened. The rain turned into a downpour which turned into a full-blown deluge. Evander threw an arm over his head while we sprinted towards the closest wall.

"There!" he called, pointing at a section of the castle where the roof stuck out slightly, providing some cover.

Our feet slapped against the wet stones as we hurried towards it. With all my attention focused on the target, I missed the puddle of water right in front of me and ran right through it. The water had made the stones slippery and I lost my footing. Careening forward, I stumbled into Evander and pushed us both the final bit into the wall.

With his arms wrapped around me, I laughed with both embarrassment and joy as we straightened underneath our temporary shelter. The world around us smelled like rain and wet stones.

I was completely soaked. The cream-colored dress had become almost see-through because of the water and my hair was plastered to my face. With the thick curtain of rain, I could barely see more than a couple of strides outside our cover but it didn't matter because I couldn't take my eyes off Evander. His eyes sparkled and the skin around them crinkled with mirth as he smiled at me.

"There was a second reason," I blurted out before I could stop myself. "For why I didn't contact you. After the equinox ball, I didn't know what to do because, well, I'm starting to feel things." I glanced up at him. "For you."

His face lit up even more brightly. Reaching up, he gently moved my rain-slick hair out of my face before cupping his hands over my cheeks. "I'm starting to feel things for you too."

My treacherous heart fluttered in my chest.

With his eyes locked on mine, he leaned down slowly, waiting to see if I would pull away. I didn't. One of his hands moved to the back of my neck and the other to the small of my back and then he drew me the final bit towards him.

His soft lips pressed against mine while his hand nestled in my hair. I drew my hands down his soaked shirt as I answered the kiss. He tasted like rain. And yet he smelled like the forest.

Calm and steady and strong. Pulling him closer, I dragged my fingers through his hair while my mouth continued exploring his.

Lightning flashed across the dark sky and thunder boomed in the distance, but the rest of the world was drowned out by the noise of the crashing rain.

Evander drew gentle fingers from the small of my back and towards my waist. It wasn't enough. I wanted him to pin me against the wall and touch me and kiss me until my mind was empty and my heart was full. Digging my fingers into his shoulders, I shoved his back into the palace wall. A surprised laugh bubbled from his throat. Before my mind could reprimand me for being too assertive, I closed the distance between us again and crushed my lips against his.

Thunder rumbled and the air around us vibrated with the force. Evander wrapped his arms around me. Closing my eyes, I lost myself in a desperate kiss with the person I was supposed to betray.

I was so screwed.

CHAPTER 25

Bundled in blankets, I lay on my bed, staring at the ceiling. Evander had left some half hour ago and I was still desperately trying to tell myself that everything that had happened today had just been part of my carefully planned manipulation. None of it had been real. I had only kissed him because I would need a way into the Court of Trees later. My mind scoffed at the pathetic lie. Rolling over on my side, I slammed a fist into the mattress.

I wasn't supposed to fall for the mark! For spirits' sake, I was a spy. It was my job to manipulate other people's feelings until they gave me what I wanted. Not to have my own feelings swayed by someone who was supposed to be nothing more than a job assignment. But I had let my guard down, and now I actually cared about Evander.

Drumming my fingers against the crisp sheets, I stared at the smooth white wall on the other side of the room. I wasn't supposed to like the mark, but I did. And he liked me. Maybe I should actually tell him what I was doing. Not everything, of course. Not that I was a spy or that I could walk through walls or anything that could hurt me. Only that Princess Syrene had the dagger and that she had tried to kill the king with it. Surely Evander wouldn't want that to happen either. If he knew that then he could help me find it in his court. I blew out a sigh. Should I tell him?

Fabric rustled as I threw the covers off me, making them flap through the air like a startled albatross before landing on the bed again, while I shot to my feet. Shaking my head, I stalked towards the closet.

What had I been thinking? Of course I couldn't tell him. That would be far too risky.

Deeming myself sufficiently dry, I got dressed in clothes that weren't soaked from the downpour of the century that Evander and I had been caught in earlier. My hair was still wet, though, so I fluffed it out until it fell down my back.

While shoving out the final bits of dumb ideas about a certain elf from the Court of Trees, I walked over to my desk and sat down to scheme again.

My body had barely touched the chair when a knock sounded at my door. Groaning loudly, I pushed myself back up and went to answer it.

"Get dressed!"

Frowning, I stared at Monette who was practically jumping from foot to foot outside my door.

"I am dressed."

"In something nicer." A conspiratorial grin flashed over her lips. "We're going out."

While she breezed past me into the room, I cast a glance at my map-covered desk. I didn't really have time to go out. Meeting Evander had already taken up time that I hadn't planned on losing today.

"I don't think I can," I said.

Monette plopped down on my bed. "Oh, come on! You never want to do anything fun."

Leaning my hip against the desk, I looked back at her with a pained expression. "I really need to work. I'm already behind on everything I have to do."

"Please." She batted her lashes at me. "I need this. Just one night of drinking. It'll be fun, I promise. Felix is coming too."

"Felix is coming? That's great. Then you have someone to go with even if I don't come."

Air puffed up and sent her hair fluttering as she threw herself back on the mattress in exasperation. "But he *likes* me. And if it's just the two of us then he might get the wrong idea." She sat back up again and shot me a hopeful smile. "Please."

I massaged my brows for a moment before heaving a sigh. "Alright. Fine. I'll come."

"Yay!" Hopping up from the bed, she strode towards my closet and began rummaging through it for something appropriate.

A glittering smile decorated her face as she threw a black dress and cloak at me. After catching the flying garments, I shot her a look across the bundles of dark fabric but then simply starting changing into them.

Sometimes I wondered if Monette ever used her powers on me. She had the ability to influence people's moods. While her power wasn't nearly as strong and as diverse as the mood control that the Prince of Trees possessed, it was still enough to sway people her way. She used it with great results on her marks, which made me wonder if she ever did the same to me.

A pang of shame hit me. What kind of friend was I to even think that? Of course she would never do that to me.

Shaking my head at my unkind thoughts, I swung the dark cloak around my shoulders and fastened the clasp at my throat. Perhaps a fun night of drinking was just what I needed to forget everything else that had happened today.

~

Rowdy laughter echoed throughout the packed tavern. I leaned forward on the scratched and stained wooden table so that I would be able to hear over the music.

"I swear it's the truth." Monette pressed a hand over her heart. "He literally walked up to me and said 'you have the most beautiful breasts in the whole city' and actually expected that to work! What kind of pickup line even is that?"

Throwing our heads back, Felix and I let out a howling laugh.

"That's insane," I said. "How could anyone think that would work?"

"Right?" Monette knocked back the rest of her wine before winking and elbowing Felix in the ribs. "Please tell me that's not how you flirt with people."

His cheeks were already red from the alcohol but the color deepened as he drew a hand through his hair. "Honestly, I have no idea how to flirt with anyone." He chuckled into his mug. "But even I know that's not how it's done."

Monette's rippling laugh drifted into the air. Smiling, I downed the rest of my drink too and then stood up.

"Come on, let's dance."

The band in the corner played a merry and fast-paced tune that blared across the whole room. No one else was dancing but who cared about that? Everyone in here would be too drunk to notice anyway.

"Here?" Monette flicked her turquoise eyes between the crowded tables around us.

"Yes." I grabbed her hand and started pulling her up from the booth we occupied. "Come on."

"No one else is dancing."

"So?"

She yanked her hand from mine with a pleading look on her face. "Kenna, please, sit down. You're embarrassing us."

Blocking out the feelings that swirled in my chest in answer, I slid back into my seat again and picked up my glass only to remember that it was already empty.

A male elf in a stained apron bustled past our table. My hand shot out and grabbed his sleeve before he could disappear further into the crowd again.

"Hey," I said. "We need shots. The strongest you have."

He gave me a nod. "You got it."

"Shots?" Felix blurted out. "Oh spirits, this night isn't going to end well."

A villainous grin flashed over my mouth as I raised a finger in the air. "Ah, yes, but isn't that the point?"

The table next to us erupted in laughter at some unheard joke and the elves around it slapped the wood so hard it almost tipped over. Wine and ale sloshed over mugs and splashed down in the laps of the people sitting on that side, making the other side howl even louder. I grinned at them right as the barkeep returned with the requested alcohol.

He placed three small glasses on the already overflowing table and filled them to the brim with a clear liquid. I eyed the bottle while he poured. Once he was done, he straightened and began lowering it to his side.

My hand shot out and grabbed his arm again. "Leave the bottle."

Surprise flitted over his face but before he could say anything, I slipped him a couple of high value paper notes. If this was going to be my night of drinking and forgetting about all the uncomfortable feelings I had, I might as well get completely wasted. The barkeep raised his eyebrows and then tipped his head from side to side while considering the money I was offering.

"Alright." Glass thumped against wood as he set down the bottle next to me. "I would say drink responsibly, but then I wouldn't make any money so…" He shrugged and shot me an appreciative smile before sauntering back to the bar.

Monette let out a baffled laugh. "Oh spirits, Kenna! You're so bossy."

"Yep." Picking up my shot glass, I nodded towards theirs across the table. "Now drink."

"As I said, bossy." She giggled and shook her head but lifted her own glass.

Felix did the same. "What are we toasting?"

A wicked smile spread across my lips and I raised the glass higher. "To being bossy!"

Both of them laughed before echoing, "To being bossy."

The clear liquor burned on the way down my throat. I relished the warm feeling that it left in its wake. While refilling our shot glasses again, I glanced up at the already intoxicated male across from me.

"Alright, Felix, tell us about the weirdest thing that's ever happened to you on a job."

"You're never going to believe it."

I grinned. "Try me."

The amount of liquor in the bottle continued dropping with each story as I refilled our glasses over and over again. When it was finally empty, my head was spinning and the tavern around us was all blurry. I squinted at the bottle as I turned it upside down and shook it. A few drops of alcohol splattered onto the messy table in front of me.

"What're you doing?" Monette giggled and lurched forward to grab the bottle, but missed by an alarming distance. "Don't pour out the alcohol."

I waved the bottle in front of her face. "It's already empty."

"We drank it all?" Felix examined his shot glass as if it could tell him how many times he had drunk from it tonight.

"Yep."

Lowering the bottle, I meant to place it on the tabletop but my ability to accurately estimate distances was apparently out of commission so it smacked into the wood at an angle instead. I jerked back in surprise as the force made me drop it. It clattered as it toppled over and rolled across the scratched surface before Felix caught it on the other side.

"Where did this come from?" He lifted it to his face and squinted at it. "It looks familiar."

Monette and I both burst out laughing.

"Okay, now I wanna go dancing," she announced and pushed herself up. "Let's go somewhere else."

Before anyone could protest, she grabbed Felix's arm and pulled him up with her. I blinked to clear my head but it didn't work, so I just slid out of the booth and stumbled after them.

Cold night air wrapped around us as we left the crowded tavern behind and staggered onto the street outside. Tipping my head up, I drew a couple of deep breaths while holding on to the wall for support.

"Come on, let's go." Monette was already marching up the street towards whatever destination she had picked.

Felix and I exchanged a glance before hurrying after her. The houses swayed like waves around me when I turned my head so I tried not to move so much. Which was of course entirely impossible when one was walking.

A strong fall wind whistled down the street. I shuddered and drew my cloak tighter around me. Or so I thought. Stopping in the middle of the street, I stared uncomprehendingly at my bare arms for a few moments.

"I forgot my cloak," I mumbled to myself. Looking back up at my friends who were still moving ahead of me, I raised my voice and tried again. "I forgot my cloak."

"What?" Monette called back.

"I forgot my cloak."

"Kenna," she complained, drawing out each vowel. "Alright, fine. We're going ahead. Come to the Purple Crown when you've got it."

Felix looked from me to Monette, which made him stumble a step forward. He opened his mouth to say something, but before he could, she grabbed his arm and steered them both back up the street.

"Hurry, Kenna!" Monette called over her shoulder.

Heaving a sigh, I spun around and trudged back towards the tavern. The road back seemed endless and I was just starting to worry that I had walked past it when the faded sign finally swung before me. Cursing my forgetful brain, I shouldered open the door and entered the warm room again.

Thankfully, our booth was still empty and my cloak was still there. Leaning down over the worn wood, I snatched up the heap of black fabric in the corner. After shaking it out, I draped it over my shoulders and turned around.

Gray eyes watched me from across the crowd.

My heart leaped into my chest. The Void. He was sitting alone at a table by the opposite wall with a mug in front of him. How long had he been there? Had he been sitting there while the three of us were here as well? His words echoed through my mind. *I'll be watching you.*

Tearing my gaze from him, I hurried back out the door. My mind spun as I made my way back up the street again. Had I said anything incriminating tonight? Was it even possible to hear what we had said from across the room? I chewed my bottom lips while I stumbled forward with one hand on the wall next to me for support. With the Void, you never knew. Since he kept his power a secret, there was no way of knowing exactly what he could do. Cold stone scraped against my palm as I continued along the wall. No, I decided, there really was nothing to worry about.

"Scream and you're dead."

I dragged my eyes from the stones in front of my feet and towards the sound of the voice. A male elf with dirty blond hair was blocking the alley before me. With one hand still on the wall, I frowned at him.

"What?"

"I said, scream and you're dead." He took a threatening step forward and raised the knife in his hand. "Now, give me everything of value you've got."

"Do I look like I carry anything of value?" I spread my arms wide.

He nodded towards my body. "With clothes that fine, yeah you do."

"Oh." Glancing down at my well-tailored black dress and cloak, I tipped my head from side to side. The motion made the buildings around me sway. "Yeah, maybe you've got a point. So I'll be going now."

Whirling around, I walked right into the wall next to me.

Pain cracked through my skull. Stumbling back, I pressed a hand to my forehead in order to stop the throbbing in it. My powers didn't work. I was far too drunk to be able to concentrate enough to phase through a wall.

"The hell is wrong with you, lady?" the male elf said from a few strides away.

"I walked into a wall." An incredulous laugh bubbled from my throat. Throwing my head back, I laughed like a lunatic up into the dark sky. "I just walked into a wall."

"Enough!" He closed the distance between us in a few quick strides and shoved me backwards into the wall again. "I don't have time for your drunk ass. Just hand over your money."

"You're mugging me?" Another laugh ripped from my chest. "You're seriously mugging me? Oh, the universe sure has a sense of humor."

Anger flashed over his face and he raised his knife. "This is your last chance."

My hands shot towards my weapons. I blinked in surprise when I remembered that I wasn't wearing any. The reality of the situation started trickling in as I took in the mugger's serious face. He had me at knifepoint. I was alone and unarmed and so damn drunk that I could barely stand, let alone actually put up any kind of resistance. I swallowed.

Felix had been right.

This night wasn't going to end well.

CHAPTER 26

"Hand it over," the mugger ground out between gritted teeth.

Spreading my hands, I shook my head. "I don't–"

"Now!"

"I believe the lady said no," came a midnight voice from the darkness beside us.

The thief before me jumped back and whirled towards the sound of the voice. I squinted against the poor light and my own drunken eyesight but I couldn't make anything out in the dark alley.

"Show yourself," the blond elf snapped and raised his knife before him.

"Gladly." A figure dressed all in black with a hood obscuring his face glided out of the darkness.

The mugger crouched into an attack position and then leaped. Or he meant to, at least. Shock slammed onto his features when he realized that he was still standing in the same spot as before.

"W-why can't I move?" he stammered.

Staying silent, the newcomer sauntered up to him and plucked the knife from his hand. I stared at the two of them, trying to figure out the same thing that the mugger wanted to know. Why couldn't he move?

After gripping the elf's shoulder, the stranger turned him around so that he faced me instead. Panic flashed across his features now that he was standing with his unprotected back to the male behind him. While remaining out of sight from the mugger, the dark figure pushed his hood down.

My eyes widened.

Mordren Darkbringer smirked at me from behind the thief's shoulder.

Of course. Now that I knew what to look for, I could see the black tendrils snaking along the dark street before wrapping around the mugger's limbs, holding them immobile.

"Ambushing drunk ladies is bad manners." The Prince of Shadows lifted the stolen knife and placed it against the male's throat from behind. "Apologize."

"What?" he blurted out.

"Beg her forgiveness." His silver eyes glittered as he pushed the blade harder against his captive's throat. "On your knees."

My mouth dropped open as the blond elf lowered himself to his knees. Mordren kept the knife in place the whole way down.

"Beg," he ordered.

The mugger swallowed. "I beg your forgiveness."

"Good. Now you get to live." Mordren flipped the blade over and hit him in the back of the head with the hilt.

I stared at the Prince of Shadows. "Fuck, that was hot."

A curious expression drifted over Mordren's face as he looked up at me and arched an eyebrow. I slapped a hand over my mouth. Had I said that out loud? When a satisfied smirk spread across Mordren's lips, I considered taking the knife and stabbing myself with it.

He huffed a quiet laugh before jerking his chin at me. "You're drunk. Let's go."

Since I was still too mortified by my outburst, I simply did as he said and walked over to him. He wrapped an arm around my waist, and before I could protest, worldwalked us away.

Only then did it occur to me that he could be taking me anywhere. To Prince Edric. To the Court of Shadows. To some kind of torture dungeon. Before my mind could conjure up even worse places, the world righted itself around us again.

My stomach turned, as it always did when I worldwalked, except now the feeling was amplified by my drunkenness. I pressed a hand against my mouth while stumbling a step away.

"If you vomit, I'll make you clean it up," Mordren threatened when he noticed my expression. "Got it?"

I swallowed twice before dropping my hand. "Got it."

"Let's go."

Glancing up, I found the coffeehouse I had met him in once before. The White Cat. A key appeared in his hand and he slid it into the lock. Wood creaked as he swung the door open and motioned for me to enter. While wondering what kind of arrangement he really had with the owner of this place, I walked across the threshold and into the dark room beyond.

"Sit at the bar," he ordered.

Being far too drunk to disobey, I slumped down on a barstool while Mordren disappeared into a back room. He returned a minute later with a glass, a water pitcher, and a lit candle. After placing the glass and the candle in front of me, he poured the water. Once the glass was full, he slid it towards me.

"Drink."

"And people say I'm bossy," I muttered but picked up the glass and emptied it in one go.

Mordren filled my glass again. Water ran down the side of the pitcher when he tipped it back up. He wiped it off with a linen napkin before placing them both on the counter. Resting his forearms against the pale wood, he leaned forward and locked eyes with me.

"Why haven't you been answering the traveling book?"

"Oh." I let out a chuckle and scratched the back of my neck. "About that. It might have gotten drenched in blood during that fight in my parents' house."

Blowing out a breath, he shot me an exasperated look.

I shrugged. "Why do you think I wrote in the very corner of the page when I asked you to come that day?"

"And you didn't think to tell me?"

"I'm telling you now."

Heaving another sigh, he stuck a hand inside his dark jacket and withdrew two small leather-bound books. He handed me one. "Here. We'll use these instead. I suspected that something had happened to the previous one because not even you would be foolish enough to actually ignore my messages."

"I may have considered it at one point." Flashing him a mischievous grin, I picked up my new traveling book and pulled out the small pen from the spine.

"What are you doing?"

"Making sure it works."

The pen scratched against paper as I wrote a short sentence on the first page. After shaking his head, Mordren picked up his book and flipped it open. I had the pleasure of seeing his eyes widen as he read the rather scandalous message I had scrawled. Then he cleared his throat and jerked his chin towards my glass again.

"You're still drunk. I only came to confront you about not answering the traveling book, but you need to sober up a bit before I can let you leave. Can't have my little traitor spy get knifed to death in a mugging, now can I?"

I muttered something rude under my breath that sober me would never have dared say to the Prince of Shadows, but sipped some more water. Mordren watched me intently from across the counter. Outside the tavern, the night lay still. Only a strong wind rattled the shutters on the windows and broke the quiet. Grabbing the linen napkin from the bar, I pressed it to my lips while trying to force the alcohol to stop muddling my mind and messing with the filter that usually kept me from saying things I shouldn't. It didn't work.

"Your friends suck," Mordren said suddenly.

"Excuse me?"

"You heard me. Your friends suck."

Drawing my eyebrows down, I brandished the napkin between us like a weapon. "I won't let you stand there and insult my friends."

"You're threatening me with a napkin? Really?" He gave me an incredulous look before snatching the white linen cloth from my hand and putting it back on the bar. "I'm serious. You have shitty friends. They let you walk around alone, completely wasted. If you had been one of my friends, I would never have let you walk the streets alone like that."

I blinked at him. "You have friends?"

"That surprises you?"

"Yeah, I thought you only had minions."

Mordren frowned at me. "Minions?"

"You know, people you can boss around."

A surprised chuckle slipped his lips but all he said was, "I see."

Reaching over, I grabbed the water pitcher and refilled my glass. The wind howled outside while I sipped at my water again. Mordren was still leaning his forearms against the counter, watching my every move intently. Wood creaked as I shifted my weight on the chair.

"Why do you let people use you so much?" An unreadable mask had slipped onto his features.

"What do you mean?"

"Your family is using you to clear their debt and these friends you were out with tonight don't seem to care much either, as long as they get what they want. Why do you let them use you like that?"

Feelings that I didn't want to examine too closely swirled through my chest. I shoved them down and instead shot a glare at the Prince of Shadows. "That's pretty rich coming from you. You're using me too."

"Yes, but the difference is that I have never pretended to be your friend." Without taking his eyes off me, he started tracing the rim of the now empty pitcher with his finger. "You do what I say because I have the power to end you if you don't. But they pretend to care about you."

A vicious retort formed on my lips but it died before I could spit it out. Instead, I tipped my head back and raked my fingers through my hair while heaving a deep sigh. "Maybe I just want to belong somewhere." Tilting my head back down, I met his gaze. "Do you have any idea what it's like?"

"What what's like?"

"To be a bastard born half-elf who most people just see as

Prince Edric's plaything." A harsh laugh ripped from my throat. "Yes, my friends and family might say mean things sometimes, but at least with them I have a place."

"It's a shitty place."

"It's better than being alone."

Mordren cocked his head. "Is it? If they prevent you from being who you really are, is it truly better?"

"You have no idea what it's like." I slammed the glass back onto the bar. "You have no idea what it's like being around this elite, these envied people that everyone wants to be like, while always knowing that you will never be one of them. They're beautiful and they're rich and they have the right last name. And all you have are your wits. So you use that to try and win your place there too, but you never will. You're always the plus one, the person who only gets to come because one of these elites deigned to bring you along." Shaking my head, I tightened my grip on the glass until it almost shattered. "Constantly being around these people but always knowing that you will never be one of them. That you will never be enough. Do you have any idea what that's like?"

Silence descended on the coffeehouse. I watched the light from the candle flicker over Mordren's face while the reality of what I had just admitted crashed into me. Horror sluiced through my chest. The Prince of Shadows opened his mouth but before he could reply, I cut him off.

"Don't say anything. Just pretend I didn't say that." I didn't even try to hide the pleading note in my voice. "Please."

Propping up my elbows on the countertop, I buried my face in my hands. I hadn't meant to say any of that but the words had just tumbled out of me. His incessant questions had drawn the first couple of answers out of me, and once I started, I hadn't been able to stop. What I had told him had been the raw truth of how I felt, but I had never admitted it to anyone before. Not to my family. Not to Monette. No one.

"Mordren," a voice said behind me. "It's been taken care of."

I jerked up and whirled around to face the newcomer. A gasp escaped my throat and I fell off the barstool as the surprise made me forget to stop my movement.

Before me stood the most stunning elf I had ever seen. Long black hair flowed down his back and sparkling light green eyes were set into a face so beautiful it defied nature.

"Whoa," my drunk and still completely filterless mouth blurted out while I slid back onto the barstool. "Who is this? Who are you?"

A half-smile tugged at Mordren's lips. "This is one of those friends you were so surprised I had."

"Oh." I continued gaping at the gorgeous elf. "You're beautiful."

"Thank you." His brilliant smile turned into a smirk when he shifted his gaze to the Prince of Shadows.

Mordren blew out a sigh. "Great, I'll never hear the end of this."

I flicked my gaze between the two of them. A rather ridiculous drunk giggle slipped from my lips as I turned to Mordren. "He's even prettier than you."

While the newcomer chuckled behind me, Mordren let out a pained groan. "Please stop, or his ego will grow so large he won't fit through the door."

"You're one to talk," his friend shot back.

The Prince of Shadows lifted his hand and gave him a rather rude gesture in reply. Incredulity filled me as I watched their exchange. I had never seen the prince behave... like an actual person. It was almost a bit jarring.

Mordren caught the look on my face and wiped all trace of emotion off his features. After blowing out the candle, he rounded the bar and sauntered towards the door.

"You're clearly still drunk, but I don't have time to babysit you all night." He jerked his chin at me. "Let's go. I'll worldwalk you back to the castle walls instead."

Too stunned to argue, I simply hopped down from the barstool and followed the two exiting elves across the white stone floor. The room swayed around me. Throwing out a hand, I steadied myself on a pale wooden table before continuing towards the door again.

When I stepped into the cold night, the gorgeous elf was already gone. Mordren twitched his fingers at me. I considered flipping him off but thought better of it and stalked towards him instead. After locking the door to the White Cat, the Prince of Shadows wrapped an arm around my waist and worldwalked us out.

Gleaming white walls rose before me a second later.

Taking a step away from me, Mordren straightened his dark clothes and ran a hand through his long black hair. His silver eyes were hard as they locked on me. "Next time I contact you through the traveling book, you'd better answer."

"Yeah, yeah, I got it," I muttered and made to turn around, but before I could, his hand shot out.

Holding my jaw in a firm grip, he stared me down. "Don't make me come get you again."

"I said I got it." When he still didn't release me, I blew out a sigh. "I understand, my prince."

"Good." He let his hand drop and took a step back.

"Hey," I said before he could worldwalk away. "Thanks for helping me out tonight."

Something blew across his face but he simply gave me a nod and then disappeared into thin air. I shook my head.

How drunk was I? Had everything that had taken place at the White Cat actually happened? Given his cold dictatorial manners these past couple of minutes, it didn't seem likely. While keeping one hand on the stone wall for support, I trudged towards the main gate.

My head was pounding, my mouth was dry, my mind was incredibly confused, and I regretted about half of everything I had said tonight.

Glaring at the stones before my feet, I stalked forward.

I was never drinking again.

CHAPTER 27

The White Cat coffeehouse lay dark and empty. I cast a glance at its pale wooden door as I moved down the street and towards the shadier parts of town. Lingering embarrassment flared up inside me at the sight of it. The worst part of last night wasn't the massive hangover I'd had today. Or that I had almost been mugged and stabbed. It wasn't even that Monette and Felix had forgotten that I was supposed to meet them at the Purple Crown and hadn't remembered me until this morning. No. The worst part was realizing what I had actually said to the Prince of Shadows.

In addition to rather pathetically admitting that I felt like I didn't belong, I had also told him that he was hot. Hot. Heat seared my cheeks at the mere thought of it. And don't even get me started on the wholly inappropriate thing I had written to him when I tried out the new traveling book. I dreaded having to face him after that. But I hoped that if I kept my mouth shut about the fact that he had almost behaved like an actual person there for a few minutes, he would keep my words to himself as well. Then again, this was Mordren

Darkbringer we were talking about. I wouldn't put anything past him.

"Fancy a trip, love?" a human man said to a woman on my right.

He was standing outside a three-story house. All the windows had been thrown open and sweet-smelling white smoke hung like a cloud over the whole establishment. The woman he had addressed hesitated for a moment but then slunk across the threshold.

Returning my gaze to the road ahead, I continued towards my destination. I had reached the rougher parts of town and if I'd been dressed the way I was yesterday, I would've had to watch my back very carefully while traversing these streets. Now, however, people took one look at the black mask across my face and the sword strapped to my back and decided that there were far easier people to target.

I ran a hand over the hilt of my knife while veering into a side alley. Unmarked buildings stood crammed side by side, but I had scouted out this place earlier so I knew where to go. A thick wooden door appeared on my right. As a courtesy, I actually opened it before going inside.

"I'm here to see Liveria Inkweaver," I said as I closed the door behind me.

A muscled elf with silvery white hair rose from a chair next to the wall. "Who referred you?"

"I referred myself."

Taking a step to the side, he crossed his arms and blocked the doorway behind him. "No one gets to see her unless they've been referred by a previous client."

"I think you'll make an exception for me."

"No exceptions." He stabbed a hand towards the front door. "Get out."

While drumming my fingers against my thigh, I considered whether it would've been better to just walk through the walls from the adjacent building. But from what I'd been told, even if I got to the Inkweaver, I needed some kind of pass from this guard for her to actually do any work for me. Blowing out an irritated sigh, I stalked towards the silver-haired elf.

"Look, I didn't want to do this…" I began.

He shot forward. Moving with speed that I hadn't expected from someone of that size, he smacked aside the arm I had been raising and grabbed a fistful of my jacket. With a whirl, he slammed me into the wall.

Air exploded from my lungs and I barely managed to draw a breath before his right hand was around my throat. The other pinned my wrist to the wall beside me. I lifted my other hand to pry his off but his fingers didn't so much as twitch. Glancing down, I understood why. His arms had morphed into stone. Very unbreakable, immovable stone.

"No one gets to see Liveria unless they have been referred by a trusted client. And now you are going to leave."

His grip on my throat tightened until I was choking. I clawed uselessly at his stone-covered hand while panic blared in my mind but he didn't let up. My vision was starting to blacken.

"When I release your throat, your first words had better be 'yes, sir.'"

I collapsed to my knees when he finally withdrew his hands. Pressing my palms to the cold stone floor, I sucked in desperate gasps while trying to force the remaining panic away. After a few broken coughs and some more gulps of air, I craned my neck to look up at the muscled elf. His arms had returned to their normal state but his gaze was still hard as rock as he waited for me to say 'yes, sir.' I didn't.

"Does Liveria know that you're stealing from her?" I croaked instead.

Fear flashed in his eyes and he cast a quick look through the doorway behind him. Stone started spreading over his arms again as he whirled back and reached for me, but before he could snap my neck, I pressed on.

"If you kill me, she will definitely find out. My associates have explicit instructions."

He stilled.

Earlier this week, I had found out where he lived and gone through his rooms until I found something to use as leverage to solve this exact problem. I needed the Inkweaver's skills because she was the best at what she did but she only worked with a very small and exclusive group. There was no way I would be able to get in on that. Unless I blackmailed my way into it. And fortunately for me, her trusted guard was also stealing from her.

Drawing another deep breath, I pushed myself off the floor and straightened in front of the muscled elf. "And unless you give me a pass and let me go see her right now, she is going to find out as well." When uncertainty blew across his features, I leaned closer to his face and smirked at him even though he couldn't see it behind the mask. "Your next words had better be 'yes, my lady.'"

Silence fell over the hallway. I took pleasure in seeing the worry in his eyes as they once more darted towards the doorway behind him. One word from me and he would be ruined. I knew that it made me a truly awful person but that kind of power and control made my soul sing.

After heaving a resigned sigh, he shoved a hand inside his

jacket and withdrew a metal token the size of a large coin. An inkpot with a quill in it had been stamped on both sides. Without a word, he dropped it into my waiting palm.

"I assume I can keep this." My fingers curled around the coin. "For when I need to see her again."

He gave me a curt nod. "And your side of the bargain?"

"I'm a blackmailer of my word." Flashing him another evil smile that he couldn't see, I started towards the open doorway behind him. "She will never know."

The staircase beyond the doorway led to a small landing with only one door. I made sure that my mask was still in place before pushing down the handle and slipping inside.

"You're new," Liveria Inkweaver said from behind a gigantic marble desk.

With her brown hair, brown eyes, and bland face, she looked very unassuming. But despite her misleading looks, I knew that when it came to her particular magical skills, she was second to none.

"I am." I held up the metal coin as I moved closer. When she gave me a nod in acknowledgement, I pocketed the token and instead pulled out some other items. Paper rustled as I placed them on the desk before Liveria and then pointed at them in turn. "I want you to write this, on this, in this handwriting."

Her eyes scanned the text before her. She arched an eyebrow at me in surprise but then simply motioned for me to sit down. "Not a problem. Please have a seat."

Wood scraped against stone as I pulled out the chair across from her and dropped into it. Making myself comfortable, I settled in to wait while the best document forger in the whole Court of Stone worked her magic on the pages before her.

It was finally time to put all my plans into motion.

CHAPTER 28

*L*eaves rustled around me as strong winds blew through the forest, bringing with them the earthen smell of damp soil and moss. I adjusted the scarf covering my hair and rolled my shoulders forward into a more submissive pose as I approached the guards at the entrance to Prince Iwdael's palace in the Court of Trees.

"State your business." The red-headed guard on the right frowned as he flicked his eyes up and down my paint-splattered dress.

While wringing my hands, I lowered my eyes to his chest and kept them there. "Princess Syrene has requested a redecoration of her royal quarters. I'm here to take measurements and sketch the layout."

"Right, I remember her giving us a heads-up about that," the other guard said.

Of course you do, I thought because the princess actually had plans to redecorate. Blackmailing my way into that particular piece of information had taken most of the week, but it had been worth it. There was no way I would be allowed entry into the royal chambers with a fabricated excuse. The only viable option had been to steal someone else's appointment.

"You've got the work order?" the first guard said.

"Right here."

After withdrawing a rolled-up parchment from my satchel, I handed it to him. I had to resist the urge to hold my breath as his eyes scanned the pages. Just when I thought he was going to challenge the authenticity of them, he nodded to himself and gave them back to me.

"It checks out." Tipping his head to the side, he motioned for me to enter. "Go ahead. And make sure you show these to the guards outside the royal wing too."

"Thank you. I will."

Warmth enveloped me as I left the cold fall day behind and moved into the castle. A small sigh of relief escaped me as I slunk through the first hallway. Keeping my shoulders curved inwards and my posture unassuming, I made my way towards the royal quarters in silence.

When I passed the route to the throne room, I had to force myself to walk with the same unhurried pace as before, but my heart hammered in my chest. If Princess Syrene spotted me, I was dead. Even with my paint-splattered dress, demure posture, and the scarf covering my red hair, I had no doubt that she would be able to recognize me if she saw me. Elves bustled past me in the corridors. I kept my eyes on the ground while praying fervently to whatever gods or spirits might be listening that none of them would turn out to be the princess.

"Halt," a voice said up ahead. "This is the royal wing."

"I know." I pulled out the work order again and held it out before me while approaching the line of guards I had tried to sneak past a couple of weeks ago. "I'm here to take measurements and sketch the layout for the redecoration."

My fingers itched for a weapon I didn't have when the four of them stared me down. One of the two in the middle took the scroll from my outstretched hand. Paper rustled as he unrolled it. In my chest, my heart pattered against my ribs while I waited in silence for him to finish scrutinizing the documents.

"She's clear." Handing the papers back, he took a step to the side. "Go ahead, girl."

It took all my training to keep the relief that surged through me from showing on my face as I dipped my chin. "Thank you."

Every step down the hall and towards the royal rooms felt like it took forever. My pulse thrummed in my ears as I waited for the guards to change their minds and rush over to arrest me. When I finally crossed the threshold into the restricted wing, I almost sagged to my knees. I had done it. After all this time, I had finally managed to get inside the royal wing. Looking up, I took in the sight of my victory.

An airy lounge opened before me. Dark wooden walls curved around to make room for a set of couches and divans in green and gold on the left while spectacular glass cabinets covered the whole right wall. Atop the shelves were crystal bottles filled with liquor of every color. I even spotted a bejeweled water pipe on one shelf. I raised my eyebrows as I moved further in. Say what you will about the disorganized Prince of Trees, but he sure knew how to have a good time.

The lounge split into two separate rooms at the back. They were equally magnificent but decorated very differently. The one on the right was full of comfortable furniture that truly looked like it had been used, while the one on the left was more put-together. Like a carefully constructed façade. I snuck into the first and took a quick look around before doing the same in the other room.

Male clothes filled the closet in the right room and dresses occupied the pale wooden one in the room on the left. So, the royal couple slept in separate bedrooms. That at least made my job a bit easier because if the dagger was here, it would most certainly be in Syrene's bedroom. After casting a quick look over my shoulder, I got to work.

There was no knowing when the princess or the prince would return to their rooms, so I had to be quick. While staying as silent as I could, I opened every drawer and cabinet, checked every nook and cranny, and patted down each piece of furniture. Twice. My irritation as well as my stress levels rose when I still hadn't found the dagger after turning the room upside down yet again.

Swallowing a string of curses, I darted back into the lounge. Pillows flew up and down in the air as I yanked them up, patted the surface underneath, and then rammed them back down one after the other. Nothing. I turned towards the liquor cabinet. This was going to be tricky.

After casting a glance out the door to make sure that the guards were still standing in the corridor with their backs to me, I hurried over to the other side of the room. Opening the first glass door, I let out a soft breath and began checking behind each bottle and underneath every shelf.

Clinking crystal echoed across the room. I froze. With my heart slamming against my ribs, I waited to see if the guards would come and investigate. The seconds dragged on. A silent sigh of relief escaped my lips as I returned the two bottles I had accidentally dinged together to their rightful places.

When my search of the lounge produced no results either,

I looked towards Prince Iwdael's room. The princess couldn't possibly be stupid enough to keep the dagger there, but it was the only place I hadn't searched.

"How's it going in there?" one of the guards called from the hallway.

"Almost done," I replied with a confidence I most certainly didn't feel.

"Alright. Prince Iwdael and Princess Syrene will be back soon and we don't want to inconvenience them in their own rooms when they want to relax so it would be best if you were out of there before they got back."

"Of course." While sprinting towards the prince's room, I called over my shoulder, "You're completely right."

They had no idea just how right they really were.

Moving across the wooden floor like a streak of lightning, I searched every surface of the comfortable-looking room. Bed, desk, drawers, closet, sofas, chairs. On top of them, under them, on every side. Nothing.

"Hurry up," the guard called again.

Disappointment deflated my chest as I was forced to conclude that the Dagger of Orias was not here. But there was nothing more I could do about that, and I was out of time. Snatching up my satchel again, I strode back into the hallway.

"Did you get everything you need?" the same guard asked.

No, I wanted to growl but I forced a shy smile onto my face instead. "Yes."

"Good. Now hurry, they should be back any minute."

Keeping my shoulders curved and my head bowed, I moved as fast as I could without actually running.

Voices came from the corridor up ahead.

Alarm bells tolled in my mind. I needed to round the bend in the hall so that the guards couldn't see me before I took any drastic measures but if I waited too long, the prince and princess would come around the corner on the other side and see me.

While drawing soft shallow breaths, I counted down the remaining steps in my head.

The voices grew louder.

Blood rushed in my ears.

A long leg appeared from around the corner on the other side just as I cleared the bend in the corridor on my end. Not wasting a second, I threw myself through the wall on my left.

The smell of clean linen enveloped me. Pressing myself against the closest shelf, I waited inside the linen closet while the unwitting royals walked past on the other side of the wall.

Once I had estimated that they were long gone, I phased back through it and into the empty corridor.

Not daring to delay even a second, I started back towards the main entrance again. It took more effort than I wanted to admit to keep a neutral expression on my face as I walked past the guards at the gate and into the cold overcast day again.

Once I reached the storage shed I had hidden in after my failed break-in earlier, I threw my bag on the ground and took out all my frustration on the closest crate.

After all my scheming to get into the royal wing, the dagger hadn't even been there in the first place.

And now, I had to start all over again.

CHAPTER 29

This was most likely going to get me killed. But I was out of options. Drawing a bracing breath, I lifted my hand and knocked on the wooden door before me.

Surprised green eyes blinked at me as it swung open. "Kenna."

"Hello, Evander."

Leaning out, he whipped his head from side to side, looking in both directions of the hall as if uncertain where I had come from. Which he of course had every right to be since I had been standing in a storage shed, changing out of a paint-splattered dress and into this green one only a few minutes ago, before I had walked through the walls to get to his room.

"I didn't know you were coming," he said.

"I'm sorry." I motioned vaguely at the wooden hallway around me. "I can leave if you want."

"No, no." Shaking his head vigorously he stepped aside to let me in. "Please, come in." He dragged a hand through his brown hair as I moved inside. "Sorry about the mess."

Discarded clothes indeed lay scattered across the bed and the two armchairs by the wall, while a couple of empty bottles littered the surface next to the liquor cabinet. Evander quickly gathered up the heaps of garments and shoved them into his closet while I took a seat on his bed.

"I have to tell you something," I said.

Worry flashed in his emerald eyes. "Okay?"

"Please come and sit."

After raking his fingers through his hair again, he approached and sat down next to me. The mattress creaked slightly beneath his weight. Drawing one leg up underneath me, I turned so that I sat facing him.

"Do you remember at the equinox ball when I left for a while?"

"Yeah?"

Glancing down at my hands, I hesitated. "Well, I saw something I shouldn't have."

"Okay, what did you see?"

My heart thumped in my chest as I looked up and met his gaze head on again. *Here goes nothing.* "This is going to sound crazy but... Princess Syrene tried to kill King Aldrich."

"What?" Doubt filled his face as he scrunched up his eyebrows and stared back at me. "That can't be true."

"It is. She has the Dagger of Orias and she tried to use it to kill the king at the ball."

The bed groaned again as Evander pushed to his feet and took to pacing the room. Shaking his head, he frowned down at the floor while stalking back and forth. Then he stopped and turned back to me.

"Look, you know that I respect you, Kenna. And I would never call you a liar." A pained expression settled on his face. "But this just sounds a bit too... farfetched. Are you sure that's what you saw? We had been drinking, so maybe you just misinterpreted the situation."

At least him doubting me was better than him calling the guards to have me arrested for slandering his princess. Keeping my eyes soft, I looked back at him.

"Yes, I'm sure."

He was silent for a moment. "Why are you telling me this?"

"Because I need your help." I got to my feet as well. "We can't let her kill the King of Elves! It would lead to civil war. Could you imagine how many lives that would be lost as a result of that? We can't let that happen."

"No, of course not." Helplessness washed over his handsome features as he spread his arms. "But what are we supposed to do about it?"

"We have to find the dagger and give it to the king."

Frowning, he waved a hand towards the closed door. "Why don't we just tell Prince Iwdael? And then he can deal with it."

"Because he might be in on it," I lied smoothly. "If he is, and we tell him, he'll have us executed."

"So tell the Prince of Stone! Or someone else who is more equipped to deal with something like this."

"We can't." Reaching out, I took his hand in mine and squeezed gently. "If any of the other princes find out about this, they could use that against your court. And I don't want you to get hurt."

Evander pulled his hand from mine and took a step back while shaking his head. "I just…"

"Please." I took a step towards him but he retreated again. "I can't do this alone. You have access to the castle all the time so you can easily tail Princess Syrene without drawing attention. We can find the dagger together and bring it to the king. We can stop an assassination and a war and–"

"Stop," he interrupted. "Please, Kenna. I just… I need some time." While raking his finger through his hair once more, he backed towards the door. "I need some time. I need to think."

"Okay." I watched as he shook his head one more time before opening the door and disappearing into the hallway beyond.

Once it had shut behind him with a soft click, I slumped down in one of the armchairs and heaved a deep sigh.

Sometimes I forgot that stopping assassination plans wasn't a common activity for normal people. I supposed I couldn't blame him. He had come here from a quiet life at the edge of the forest and now I had just informed him that his princess had tried to kill the King of Elves with a magical dagger that was believed to be lost. Resting my head against the back of the chair, I closed my eyes.

At least now he knew the truth about the dagger. He knew that I needed to find it and give it to King Aldrich, and that was the important part. The fact that I was going to use it to get my freedom too wasn't something that he would count as a betrayal. Not in the way that just using him to find the dagger and then leaving would have been. But even sharing this much had been a gamble.

If he told anyone else about this, about me, I was as good as dead. Trusting Evander was the riskiest thing I had done in quite some time, but if I was going to have any chance of finding this dagger then I needed his help. All I could do was hope that his feelings for me were stronger than his fear.

My heart pattered in my chest as I waited to see if Evander would come back to help or to sentence me to death.

Drumming my fingers against the velvet armrest, I prayed that I had been right to trust him.

I shot to my feet as the door finally creaked open. With my pulse beating wildly, I waited to see who would walk across the threshold.

When a brown-haired elf in a green shirt was the only person to enter the room, I almost sagged back into the armchair. Evander closed the door behind him before leaning back against the dark wooden surface. A small smile tugged at his lips.

"Alright, I'm in."

My face lit up. "You are?"

"Yeah." Pushing off the door, he closed the distance between us. "I'm sorry I freaked out. I'm just not… used to stuff like this."

"Completely understandable. I freaked out too at first. I think anyone would."

He brushed his fingers over my cheek. "But I'm here now. So, how do we start?"

"Grab some paper and a couple of pens." A mischievous grin spread across my lips as I moved back towards his bed. "Now, we scheme."

Time flew past as we discussed potential hiding places and strategies before I moved on to teaching him all I knew about how to tail someone without them noticing. He wrote everything down, and thankfully never questioned how in the world I happened to be in possession of that particular knowledge. When I had finally exhausted my rather deep well of information, I flopped down on my back and rested my head against his soft pillows. The mattress bounced underneath me as Evander did the same.

"Do you really think this will work?" he asked while turning his head to look at me.

I rolled over on my side to meet his gaze. "Yeah, I do."

He nodded against the mattress before propping himself up on one elbow and twisting his body towards me. Lifting his other hand, he reached out and pushed a loose lock of hair back behind my ear. "I'm glad you told me."

A pleasant shudder went through me as he trailed his fingers down my cheek. "Me too."

For a moment, we only continued staring into each other's eyes in silence. Somewhere outside, rippling laughter drifted through the air.

"I can't stop thinking about that kiss," Evander suddenly blurted out.

I blinked in surprise before a smile spread across my lips. "Same here."

"Can I...? I want to..." A nervous chuckle bubbled from his throat. "Can I kiss you again?"

"Yes," I breathed.

While moving his hand to the back of my neck, he leaned forward and brushed his lips against mine. I grabbed the front of his shirt and rolled over on my back while pulling him on top of me.

He laughed against my mouth. "Easy."

I didn't want to take it easy. I wanted to feel his body against mine, his hands on my skin, his mouth against mine. Releasing my grip on his shirt, I ran my fingers down his chest until I found the first button. While still ravaging his lips, I started unbuttoning his shirt. His hands trailed down my body until they reached the edge of my dress that had gotten all bundled up around my thighs. With gentle fingers, he pulled it upwards.

The final button on his shirt came loose and I pushed his dark green shirt off his shoulders. Pausing briefly, he took his hands from my body and shrugged out of the garment. While he shimmied out of his pants as well, I yanked my dress over my head.

Fabric rustled in the air as we both threw our clothes across the room.

His eyes shone with affection as he leaned down over me and traced his hands over my ribs. My skin prickled at his touch. Reaching up, I put a hand behind his neck and yanked him towards me until his lips met mine. He rocked his hips gently while I raked my fingers down his shoulders. I wanted more. Arching my back, I moaned into his mouth until an answering one ripped from his throat.

The problems of tomorrow fell away as my body joined his in a gentle rhythm there among the rumpled sheets in a foreign court.

After release finally surged through his body, Evander slumped back on the mattress beside me. His chest heaved. Twisting to the side, I watched the astounded expression on his face.

"That was… Wow." He rolled over on his side to face me as well. Leaning forward, he placed a hand on my cheek and gave me a soft kiss before drawing back slightly again. His eyes were locked on mine. "You're so beautiful. And caring and selfless. I can't believe how lucky I am to have met you."

Strange feelings pricked my chest at his words. I really wished he had said something else. Complimented me on something other than being caring and selfless. Maybe because I knew that it wasn't true. Or perhaps because, deep in my wicked heart, I knew that I didn't want to be caring and selfless.

If he only knew the real me, the one who had just straight out manipulated him for weeks before I had finally grown a conscience and stopped, then he wouldn't be saying things like that. Scooting closer, I buried my face in his neck. He wrapped his arm around my back and pulled me closer. While resting a hand on his still heaving chest, I tried to smother the voices in my head.

I might be an awful person sometimes. But by all the gods and spirits, I was so glad that I at least didn't have to betray him anymore.

CHAPTER 30

*P*erfume hit me like a brick to the face. While stifling a cough, I closed the door behind me and moved further into the hut. Beads clinked.

"The Black Mask, back so soon."

"Hello, Stella." I smiled at the old woman even though she couldn't see it beneath my disguise.

Her thick glasses glinted in the light from the flickering candles as she tilted her head to study me. "I trust my previous information panned out."

"It did indeed. And now I need some more."

A chuckle shook her plump frame before she motioned for me to sit down at the table. I tried to breathe through my mouth as much as possible while moving through the perfume-drenched cottage and sliding into the chair closest to the door. Stella lowered herself into the one opposite me. Reaching into my jacket, I pulled out several sheets of paper and placed them on the table between us.

"I need to know everything there is to know about these

people." Grabbing the top half of the pile, I slid the drawings towards her. "And the juicier the better."

"Busy, busy girl." The wrinkled skin around her eyes creased even more as she grinned at me before picking up the first sheet of paper. "Let's see what we've got."

Wind chimes tinkled outside and filled the silence while Stella examined the drawings I had brought. The occasional *hmm* and *ah* were her only comments. I absentmindedly pushed the other stack of papers around the tabletop while she pondered.

"Oh!"

I jerked up at her outburst. Paper fluttered through the air as the motion sent the stack I had been poking at clean across the edge. Scrambling up from my chair, I whirled around in an attempt to locate whatever had caused her exclamation.

"What is it?" I asked, whipping my head from side to side.

"Jumpy little thing, aren't you?" She chuckled and waved me back into my seat. "No one is attacking us. I just finally made the connection between all these people you're showing me." Leaning forward, she fixed me with a knowing look. "All of them work as guards at the castle."

Dropping to one knee, I started gathering up the scattered papers that had flown across the floor while I casually tossed over my shoulder, "They do?"

"As if you didn't know." Wood creaked as she leaned back in her chair again. "This wouldn't have anything to do with any kind of treason, now would it?"

Satisfied with my paper hunt, I dumped the stack on the table again before dropping into my chair in a carefree manner. "Of course not. Quite the opposite, really."

"Uh-huh."

I reached into my jacket again and withdrew a rather

impressive amount of money. After running my thumb over the edge and making the bills flap with an enticing sound, I set it down on the wooden tabletop and pushed it towards her. This time it wasn't just the candlelight that glinted in her eyes. With her gaze locked on the pile, she sucked her teeth. Then she reached forward and grabbed it.

She huffed while stuffing it into one of her own pockets. "You're lucky my love of money is stronger than my love for the crown."

Since I knew she couldn't see it behind the mask, I let a knowing smile spread across my lips before simply inclining my head.

"Alright, here's what I know…"

While Stella launched into a lecture on everything she knew about the guards I had selected, I listened and made mental notes about the things that I might be able to exploit for my own gain. The wind chimes outside continued clinking merrily as a gentle breeze swirled through the forest.

"And there you have it," she finished with a satisfied nod. "Got what you needed?"

"Always." After gathering up all the sheets of papers on the table, I rolled them up and stuck them back into various pocket of my black jacket. "Thank you, Stella."

"Now, I'm taking your word for it that I won't wake up tomorrow to hear that the prince and princess have been assassinated in the night."

I chuckled. "I have no intention of assassinating anyone. Promise."

"Good. Until next time then, Black Mask."

"Until next time."

With one final nod, I turned around and slipped back into the bright fall day outside. Crisp air smelling of moss and pine met me. I drew a couple of deep breaths to clear the perfume from my lungs before starting back towards the spot where Felix would be waiting for me. It was time to pay a visit to a group of guards.

∼

Red eyes stared down at me. I stood my ground as the muscled guard shifted his gaze from the paper in his hand, to my face, and then back again. Clanking swords came from further inside the barracks. Once he had finally finished reading the document I had given him, he looked back up at me.

"The buff black-haired dude, right?"

"Yeah."

"Alright, seems straightforward enough." He raised a bushy eyebrow expectantly. "And the money?"

I pulled out a stack of bills and placed it in his waiting palm. "I cannot stress enough how important it is that this is kept secret. Prince Edric will have all our heads if anyone else learns about this. Do exactly what it says in the instructions and don't tell anyone about my involvement. It could jeopardize the whole mission."

"Got it." A serious expression blew across the guard captain's face. "The prince can count on me."

"Good."

After giving him a somber nod, I spun on my heel and strode back out into the stone courtyard. White marble gleamed in the sunlight. Turning up my collar against the brisk fall winds, I started towards the Court of Stone's so ironically named garden.

I wasn't even sure why I was going there, only that I wasn't ready to go back into the castle yet. Nervous energy bounced around inside of me. So much depended on this. *Everything* depended on this. And I couldn't help worrying that it wouldn't be enough. That I had missed something.

As I reached the edge of the garden, I stopped and leaned against the cold stone wall. Strong winds ripped at my hair. A shiver coursed through me. The sun shone in the bright blue sky, but since I was standing beneath the twisting palace spires, I felt none of its warmth. Even though the skies were clear here, I knew I couldn't stay long because black clouds were rolling in from the west and would soon blanket the city. Tipping my head up, I took a few deep breaths to steady my nerves.

The most stressful part of this scheme was that I wasn't in control of the timeline. I hated not being in control. Normally, *I* wanted to be the one who decided when things happened, but right now that was impossible. I had set up all the pieces to fall in a prearranged way, and now all I could do was wait for the first one to tip over. And then hopefully, the rest would follow.

Standing in the shade, I watched the oncoming storm on the horizon.

This had better work.

CHAPTER 31

When four days had passed and no pieces had started falling into place yet, I was about ready to crawl out of my skin. Pacing back and forth inside my room, I tried to think of things I could do to speed things up without showing my hand. No magical solution presented itself.

A knock sounded at the door. I jerked up and almost ran over to answer it before I remembered that I was supposed to be playing it cool. Forcing myself to move casually, I sauntered over and swung the door wide.

The disinterested face of an attendant who was usually stationed in the throne room met me on the other side. "Evander Loneleaf is here to see you."

My heart leaped into my throat but I kept the neutral expression on my features. "I see. Thanks."

He gave me a nod before turning and striding back towards his post.

This was it. If it had been anything else, Evander would have simply written a letter. But if he had come here in person, it could only mean one thing. He had found the Dagger of Orias.

With my heart thumping in my chest, I grabbed my dark green cloak and then locked the door behind me before hurrying towards the throne room.

Evander had a calm expression on his face where he stood just inside the main entrance, which I was incredibly grateful for since I had been worried that his inexperience might give it away. Plastering a carefree smile on my lips, I approached him.

"It's so good to see you!" I gave him a quick kiss on the cheek. "I've been cooped up inside all day and I'd love to take a stroll and get some fresh air."

Thankfully, he smoothly picked up on what I was doing and offered me his arm. "Sounds like a plan."

After taking it, I started us back down the passageway filled with statues. While filling the silence with meaningless small talk, we made our way across the courtyard and then out the gates.

The city was bustling with people who braved the cold winds in search of wares or simply a good time. From atop the hill, they looked like colorful ants milling around the white stone city.

"Here," I said when we had reached a secluded spot. "We can talk here."

With tall castle walls behind and an unobstructed view of the area on all other side, I felt confident that I would be able to spot any potential eavesdroppers before they ever got within earshot. Standing side by side, we pretended to simply be enjoying the view while we finally got to the part we had been waiting for.

"I found it."

My mouth went dry. "You're sure?"

"Yes. I've been following Princess Syrene these past few days and this morning, I finally had a breakthrough." Evander shuddered and took a step closer as crisp winds tugged at our clothes. "She told Prince Iwdael that she was going for a walk, but she sent her guards away and went straight to the mausoleum instead."

"The mausoleum?" I frowned up at him. "I thought the Court of Trees burned their dead and returned the ashes to the forest."

"We do now. But it wasn't always like that. There is an old mausoleum at the back of the hedge maze where, long ago, the royal family apparently stored the ashes of their loved ones." He shrugged. "From what I've been told, it's empty now, but the building is still there."

"And you're sure the dagger is in there? She wasn't just there to… you know, visit her relatives?"

Evander snorted and shot me an amused look. "Visit her relatives." Chuckling again, he shook his head. "No, there would be no reason for her to be there. For one, the ashes that were there have apparently been scattered in the forest to rejoin nature, like they should have been in the first place. And two, even if they hadn't been, Princess Syrene isn't actually related to anyone from any of the previous royal families."

"Huh. And there's really no other reason why she would be down there?"

"Well, I guess there could be." Scrunching up his eyebrows, he tipped his head from side to side. "But she also lied to the prince and ditched her guards before going there. I don't know. It just sounds a bit too suspicious not to be it."

"True."

Silence fell across the hill as I pondered what he had told me. I didn't like going in without having visual confirmation that the dagger was actually in there, but Evander did have a point. What other reason could the princess have for visiting a decommissioned mausoleum in secret? And if Evander tried to sneak in to make sure, he might get caught. Tailing someone and breaking into a guarded hiding place were two completely different things. Which meant that it would be up to me. And if I was going to go to the trouble of sneaking inside just to see if the dagger was there, I might as well steal the damn thing too.

"Alright," I said, making a decision. "We'll have to assume that the dagger is in there. Now, we just need to make a plan. It would really help if I could see where the mausoleum is and what it looks like."

"Here."

Paper rustled as Evander drew out two rolls of paper. Turning his back to the wind, he unrolled the first one. It was a crudely drawn map of the hedge maze with an X marking our target. The second one was a rough sketch of the building from the outside.

Taking them, I raised my eyebrows. "You drew these?"

"Don't look so surprised." He swatted me on the arm while a proud smile flashed over his lips. "I like to come prepared."

"Good to know." I winked at him before turning my attention back to the drawings. "How did she get in? Did she use a key or something?"

"No, she just knocked on the door and then it opened. So my guess is there's someone in there keeping guard."

"Makes sense." A rogue breeze snatched at the papers so I rolled them up and stuffed them inside my cloak. "Alright, I'll study these and make a plan for getting to the mausoleum."

"And once we're inside?"

"We'll play it by ear."

Worry flashed over his face as he raked his fingers through his hair and started pacing back and forth. "Should we really be doing this alone? You're a courtier and I'm the son of a woodcarver. Doesn't it feel like we're just a little bit out of our depth here?"

If he only knew what I really was. But I couldn't tell him. Not yet. Not until I was free and could make my own choices and actually start building a life that wasn't based on lies and manipulation.

"Who else could we tell?" I spread my arms. "Do you know anyone you trust enough with this information?"

"Well, no. But I don't really know anyone at court." A tiny spark of hope lit his eyes. "But you do. Don't you have someone in your court who knows their way around stuff like this? Someone who could help us break in? We wouldn't even need to tell them why we're doing it."

I most certainly did. Several people, in fact. But if I was to use the dagger to blackmail King Aldrich, then none of them could ever know.

"No, I don't." I gave him a sad smile. "The people I know here are also courtiers, or nobles. They wouldn't know how to do this any more than we do."

His shoulders slumped but he gave me a tentative nod. "Alright, I guess it's up to us then. When are we doing this?"

"Tomorrow."

"Oh." Evander wrapped his arm around my back and pulled me close. Resting his chin on my shoulder, he heaved a soft sigh. "Will you think I'm a wuss if I tell you that I'm kind of scared?"

My heart ached for his innocent soul as I held him tighter. "Not at all. To be honest, I'm worried too."

"What if it doesn't work?"

"Then you run like hell and leave me to deal with the fallout."

He jerked back. With a firm grip on my shoulders, he locked eyes with me. "Not a chance. I know I freaked out in the beginning, but we're in this together now. I'm not leaving you behind. We are going to find the dagger and we are going to stop an assassination. Together."

"And a war."

Chuckling, he drew me into a tight hug again. "And a war."

I held him close and savored his steady warmth while winds ripped around us.

Tomorrow, we would be walking into unknown dangers in the hopes of finding a magical dagger and stopping a princess from killing the King of Elves. There was of course also the tiny detail of blackmailing said king to give me my freedom. And I still hadn't told Evander about that.

Heaving a sigh, I rested my cheek against his chest.

One problem at a time.

CHAPTER 32

Dark clouds blew across the moon. After phasing through the final wall, I remained standing pressed against the white stone while I scanned the courtyard. Nothing moved. I checked my weapons again before straightening my black jacket. Leaving the hood down, I snuck across the empty part of the palace grounds and towards the high defensive walls before continuing towards the city beyond.

Since I couldn't tell anyone that I was heading to the Court of Trees to steal the Dagger of Orias, I also couldn't rely on Felix to get me there. Instead, I would have to use a rogue worldwalker for hire who I knew operated out of the part of town that Collum and his gang controlled. Even though they hadn't seen my face, I didn't exactly relish the risk of running into them. But I didn't have any other options either. Keeping my head down, I left the castle hill behind and veered into a narrow alley that would take me towards the shady parts of town.

"Going somewhere?"

I jumped to the side and reached for my weapons. A figure was leaning against the gray stone wall right inside the alley mouth and staring at me with hard eyes.

"You?" I blurted out. Frowning, I took my hands from my weapons and instead crossed my arms. "What are you doing here?"

The Void pushed off the wall and prowled towards me. "Imagine my surprise when I found out that you and your little boy toy have located the Dagger of Orias and that you're planning on getting it today."

Icy dread seeped into my veins. If he already knew about that then I would have to be a very convincing liar in order to talk my way out of this mess.

"Yeah, we are. Well, we're going to scout it out today, anyway." With an appropriately curious expression on my face, I gave him a casual shrug. "How did you know?"

"Do you really think that anything happens, in any court, that I don't know about?"

Well, yes, since you still haven't figured out that I'm the traitor, I thought with no small amount of smugness, but wisely enough decided not to voice out loud. Instead, I simply said, "I guess not."

The Void had stopped only a stride away and was now glaring at me as if waiting for an answer. Since he technically hadn't asked a question, I just looked back at him with a mildly confused expression on my face. His patience ran out before mine did.

"Why didn't you tell anyone that you had found the dagger?" he demanded.

"I already told you, because we're just going to go scout it out." I gave him a little shake of my head as if that should've been obvious. "We don't know for sure if the dagger is there yet and I didn't want to say anything until I knew for sure. You know what Prince Edric is like. He would've been furious if I'd told him that the dagger was there only to come back later and say that it wasn't."

"Right," he scoffed. "Well, I'm coming with you."

"No, you're not. I've already told Evander that I'll be coming alone."

"So lie to him." A vicious smile flashed over his lips. "You're good at that."

Anger, and a tiny drop of guilt, shot through me but I ignored it and instead threw up my arms in a show of exasperation. "He'll know that something is up! You'd really risk the whole mission just to... what? Satisfy your need for control?"

"Yes, I would. Because here's the thing. I don't trust you." His eyes glinted dangerously as he jutted his chin out. "So right now, you only have two options. One, I go straight to Prince Edric and tell him that you were planning on taking the dagger for yourself. Or two, I go with you to get it, and if you don't do anything else to piss me off, I might be merciful and leave out the part about you trying to sneak off and do this on your own."

Irritation crackled through me. If he actually went to Prince Edric and said that, then there was no way in hell I would ever be allowed to go alone to the Court of Trees again. But how was I supposed to get the dagger to King Aldrich if the Void was there when I stole it? And I couldn't just lead him to an empty location and pretend that the dagger wasn't there because Evander wasn't a spy. He would never be able to convincingly sell that lie to someone like the Void. I would never get another chance like this.

My hand drifted towards the dagger strapped to my thigh.

"Oh please do draw your weapons." His grin widened. "See how that plays out."

As far as I could tell, he wasn't carrying any weapons of his own. But then again, depending on what his magic power was, he might not need any. I couldn't risk it.

"No, of course not." I let my hands fall back by my sides. "Please come with me to check if the dagger really is in the Court of Trees."

"Smart move." With a cocky smile on his face, he twitched his fingers at me. "Let's go then."

Biting back a curse, I moved over until I was standing next to the Void. As soon as he had placed his arm around my waist, we disappeared into the night before finally reappearing again outside the tall wooden walls in the Court of Trees.

An owl hooted in the trees further in. Detaching myself from the Void, I drew a deep breath of cool forest air. The whole area around the castle smelled of moss, soil, and mist.

"I assume you were planning on walking through the wall to get inside," the Void said.

"Yeah, I've told Evander I'll be meeting him in the garden." However, since I had planned on hiring a rogue worldwalker, I hadn't expected to arrive this early. "It'll be a while, though. And I don't have a plan for getting you inside."

The Void scoffed. "Don't worry about it. I'll get inside on my own."

Without another word, he turned and stalked towards the gate. I had half a mind to follow him and see how exactly he would manage that, but then thought better of it. After all, I had some last-minute, panic-fueled scheming to do.

Swallowing the rising dread in my throat, I phased through the tall defensive walls while trying to reformulate the plan I had so carefully constructed but would no longer be able to use. Now, I would not only have to manipulate Evander so that he would let me go and see the king on my own, I would also have to deal with the Void.

In the end, there really only was one option that didn't end with my execution.

I would have to outmaneuver the best spy my court had ever seen.

CHAPTER 33

*L*eaves rustled around us as we made our way through the hedge maze. Arm in arm, we looked like a couple on a casual moonlit stroll through the gardens. At least from a distance. I might be presenting a calm exterior, but on the inside, I was one more misfortune away from crumbling entirely under the pressure.

"Does it make me a scaredy cat if I admit that I'm really glad your father's friend could join us?" Evander let out a nervous laugh. "I've been freaking out all day but now I feel so much better knowing that at least one of us has had some kind of experience with something like this."

"No, not at all." I gave his arm a gentle squeeze. "I was so relieved when he showed up too. I had no idea that he'd be coming back so soon."

He beamed down at me. "I guess sometimes the spirits really do answer our prayers."

Our prayers. Right. Stifling a snort and an eye roll, I instead smiled back at him.

Finding a way to explain the Void's presence hadn't been easy, and the least ridiculous lie I had been able to come up with was that he was a friend of my father's. My real elven father. And that he was some kind of fighter who knew how to carry out secret missions and who had just gotten back from one of them. It was the only explanation that covered both the Void and the reason why I was suddenly wearing weapons.

Evander had looked absolutely flabbergasted when he had seen the sword across my back, as well as the very unladylike black pants and jacket. But once I spun a half truth about my warrior father and his friend, he had thankfully accepted it without question. I guessed that due to his worry and fear, he was more or less ready to believe just about anything that would help us pull this off without getting caught.

"Speaking of," I said as a figure of medium height and build appeared from a nearby path and stopped in front of us. "Here he is."

Silvery light from the moon fell across the Void's bland face. He didn't smile as we closed the distance to him, but at least he didn't glare at us either.

"Nice to meet you." Evander held out his hand as we stopped before him. "I'm really glad you could come."

The Void shook his outstretched hand. "Of course. I couldn't very well say no when Kenna asked for my help."

"She can indeed be quite persuasive." A smile tugged at his lips and he winked at me before his face turned serious again. "We're almost at the mausoleum. What's our plan for the guard?"

"Which guard?" the Void demanded.

I reached into one of my many pockets and pulled out the

map Evander had drawn. In my solitary scheming, I had also filled it in with markings of guards.

When the three of us had gathered around it, I pointed to the guard closest to our location so that the Void would know which one we were talking about as well. "This is him. Just give me a minute to get him out of the way, and then we have a clear shot at the mausoleum."

"What about him?" The Void stabbed a finger at the X marking the elf stationed on the other side of the building.

"Nothing." I didn't have any blackmail leverage on that particular guard, which was why I had suggested that we approach from this side. "We'll just have to leave the same way we came."

"That's a stupid plan."

"Well, do you have a better one?"

"Yeah, I get rid of him too so that we have options in case things go sideways."

I blew out a sharp breath. "Fine."

"Don't kill him," Evander said, worry coloring his voice. "Please. He's only doing his job."

Twisting slightly so that Evander couldn't see, the Void sent me a look that said 'who is this pathetic sap?' but then nodded. "I won't kill him."

After stuffing the map back in my pocket, I put a hand on Evander's shoulder and gave him an encouraging smile. When I was sure that our inexperienced civilian wouldn't freak out, or at least not for the next couple of minutes, I shifted my gaze to the Void. We exchanged a nod. And then we took off in opposite directions.

Once my back was to Evander, I raised my hood and pushed the black mask down in front of my face.

Dark bushes flashed past in the corner of my eye but were soon replaced by a stretch of open grass. A tense figure paced back and forth a short distance ahead, and behind him, a building made of white wood shone like a jewel in the night. The mausoleum.

"Hey," he called. "Who are you? What are you doing out here all alone?"

"Oh, thank the spirits! I couldn't sleep so I was out walking but then I heard a noise and got so scared," I lied breathlessly while continuing to run towards him. "I'm so glad you're here."

"Yeah, of course. What did you hear?"

As I got closer, his violet eyes flicked from the sword sticking up over my shoulder to the mask covering my face. Alarm flashed over his features and he opened his mouth to no doubt call for reinforcements.

"I wouldn't," I cut him off. "Not unless you want your mother to find out."

The shout died in his throat as hesitation blew across his face instead. It bought me the final seconds to close the distance between us. Stopping before him, I pressed on before he could do something stupid.

"You're dating a scullery maid." I lifted one shoulder in a nonchalant shrug. "I mean, she's pretty. With her blond curls and those big green eyes. But your mother would disown you if she ever found out."

His mouth opened and closed a few times but no sound came out.

Behind my mask, I was grinning like a villain while satisfaction coursed through me at the desperation in his eyes. "It would be a real shame if someone were to tell her."

Silence fell over the grass once more. Only the wind

shaking the trees beyond the walls broke the stillness while the guard and I stared at each other. Then he swallowed. Audibly.

"What do you want?"

"For you to take a hike." I jerked my chin in the direction opposite the mausoleum. "Go guard some other part of the grounds tonight."

Uncertainty flickered in his violet eyes. Since he worked for Prince Iwdael, and not Princess Syrene, he didn't know that this section of the grounds just happened to contain the building that housed the Dagger of Orias. Frowning, he most likely tried to figure out what I wanted with to do in this unimportant part of the castle gardens. Then he glanced towards the palace as if to count how many other guards were standing between me and the royal family. Apparently deciding that if I was an assassin, I was a shitty one and didn't really stand a chance, he turned back to me and nodded.

"Alright."

"Good." I nodded back. "As long as you keep your mouth shut about this, I'll keep mine shut about your dirty little secret."

From the look in his eye, I could tell that his pride was severely wounded, but he stalked away without another word. I followed him for a while to make sure that he really left before returning to the edge of the hedge maze where I had left Evander. When I was getting close, I pushed the mask back into my hood again.

Right as I turned the final corner, the Void did the same from the other direction.

"It's done?" we asked at the same time.

"Yeah," I replied.

He nodded. "Same."

Evander let out a long, shaky breath. "And now we need to get through the door."

"I assume you have a plan for that?" the Void said as we started back the way I had come.

"We do."

Well, *I* had a plan anyway. One that I hadn't, and wouldn't, share with Evander so I didn't elaborate further. The Void seemed to take the hint because he didn't press the matter.

Thick clouds blew across the moon and made the darkness around us even thicker. We slowed our advance slightly until the bright moon was back in the star-speckled heavens.

The mausoleum rose before us like a silent watcher. Symbols had been carved into the white wooden surface and it looked thick enough to be able to withstand a siege. I took in every detail as we made our way towards the massive door. There was no lock or handle on the outside, which strengthened Evander's observation that there was a guard on the other side who opened the door. It had probably been built that way so that only the Prince of Trees who had the ability to move the wooden door with his magic could get inside, but it worked rather well for sneaky princesses too, it would seem.

"Okay, I'll knock on the door and then you," Evander began and pulled out a small pouch from his pocket, "can throw this in his face."

The Void reached for it but I snatched it before he could, earning a scorching glare in the process. Opening it, I found some kind of pale powder.

"What is it?" the Void asked.

"It's a powder that people put in their tea to help them

sleep, but it's pretty potent so if you breathe in a concentrated dose, it'll knock you out."

"You're sure?"

"Yeah. They warned me about not breathing near it when I bought it."

"This'll work," I said. "But I have a better idea than knocking on the door." Turning around, I pointed at the dark bushes behind us. "Evander, could you please go and get me a branch from over there."

Surprise flitted over his face, but then he nodded. "Uhm, okay. Sure."

"Thanks."

After checking to make sure that he did indeed walk back over to the indicated hedge, I whirled towards the door again.

"Don't trust him enough to tell him that you can walk through walls, huh?" the Void huffed under his breath.

Ignoring him, I cast one final look over my shoulder to make sure that Evander's back was turned before I snapped my mask back in place and strode right through the door.

Silk caressed my skin. And then flickering candles in a white wooden room appeared in front of me, along with a mercenary with short black hair. He jerked up from the chair he had been sitting on as shock danced across his features. I leaped forward while his hand darted towards his sword. He only managed to brush the hilt before I threw the contents of the pouch in his face.

Violent coughing filled the room. It echoed off every surface in the astoundingly empty space while the mercenary tried to dislodge the powdery substance from his throat. Coughs turned into wheezing breaths as he clawed at his throat. And then his eyes rolled back in his head and he toppled backwards.

I cringed at the ruckus his body made as it connected with the floor, but I had wanted to know if there was anyone else here, hiding in the shadows. Standing in the empty room, I waited to see if anyone would come running to investigate the noise. No one did.

Once I was certain that there were no more hostiles inside the mausoleum, I pushed my mask back up and went to unlock the door. Pushing down the handle, I swung it open to reveal the impatient face of the Void and the confused eyes of Evander.

"Once this is all over, we need to talk about some things," the green-eyed elf said.

A tired smile drifted over my lips as I gave him a nod. "Yeah, we do."

"Save your lovers' quarrel for another time." The Void bustled past me and strode inside. "We're on the clock."

After ushering Evander inside as well, I closed the door and locked it behind us. The Void had already started searching the room, so I avoided Evander's suspicious glances and did the same.

The mausoleum was essentially one large room. Straight walls framed the rectangular shape, and symbols had been carved into them on the inside too, but other than that the space was completely empty. Save for the toppled chair and the unconscious mercenary, that is. I drew my fingers along the wall while walking one side of it.

"Guys?" Evander had stopped a few strides inside the door and was staring at the floor with a deep frown on his face. "Is it just me or are there cracks in the wood here?"

Both of us drifted over to where he was standing. Squinting down at the polished white floor, I studied the area right in front of him.

"Yes, there are," the Void said, one second before I spotted the cracks as well. He flicked his hand at me. "Kenna, your sword."

"If you break it…" I warned.

Looking up, he only narrowed his eyes at me. When Evander glanced between the two of us and the suspicion in his eyes grew, I blew out a short sigh and yanked out my blade. Steel rang into the silent mausoleum as it slid free. After flipping it over, I handed it hilt first to the Void.

He took it without another word and wedged it into the crack. Leaning down, he put his weight behind it and pushed downwards. Wood groaned. My heart thumped in my chest as it creaked louder. Then something snapped.

I winced, but it wasn't my sword that had produced the sound. It was the floor. Sucking in a slight gasp, I stared at the trapdoor that had popped open in the white wood.

The Void shoved the blade back in my hand and then moved over so that he could open the hatch. A soft thud echoed through the room as it fell back on the floor. Leaning forward, all three of us looked down the hole.

Narrow stairs made of the same material as the rest of the building led down into the darkness. We exchanged a glance.

"Get some candles," the Void said.

Evander straightened and went to borrow some from the candleholders set into the walls. I slid the sword back in its scabbard while we waited. Rolling my shoulders, I tried to free some of the tension in my body. It didn't work.

The dagger I had spent weeks searching for might be just below this small staircase. A few steps, and then I might find the one thing that could buy me my freedom. Blood rushed in my ears. This had to work. It had to.

"Here." Evander handed me a candle before giving another to the Void.

For a moment, the three of us just stood there, staring down through the open trapdoor.

Then I took a step forward.

And walked into the dark unknown.

CHAPTER 34

Firelight danced over walls made of packed earth. With every step down into the hidden mausoleum basement, the air grew cooler and the smell of damp soil stronger. I kept my eyes moving back and forth, scanning the path ahead, but the wooden steps only led to a dark hallway. Holding out the candle, I swept my gaze through it one more time before descending the final step.

"It's empty." I had whispered the words but in the dead silence of the secret underground area, the sound echoed painfully loud in my ears.

"It might be booby-trapped," the Void said from behind me.

"I know." Keeping my back to him and Evander, I pulled the black mask down in front of my face. "So step where I step."

The ground before my feet was made of packed earth, just like the walls, so there were no false tiles to worry about. But there might still be tripwires or others triggers, so I paused to scan for any before each step. Only brown soil stared back at me. My pulse pounded in my ears as I continued down the hall.

A cloud exploded before me.

I jerked back but the pale powder slammed straight into my face before I could retreat. Alarm bells tolled in my head. It had looked exactly like that knock-out powder I had used on the mercenary upstairs. If it was, I would be losing consciousness in a matter of moments. Holding my breath, I counted down the seconds in my head while the cloud dissipated.

"Did you breathe it in?" the Void said once every trace of the pale powder was gone.

Too stunned to reply, I simply stood there, trying to figure out how I was still standing. Then I lifted a hand and drew my fingers over my mask. They came back white.

Of course. The mask had acted as a shield and had prevented me from actually breathing in the powder.

"No," I replied at last. "You?"

"No."

"Are you okay?" Evander's worried voice cut through the dark hallway. "Please tell me that wasn't a poison cloud."

Temporarily placing my candle on the ground, I wiped both hands over my mask to remove the rest of the powder and then dusted them off. After pushing the mask back into my hood, I turned to face my two companions.

There was white powder on the ground around the Void as well. I narrowed my eyes at him. He only looked back at me with the same arrogant expression he always had on his face. I'd had my mask to protect me, but how in the world had he managed to avoid the powder?

Before I could question him about it, he called over his shoulder to Evander, "We're fine. The cloud missed us."

Evander, who was the last person in our little procession, had thankfully been standing too far away to be affected by the knock-out powder. Having to carry his unconscious body out of here would've complicated my plans to screw over the Void and go blackmail the King of Elves.

"Good." His green eyes were still filled with worry as they settled on me. "Please be careful, Kenna."

I gave him a nod before turning back to the path ahead. The flickering candle made shadows dance across the walls, but didn't reveal any traps. Drawing a deep breath to steady my nerves, I took a step forward and continued down the hallway. Clothes rustled behind me, informing me that the Void and Evander were following as well.

My heart thumped in my chest. Every time I set my foot down, I couldn't help the spike of fear that flashed through me because I knew that I might have just triggered another trap that I couldn't see.

An open doorway became visible at the end of the hall. Glancing up at the ceiling, I tried to estimate how far into the mausoleum we were. It was a rather short hallway but it had felt longer because I had been walking so slowly. By my estimates, we weren't even halfway through the mausoleum yet.

Something moved in the corner of my eye.

"Down!" I screamed.

Steel rang into the darkness as I yanked the sword from my back and swung it in wide arcs above my head. It whizzed through the air as I ducked and twisted while continuing to slash around me. Soft thumping sounded as the remnants of the trap fell to the floor. My heart was slamming against my ribs when I finally straightened and took in the scene around me.

Dark vines that had been woven into a net blanketed the ground. Except in the middle. There, the sturdy ropes had been cut into pieces, forming a hole that had saved us from getting trapped in it. The candle I'd been holding lay spluttering next to my boots.

My companions looked from the severed vines, to my sword, and then back up to my face.

"Wow," Evander blurted out.

The Void, on the other hand, wasn't impressed. Irritation, and something else, swirled in his gray eyes as he stabbed an arm towards me. "How do you keep triggering every trap in here?"

"I don't know," I snapped back while returning the sword to its sheath. "I have no idea what triggers the traps!"

It was true. We had gotten lucky with the vines. If I hadn't glanced up at the ceiling to estimate the distance we had walked at that exact moment, I would never have seen the falling net on time. But I had no idea how I had managed to trigger it.

"Don't take it out on her," Evander said with surprising force. "She just saved you from that trap."

The Void looked like he was about to spit venom in his face but then he just whirled back towards me instead and flicked his hand. "Let's go."

After giving my head a quick shake, I picked up my candle and started forward again. I had this nagging feeling in my mind that something was wrong, but I couldn't quite put my finger on what it was. As if I had forgotten something. Or that there was something I should know but for some reason had missed.

Thankfully, the final steps towards the open doorway

went without incident. Stopping right before the threshold, I examined the area around it.

The door had been left open and stood pressed against the dirt wall, but it wasn't really a door as much as it was a set of wooden bars. I prodded it carefully but it didn't move. My suspicion grew. Why booby-trap the corridor only to leave the door open?

Moving slowly, I leaned over the threshold and held out my candle so that I could see into the room.

I sucked in a gasp.

The room beyond was small and mostly empty. A couple of wooden boxes had been pushed along one wall but my gaze had gone straight for the centerpiece. It looked like a cage. The bottom part was made of solid wood while everything above that was made of the same round wooden bars as the door. Steel gleamed inside the cage. There on a tall stand was the weapon everyone had thought lost. The Dagger of Orias.

The wavy blade glinted in the candlelight and the markings etched into it seemed to glow from within. Goosebumps crawled over my arms. It looked exactly the same as it had on that balcony in King Aldrich's castle.

"It's here," I breathed.

It actually was here. The dagger that could kill a king with impenetrable stone skin. A wide grin spread across my lips. My ticket to freedom.

I glanced back at my companions. Wonder shone on Evander's face as he peered over the Void's shoulder to see the dagger. Gratitude coursed through me. I was so glad that I had decided to trust Evander and ask him to help me find the dagger. If it hadn't been for him, I would never have found it. At least not before someone else did, or before Princess Syrene used it to kill the king.

"This could be a problem." The Void tipped his head towards the wooden bars that made up the door. If he was happy that we had actually found the dagger, he hid it well. "Who wants to bet that as soon as we go inside, this'll close behind us?"

Putting a lid on the excitement bubbling through me, I turned back to him and nodded. "Yeah, I was thinking the same thing."

Evander opened his mouth but before he could say anything, the Void cut him off. "I'll stay here and make sure the door stays open. You, go grab one of those boxes and bring it back here so we can wedge it in the doorway."

Hesitation blew across Evander's face as he leaned forward and cast a glance into the room. I was just about to offer to do it instead when he swallowed and walked into the room. My fingers curled around the hilt of my knife but no traps sprang to life as he crossed the dirt floor and bent to pick up one of the boxes. Turning slowly, he made his way back to us.

"Well, that was nerve-wracking." A slightly hysterical laugh slipped from Evander's lips as he placed the wooden box in the doorway. Straightening, he shot us a proud smile. "But now we know that there are no traps on the floor inside."

"Yeah." The Void shooed us into the room while repositioning the box so that it sat in a way that could truly support the weight of the door if it swung shut. "Now stop patting yourself on the back and go figure out a way to get the dagger out of the cage."

After placing our candles in a triangle around the wooden cage, we drifted closer to inspect it. There was no door, no handle, and no lock anywhere on the structure. I ran my fingers along the round poles. They were spaced too closely to squeeze through and the solid bottom part only reached as far as my knees, while the rest of it was made up of those bars, which meant that I couldn't phase through it.

"Can't you just…?" the Void said to me while waving a hand towards the cage.

"No, I can't. It doesn't work like that."

Evander glanced between the two of us but thankfully didn't press the matter. Instead, he completed his arc around the structure while staring at the floor. When he reached the front of it again, he crouched down and dug his fingers under the solid bottom. Letting out a loud grunt, he heaved upwards.

Nothing happened.

The Void scowled at him. "What are you doing?"

After blowing out a sigh, Evander sat back on his heels again. "It looks like there's some kind of hinge set into the floor at the back so I thought maybe I could just lift it off, but it's too heavy."

I hadn't gotten to the back of the structure yet, and neither had the Void, so both of us rounded the final corner to examine the supposed hinge that Evander had found.

"He's right," the Void said.

"You don't have to sound so surprised," Evander grumbled quietly from the front of the cage before raising his voice again. "Grab the sides. We might be able to lift it and then tip it over if we all do it together."

Since I knew firsthand how well the Void handled other people giving him orders, I just waited for him to snap back at Evander. But fortunately, the arrogant spy only glared in his direction before stalking back to his side of the cage. I thanked whatever gods or spirits were responsible for that small mercy as I moved back to my side as well.

Crouching down, I dug my finger as far under the solid

side of the cage as they would go.

"On three," the Void said. "One. Two. Three."

After sucking in a deep breath, I pushed upwards with my legs.

Wood creaked as the structure lifted slightly. My arms shook under its enormous weight but I kept heaving. A gap the size of my hand appeared between the packed dirt floor and the bottom of the cage.

"Good," the Void called from the other side. "Keep going. We–"

Startled cries rang out.

The wooden structure sent a boom echoing through the room as it slammed back down on the ground.

I blinked in shock at the contraption that had shot out from under the cage and now encircled my wrist. Metal clanked as I desperately yanked against it. It wouldn't budge.

Panic clawed its way up my throat as I continued staring at my left hand and the manacles that trapped it firmly to the bottom of the solid wood panel.

My heart slammed against my ribs.

I was handcuffed to the cage.

Wood rattled into the deafening silence. I jerked my head up and whirled towards the sound. Fear drew its icy fingers down my spine as I saw what had caused the noise. The door to the room was slammed shut. My mind spun. We had locked the front door behind us, so no one should have been able to get inside. But the wooden box we had used as a safeguard for the door had been kicked into the room. How could this have happened?

A face appeared behind the bars.

My mind went blank and the world stopped as Evander grinned at me from the other side of the closed door.

CHAPTER 35

"Evander?" I stared uncomprehendingly at the green-eyed elf who was now standing safely in the hallway, on the other side of the bars. "What's going on?"

"You're a spy," he stated while keeping his gaze locked on me. Then his smile sharpened. "So am I."

"What?"

"So I guess we've been playing each other."

Metal clanked as I yanked against the handcuffs keeping my left wrist trapped to the bottom of the cage. The edge chafed against my skin but my restraints remained firmly in place. Pushing myself up on my knees, I peered over the solid wood in a desperate attempt to figure out what had happened to the Void.

Brown hair was visible on the other side of the cage.

"Hey!" I banged my free hand against the wood. "We–"

"Oh, don't worry," Evander cut in from the door. "He's handcuffed too. Neither of you are going anywhere, so just sit back and wait while I go get Princess Syrene. And a dozen guards or so."

"Wait!" I called as he began turning away. Scooting over on my knees, as far as I could get, I twisted until I could face him. "I don't understand. Why are you doing this?"

"I already told you. I'm a spy."

"For the Court of Trees?"

"For *Princess Syrene*." He let out a satisfied chuckle. "Remember I said that my lowborn family suddenly came into money?" His grin widened as he spread his arms. "How do you think that happened? Now sit tight while I go get her."

Metal clanked against wood again as I tried to rise from the floor, before being forced back by the manacles. "No. You owe me an explanation."

He arched an eyebrow at me. "I *owe you* an explanation?"

"Yes." I wasn't sure exactly what the Void was doing, but since he had stayed silent, I knew he was working on getting out of those handcuffs so I needed to buy him some time. Slumping back on my knees again, I let a pleading expression settle on my face. "Please. I don't understand. Princess Syrene made you rich in exchange for you… what? Trapping me?"

Evander lifted one shoulder in a casual shrug. "For what it's worth, you weren't the target. You're just collateral damage."

"What do you mean?"

He nodded towards the Void. "*He* was the real target. You see, Princess Syrene figured out that one of the other courts possessed an incredibly skilled spy. Someone who somehow knew that the dagger had been found. And that could of course mess up her plans to kill King Aldrich, if they realized that she was the one who had it. So she set a trap."

"To see which court miraculously showed up right after someone had gotten wind that the Dagger of Orias had been found," I filled in.

"Exactly." Leaning against the bars, Evander waved a hand in my direction. "And then the Prince of Stone, someone who never attends a party unless he has to, showed up with you in tow. So that's when we knew that the spy was from the Court of Stone, and now all we needed was for you to lead us to the elite spy in your court. Because, no offense, you weren't good enough to be the original infiltrator."

Something clinked faintly from the Void's side of the cage but I kept my eyes on Evander. I had to keep him talking. "But if you were using me to lure out the person who had infiltrated your court, then why did you send assassins to kill me after the ball?"

"Because after the ball, King Aldrich was supposed to be dead and catching the spy would no longer matter since the mission would have already been carried out."

"But then I saw her with the dagger."

"Yes, then you saw her with the dagger." He shrugged. "Which meant that you had to die before you could tell anyone else that Princess Syrene was the one who had it."

"But I didn't, and there was no second attack."

"No, there wasn't. Because for some reason, you never told anyone else that you had found the dagger. I still haven't really figured out why yet." Tipping his head from side to side, he considered. "But I guess we'll find out soon enough. Anyway, so then the plan to capture the real threat was back on. Fortunately for me, you decided to ask for my help, which of course allowed me to set this all up."

"But you couldn't possibly have known that I'd bring him along," I protested. "Even I didn't know he was coming until the last second."

A triumphant smile spread across Evander's lips. "Who do you think leaked it to people we knew would tell him?"

Another soft clink sounded from the Void's side. He shot me a quick look over the top of the solid panel. I yanked out my knife and slid it across the floor right as he leaped up and sprinted towards the door, snatching up the blade on the way.

Wood vibrated as the Void threw himself against the bars of the door and reached for Evander. The green-eyed elf let out a startled yelp and leaped backwards. From my position, I couldn't see what was happening on the other side, but the Void was banging furiously against a completely unmoving door. A haughty snicker sounded a moment later.

"Clever." My heart sank at the smugness in Evander's voice, because that meant our attack had failed. "Keeping me distracted while your little friend got out of his handcuffs. I guess story time is over now."

"Evander." I wasn't even sure what I was hoping to get from this but I had to know. "Was any of it real?"

His face appeared over the Void's shoulder from a safe distance inside the hallway. "I could ask you the same thing."

Normally, I didn't take this kind of double-crossing very personally. I was a spy. Betrayal was part of the job. But this was different. He had pretended to truly care about me. I mean, yes, I had been playing him too in the beginning, but then I had actually started to feel something for this damn elf and had stopped simply manipulating him. I had trusted him. Confided in him. Laughed with him. Hell, I had even slept with him. And not because it was my job, but because I had actually wanted to sleep with him. For me, that had been real. But *all of it* had just been an act for him. I could almost feel a piece of my heart cracking and going cold.

Evander threw me a smirk from the other side of the bars. "It was good sex, though."

A harsh laugh ripped from my throat. "No," I said and truly meant it. "No, it wasn't."

"Whatever you need to tell yourself."

His face disappeared from view. A moment later, footsteps sounded down the hallway.

Yanking against my manacles, I called after the traitor spy, "You'd better sleep with one eye open from now on."

No response came. Once the footfalls had died down as well, the Void whirled around and advanced on me instead. Anger, and what looked a lot like panic, danced in his gray eyes.

"How could you not know that he was a spy?" Stopping a mere stride away, he threw his arms out and glared down at me. "You've been working him for weeks! How could you have missed that he was playing you too?"

Since I was still handcuffed to the cage, I was forced to crane my neck to meet his furious eyes where I sat on my knees before him. "How could *I* not know? How could *you* not know? I thought nothing happened in any court that you didn't know about!"

"I keep track of every single one of Prince Iwdael's spies. Every one of them. But no one even knew that *Princess Syrene* had recruited a spy of her own. She's not supposed to have any spies!"

"Well, apparently she did. And they played you as much as they played me." Metal clanked as I shook my wrist and glared from the manacles keeping me trapped on the floor to the pissed-off spy above me. "What are you waiting for?"

He stared down at me. "For you to pick the lock."

"I don't know how to pick locks."

"Are you serious?"

"I can walk through walls! Why would I need to know how to pick locks?"

The Void scoffed. "And how is that skill working out for you right now?"

Biting back a vicious retort, I rattled the handcuffs again. "Are you going to help me out of these or not?"

"I should leave you there as punishment for your incompetence." Dread sluiced through me when I realized that he might actually do it, but before I could say anything, he pressed on. "But if we're going to get out of here before the guards come back, I might need you."

Crouching down, he got to work on my manacles. They fell open with a soft click. While massaging my wrist, I straightened before him.

"Good choice," I said. "Because while you were busy being too slow to get Evander, I actually figured out how to get the dagger."

The Void look like he had gotten stuck between hitting me and asking me to elaborate. Apparently deciding on neither, he simply snapped his mouth shut and scowled at me while I took a couple of hurried strides towards the wall. Dropping down on the ground, I placed my feet against the packed earth wall and curled into a ball. Then I pushed off and launched myself across the floor.

Since I could only phase through something if all of me fit through it, I hadn't been able to walk through the cage's bars. But there was nothing stopping me from simply gliding along the floor and straight through the knee-high panel of solid wood at the bottom that they had used to hide the handcuffs.

Soft fabric brushed against my skin. And then my palms slammed into the panel on the other side. Pulling my legs the final bit with me, I curled back up until all of me was inside.

After unfurling my limbs, I stood up. Or at least as much as I could inside the cell.

The Void stared at me from the other side of the wooden bars.

"Don't ask why," I said before he could. "Because I'm not going to tell you."

Everyone's powers had limits, and I didn't want him to know what mine were.

Keeping my back slightly bent, I turned towards the item beside me.

The Dagger of Orias gleamed in the flickering candlelight. The weapon that could cut through magic and kill the King of Elves rested atop the wooden stand, its magical markings glowing faintly from within. My heart pattered against my ribs.

So as to not give myself enough time to reconsider, I threw my hand out and snatched it off the stand without thinking.

CHAPTER 36

I half expected it to burn me when I touched it, but it didn't. In fact, aside from a slight aura of magic to it, holding it felt just like holding a normal dagger. After allowing myself a moment to stare at the item that would finally give me my freedom, I stuck it into one of the deep magical pockets of my jacket where I knew no one could take it unless I wanted them to. The Void watched me intently.

"What are you doing?" I snapped. "Stop staring at me and go figure out a way out instead."

"Do not give me orders," he ground out but stalked back towards the door.

My heart thumped in my chest. The cage around me was starting to feel incredibly claustrophobic and gave rise to the irrational fear that my magic wouldn't work on the way out and that I would be stuck in this small cage forever.

Shaking my head, I sucked in a desperate breath to calm myself while dropping down on the floor again. After curling myself up as best as I could by one wall, I pushed off with my legs and slid towards the other side.

Relief washed over me when I phased through the wooden panel and glided across the ground outside.

I was out of the cage. And I had the dagger. Now, all I needed was to find a way out of this mausoleum. Well, and then ditch the Void, and then somehow get to King Aldrich's castle, get past all the guards there and get to his room, and then blackmail him. The odds of pulling that off were slim. Dusting myself off, I hurried over to the Void. But one thing at a time.

"Anything?" I asked as I skidded to a halt next to him.

"No. There's no lock, no handle, no nothing." He grabbed the wooden bars and yanked hard. They didn't budge. "It can't be opened from inside the room. There's a small lever out there in the corridor but there's no way we can reach it from here."

A lightning bolt struck and I shoved a hand into my jacket. "What about the dagger? If it can get through King Aldrich's stone skin, it must be able to cut through some wooden bars."

The Void pinched the bridge of his nose. "The dagger is spelled so that it can cut through *magic*. It doesn't make the actual blade extra sharp." Taking the hand from his face, he waved it towards the door instead. "But sure, try it."

Pulling out the Dagger of Orias, I started sawing into the side of the closest piece of wood. Panic and hopelessness crashed into me when my frenzied sawing barely even scratched the surface.

"It won't work," I said, desperation coloring my voice. "We'll never get through it before they come back." Sticking the dagger back into my pocket, I whipped my head from side to side. "There has to be another way out."

Both of us sprinted to the packed earth walls and started furiously tapping against it. No hidden exit revealed itself.

Blood rushed in my ears. Evander and the guards could be returning any moment now.

"I'm so stupid!" A frustrated howl ripped from my throat and I kicked the wooden box we had used to wedge the door. It flew across the floor before crashing into the opposite wall. "I've been dealing with too much shit! It's made me sloppy. If I'd only had my own problems to worry about then this would never have happened. But I've spent so much fucking time trying to solve everyone else's problems too that I couldn't focus on my own. If I hadn't spent all that time and energy on everyone else, I would've seen the signs. Seen that Evander was a two-faced bastard who was planning to betray me from the very beginning." Raking my fingers through my hair, I shook my head. "I should've just said no and focused on my own problems."

"Yeah, you're stupid," the Void snapped. "But we don't have time for your soul searching right now, so get your head back in the game." He flicked a hand towards the closest wall. "Can't you just walk through it? Or the door?"

"No." I blew out a sharp breath. "I already told you. It doesn't work like that."

He slammed a hand against the wall in frustration. "What a useless skill!"

"I don't see you helping either," I shot back. "What even is your skill anyway?"

Another fist against the packed dirt was my only reply.

There was no way out. We were trapped here. And we had already wasted precious time we didn't have. Evander had left five minutes ago, and should be on his way back with the guards any moment now. Tipping my head back, I drew my fingers through my hair again and released a shaky breath. I was going to die here.

I blinked. My arms fell back down by my sides as I stared up at the white wood above me.

"The ceiling," I breathed.

"What?"

"The ceiling." Snapping my head back down, I stared at the Void. "I can phase through the ceiling. If you help launch me into the air, I can get through it and land back up in the mausoleum. Then I can run back down the stairs and pull the lever to open the door for you."

He stared at me for a moment. I could almost see the calculations going through his head. Then he nodded.

"Alright." Getting down on one knee, he laced his fingers together and held them in front of him. "Let's do this."

I backed as far away as I could in order to get a running start. Just before I was about to take off, the Void spoke up again.

"Kenna?" Hesitation swirled in his gray eyes and his voice was the gentlest I had ever heard. "You will come back for me, right?"

"I should leave you here," I echoed his words from earlier with a slight smirk on my face, "but if I'm going to get out of this court in one piece, I might need you."

He huffed a laugh and then jerked his chin. "Let's go."

I sprang forward. Leaping the final step, I placed my foot into his interlocked hands right as he straightened and threw me upwards.

Air rushed in my ears and my heart beat wildly in my chest. Phasing through a ceiling was something I very rarely did because it could be incredibly dangerous. I needed enough momentum to carry me all the way up through the surface. Otherwise, I would just slam straight into it and fall back down again. Praying to whatever gods or spirits might listen to a wicked little blackmailer, I stared straight at the white wood as I flew towards it. This might hurt.

When the feeling of passing through a curtain of sheets enveloped me, followed by the sight of a white mausoleum filled with lit candles, I almost wept with relief. I flew a couple of strides into the air before I lost momentum. My boots slammed into the wooden floor as I landed in a crouch in the middle of the carved hall.

For a brief moment, I actually entertained the idea of leaving the Void down there since it would be easier to blackmail the king without first having to ditch an inconvenient spy somewhere along the way. However, there was one problem with that plan. I couldn't worldwalk. And the rogue worldwalker I had planned on hiring before the Void showed up was not an option since he was still in the Court of Stone. And I didn't actually know any worldwalkers in the Court of Trees so unless I took the Void with me, there was no way for me to get to King Aldrich's mountain castle.

Cursing my inability to worldwalk, I sprinted back down the stairs while snapping my mask into place.

No knock-out powder was deployed, though. As I ran past the shredded net on the ground, I realized what had felt off the first time we had walked through here. None of the traps had been trying to kill us. Only capture us. I really should've noticed that. And I wasn't the one who had been triggering them. Evander had.

The Void was standing right on the other side of the bars. I threw him a glance before pushing down the small lever I had also missed last time. Wood groaned as the door swung outwards. Relief flowed through me and I swore it was mirrored in the Void's eyes too.

"Hurry," I snapped instead and took off back up the stairs.

Our boots thudded against the steps as we sprinted up them three at a time. The candles in the mausoleum fluttered in a breeze that snuck in through the gap in the front door that Evander had left open.

Raised voices came from outside it.

My pulse pounded in my ears as I threw the door wide and darted into the cool night outside. Dark figures were closing in across the grass. Shouts rang out as they spotted us.

"Go through the wall." The Void stabbed a hand towards the high defensive walls. "I'll meet you outside. Storage shed."

Without waiting for a reply, he sprinted into the darkness. The shouts grew in intensity and the cluster of guards split up to chase after the fleeing spy. I whirled around and ran in the opposite direction.

The mausoleum was fairly close to the wall, I just needed to make it there first and then I'd be in the clear.

Air exploded from my lungs.

I slammed into the damp grass as a body connected with mine from the side. While still trying to figure out how I had missed the guard that had jumped out of the hedge maze from the other side, I ripped out my knife and stabbed it into the first area I could reach.

A cry tore from my attacker's throat as the blade buried itself in his arm.

Yanking it out, I use the moment of reprieve to scramble out from under him and jump to my feet. The guards chasing me were getting closer with each second. As soon as I was up, I spun around and started towards the wall again.

I let out a yelp.

The elf on the ground had grabbed my ankle and pulled it

towards him. Desperately, I tried to yank it free but his grip was like iron. The other guards were almost upon me now.

Bending down, I swiped my knife across his forearm. Blood welled up from the cut and another pained cry split the night but his grip on my ankle loosened. I whipped my foot away from his fist and smacked it into the side of his head before darting away.

My heart pounded in tune with my panic as I hurtled towards the wall. The guards were only a few strides behind me. Pushing my legs as fast as they would go, I ran with everything I had towards the dark wood before me.

Hands snatched at the hem of my jacket. My throat burned and my ribs ached from the previous hit but I shoved it to the back of my mind and pushed myself harder. Only a little more.

Silk brushed against my skin.

And then I was through.

Shouts rose from the other side of the wall as the guards realized that I was gone and that they couldn't follow me. I rammed my knife back in its sheath.

Not daring to slow down, I set course for the storage shed I had used on multiple occasions and ran towards it. Praying that the Void was already inside, I leaped through the wall and skidded to a halt among the wooden crates.

It was empty.

Panic clawed its way up my throat.

Pushing it down, I forced myself to take deep breaths. I had been able to take a shortcut by going through the wall. The Void would have to get out another way and then make it all the way here. Of course it would take longer for him than for me to get here. I kept that thought on repeat in my head as

I pushed my mask back into the hood of my jacket and then took to pacing the room.

The minutes dragged on.

Then the door creaked open.

My hands shot to my weapons as a dark figure slipped into the room.

CHAPTER 37

"You're here. Good."

I relaxed as the Void became visible in the moonlight filtering in through the window. "Where are the guards?"

"Not here yet, but it won't be that long until they search this part." He stalked across the floorboards until he was standing right in front of me. "We have to go. Now."

"I know. But we can't go back to the Court of Stone."

He blinked at me in surprise. "Why not?"

"Because I overheard the guards that were chasing me," I lied effortlessly. "Evander told them who we are and they worldwalked people to intercept us outside the Prince Edric's castle. If we go there now, we'll be captured before we can get inside the walls."

The Void raked his fingers through his short brown hair and let out a string of curses. "It's in moments like this that I really hate the wards keeping people from worldwalking directly into the castle." He met my gaze. "So what do we do?"

"If we worldwalk to King Aldrich's castle, we can have his

people contact Prince Edric and get him to come meet us there. And then we can give him the dagger and then he can give it to the king, so that when we go back to the Court of Stone, there is no dagger for them to steal back."

He narrowed his eyes at me. "That sounds awfully risky."

"Well, do you have a better idea?"

Silence descended on the room while I fervently hoped that he wouldn't come up with a better idea. Or see through my lies.

The Void blew out a resigned sigh. "Alright. But if we just worldwalk to the landing area completely unannounced, they might attack first and ask questions later."

"Okay, so drop us at some other spot along the plateau and then we can just walk there."

Drumming his fingers against his thigh, he considered in silence for another few moments. Raised voices echoed from outside as the guards drew closer.

"Fine," the Void finally said. "There's a small cabin a bit further away that might work."

"Great, then let's go!"

The shouting in the forest outside grew louder. I didn't hesitate one second as I closed the final distance between us and threw an arm around his back. Once he had done the same, I sucked in a deep breath. And then we were gone.

My body folded in on itself and the world around us blurred.

A few moments later, the area around us came back into focus.

We were once more standing in a small wooden room, but instead of having piles of stacked crates, it was completely empty. I staggered away from the Void and shook my head to clear the nausea from my stomach.

Cold mountain air leaked in from the cracks in the walls and the lone window showed a breathtaking vista of a star-speckled night sky and dark jagged rocks below it.

I had made it to King Aldrich's mountain. The Void watched me from a few strides away while I took longer than I really needed to recover from the worldwalking. Now that I was here, I needed to find a way to give him the slip and get inside the castle on my own. Bracing my hands on my knees, I pretended to take a few deep breaths while I considered my options.

Since I didn't know where on the mountain the Void had dropped us, I might need to keep him around a little longer. At least until we were so close to the castle that I could starting plotting a way inside. When he wasn't looking, I ran my eyes over the Void's body. He still didn't look like he was carrying any weapons and he hadn't used any tonight, so he probably wasn't. His magic could be a real problem, of course, but if I simply walked behind him the final stretch then I could just whack him over the head with the hilt of my knife and knock him out.

As far as master plans went, it wasn't my best work. But it would have to do for now.

"Are you coming or what?" the Void snapped and jerked his chin towards the door.

"Yes." I stalked forward while irritation that wasn't faked flashed through me at his rude tone. "Excuse me for not being that used to worldwalking."

"What kind of spy doesn't know how to worldwalk without throwing up?"

"Not everyone is born with that blessed power, you know." Throwing a glare at him over my shoulder, I yanked open the door. "So maybe you–"

"Hello again."

My blood froze in my veins and it had nothing to do with the biting wind that whirled in through the open door. Moving slowly, I twisted my head back towards the door and the midnight voice that had come through it.

Mordren Darkbringer smiled down at me from the other side of the threshold.

Leaping backwards, I drew my blades and sank into a defensive position. The Prince of Shadows seemed to take that as an invitation because he followed me into the room and closed the door behind him. Alarm bells blared inside my skull. How were we supposed to get out of this?

"Kenna," the Void snapped behind me. "The wall!"

I whipped my head to the right. Of course. He wanted me to run through the wall and disappear before Mordren could get his hands on the dagger. Hesitation flashed through me. Would I really leave the Void here alone to face the wrath of Mordren Darkbringer?

Yes. Yes, I would.

Without a second look back, I darted towards the closest wall.

Shadows shot out.

I launched myself into the air to avoid the black tendrils snaking across the wooden floorboards. Victory coursed through me as his shadows flew past underneath me. Two more strides and then I would be through the wall. I pushed off with my legs and threw myself towards it.

Agony pulsed through me. It was followed by even more tangible pain as I slammed into the wall without phasing through it and collapsed on the floor. His wave of power had crippled my ability to focus, rendering my own power useless.

Metal clattered against wood as my blades bounced down beside me.

I balled my hands into fists as another wave of pain rolled over me. Once it disappeared, I snatched up my weapons and shot to my feet again. Only to realize that shadows now encircled my ankles. The Void was on his knees a few strides behind me, his face contorted in pain. I gripped my blades tighter.

Mordren tutted. "Oh, come now. None of that. I'm just here to collect what you owe me, and then I'll be on my way."

"I don't have it," I said with as much confidence as I could muster.

Pain spiked through me, making my vision blacken for a second. I gasped in a breath as the agony ebbed again.

"Don't lie to me," Mordren warned. "Now, hand over the dagger."

"No."

A dark laugh drifted through the cabin. "No?"

My gaze darted around the room. With his shadows attached to me, I couldn't phase through the wall which severely limited my options.

The Prince of Shadows took a step towards me. I took a step back, the black tendrils around my ankles coming with me. The wicked smile on Mordren's face made me think that he only allowed me to do so because he enjoyed seeing me retreat.

"You don't think I can take the dagger from you?" he said, that smile still on his face.

"You will never be able to find it." I backed another step towards the Void. "Not unless I want you to."

He let out another dark laugh. "Oh, I do enjoy a challenge.

I will take you back to my court and make you beg for the pleasure of handing it over."

Agony pulsed through my body until my knees buckled. Metal clattered against wood again as I dropped my weapons and collapsed to the ground next to the Void. The pain intensified.

"How long do you think you can last?" Mordren said but the pain let up slightly.

Bowing my head, I twisted towards the Void and breathed, "When I say run, you worldwalk out of here and tell Prince Edric what I did."

His face was still set in a mask of agony but he managed a nod.

"I said, how long do you think you can last?" Mordren pressed. "Huh?"

Another wave of pain rolled over me.

"Okay," I gasped out. "Okay, I'll hand it over."

His power withdrew. Beside me, I felt the Void relax as well. Pushing myself up onto my knees, I lifted my head and met Mordren's gaze head on while I stuck a hand inside my pocket. With calculated slowness, I withdrew the Dagger of Orias.

A triumphant smirk curled Mordren's lips at the sight of it.

I held it in front of my chest.

And then I threw it into the Void's waiting hands. "Run!"

He disappeared into thin air.

Releasing a long breath, I sat back on my heels. If I couldn't use the dagger to blackmail King Aldrich into giving me my freedom, I could at least make sure that Prince Edric got it. That way, I at least had a small chance at earning my freedom anyway. If the Void told Edric what I had sacrificed to get the dagger to him, then maybe he would agree to set me free in repayment of that. But that was of course all dependent on me surviving the next couple of minutes. Looking up into Mordren Darkbringer's face, that didn't seem like a very probable outcome.

"Oh, Kenna." He shook his head at me. "You really should have just handed it over."

"Too bad." I raised my chin defiantly as I pushed to my feet. "Now you'll never get it."

His answering smile was a slash of white in the moonlit cabin. I glared back at him but my heart thumped in my chest as I waited for him to exact his revenge.

The air next to him vibrated.

And then the Void appeared beside him.

My mouth dropped open in complete and utter shock as the gray-eyed spy chuckled and handed the Dagger of Orias to the Prince of Shadows.

CHAPTER 38

"I told you. You really should've just handed it over yourself." Mordren twirled the dagger in his hand in a nonchalant gesture. "Then I might have actually shown you mercy."

Still unable to comprehend the events of the past few seconds, I whipped my head between the two of them. The Void lifted one shoulder in a casual shrug. And then my mind finally caught up.

"You." I stared straight at the Void. "You work for him?"

"Yep."

"All this time?" Dragging a hand through my hair, I shook my head. "All this time that you've been hunting for a traitor in our court… and it was you all along."

His lips tugged upwards in a smirk. "Well, it was me *and you*, wasn't it?"

"Why?" I flicked desperate eyes from the Void to Mordren. "Why go to all this trouble to involve me in this when he already worked for you?"

The two of them exchanged a look, some kind of silent

communication passing between them as if debating whether I deserved an explanation or not. When the Void only shrugged, it was down to Mordren to decide. He strode towards me.

On instinct, I tried to retreat but his shadows kept me firmly in place.

Stopping a mere stride in front of me, he reached out and drew two fingers along my jaw. "I was rather impressed by your scheming, even though you lost." His fingers came to a halt under my chin and tilted it upwards so that I faced him. "So I'd say you have earned an explanation. You'll never be able to share it with anyone anyway."

Behind him, the Void let out a huff that I couldn't quite interpret but I kept my eyes on the Prince of Shadows.

"You see," Mordren began, "the Void here is very good at what he does and he found out that the Dagger of Orias was hidden somewhere in the Court of Trees. But the problem was of course that I was the only one who knew that. If I had gone after the dagger on my own, then they would know that I was the one who had infiltrated their court. So I needed a buffer. Someone to take the blame while my own spies stayed anonymous."

"The Court of Stone," I filled in.

He took his hand from my chin. "Correct. I knew that Edric, that insufferably honorable workaholic, would never actually use the dagger to kill King Aldrich, so I had the Void leak the news about the dagger to him and only him. Then he would send his own spies to look for the dagger and I would put pressure on the one he sent to the Court of Trees." His smile widened. "Fortunately for me, you took care of that for me when you blackmailed one of my informants."

"So even if I hadn't done that, you would've found

something else to blackmail me with?" I blew out an annoyed breath. "Great."

"Yes, you really were doomed from the start." His silver eyes glinted in the moonlight as he leaned forward slightly. "And then I just needed an excuse to keep a close eye on you."

Silence fell across the empty cabin as Mordren waited for me to connect the dots on my own. A cold wind whirled outside and sent a fresh puff of mountain air into the room. I glared up at the Prince of Shadows. And then the final piece clicked into place.

"The traitor hunt." Closing my eyes, I rubbed my forehead for a few seconds before looking back up at him. "You started it on purpose. You picked one of the random pieces of information I gave you and then you made sure to almost get caught so that Prince Edric would know that someone else had been given that information as well. Because you knew that he would call in his most trusted spy to root out the traitor, which meant that you could have the Void keep a very close eye on me inside my own court."

"Indeed."

"So your first plan was for me to hand over the dagger in exchange for you keeping quiet about my blackmailing scheme, and if that failed, the Void would make sure you got the dagger anyway." I let out a long breath, followed by a surprised chuckle. "Damn. And here I was, making plans to betray you separately. I didn't even consider that you might be in this together. That changed everything."

The Void arched an eyebrow at me from across the dusty floor. "I thought you'd be more pissed. When Evander betrayed you, it really got to you but you don't even seem all that angry now."

Shifting my gaze to the traitor spy, I shrugged. "Evander

pretended to care about me. He messed with my feelings, and that's unforgivable to me. The two of you have been dicks to me since the beginning, so I don't take that as personally." A vicious smile spread across my lips. "Though I'd still watch my back if I were you."

Shadows snaked from Mordren and twisted around my limbs. He leaned closer to my face as one dark tendril slithered around my throat. "Is that right?"

I kept my mouth shut but held his gaze. He continued staring into my eyes for another few seconds before letting out a soft chuckle and taking a step back. All his shadows retreated with him.

"Well, goodbye then, Kenna," he said as he turned around and strolled towards the door.

The Void fell in beside him as he passed. I watched the silvery moonlight play across Mordren's long black hair as he made his way towards the door. Bending down, I picked up my weapons. For a moment, I considered stabbing them both in the back, but then thought better of it and simply returned the blades to their sheaths.

Mordren had just pushed down the handle on the door when a sudden thought struck me like a shovel to the back of the head.

"Wait!" I called out.

Moving with calculated slowness, he closed the door again and took a couple of steps back towards me. The gleam in his eyes told me that he had been waiting for me to figure this part out. "Yes?"

I swallowed. "I can't worldwalk."

"I know."

Panic washed over me. There was no other way off this mountain. The only possible way to get here or to get back down was to worldwalk, and only people who had previous clearance from the king were allowed to do so. If I was found here alone, with no one to verify my presence, then there was no way anyone would believe that it was anything but treason.

"If you leave me here, I will be executed." My breathing was coming in fits and starts.

"I know." Mordren cocked his head. "Why do you think I said that you wouldn't be able to share what I told you tonight anyway?"

My heart slammed against my ribs. "Don't leave me here."

The Prince of Shadows closed the distance between us while a malicious smile curled his lips. Stopping a few strides before me, he looked pointedly at the floor before locking eyes with me again. "Go ahead. Grovel."

"Please."

He simply continued staring me down. Working my tongue around my suddenly parched mouth, I swallowed. Mordren held my gaze. I was out of options. We all knew it. So after drawing a shaky breath, I swallowed my pride and got down on my knees.

His smile widened as he watched me lower myself to the floor before him. Even through the fabric of my pants, the floorboards were cold beneath my knees. Another mountain breeze blew in through the crack under the door. I suppressed a shiver as I looked back up at the Prince of Shadows.

Keeping my eyes soft, I met his gaze. "Name your price."

"Oh I could get used to this." He ran his eyes up and down my body. "You on your knees before me."

I said nothing as he cocked his head. A curtain of glossy black hair slid over his shoulder with the movement.

Even though my life was hanging in the balance, or

perhaps because of it, I couldn't help the rush of envy that shot through my body at the power he held in that moment. One word from him could either save me or condemn me. And all I could do was get down on my knees and beg him for mercy. Another flash of envious desire coursed through me. I wanted that kind of power too.

Mordren let the silence stretch for another few seconds before a smile drifted over his lips again. I drew in a soft shaky breath as I waited to hear his judgement.

"Tell you what," he said at last. "Since you asked so nicely, I think I'll be merciful. If you keep your mouth shut about the fact that the Void works for me, then I'll get you off this mountain."

"Deal," I blurted out.

"So desperate." Another dark laugh drifted through the cool air before he turned serious again. "But know this, if you ever break this bargain and tell anyone about the Void, then I will destroy you and everything you have ever touched. Am I making myself clear?"

"Yes."

"Yes, what?" he coaxed.

"Yes, my prince."

"That's right." Mordren shifted his gaze to the Void. "Get her back to the Court of Stone."

The Void simply inclined his head.

Glittering silver eyes slid back to me. "I'll see you soon, Kenna."

And with that, the Prince of Shadows disappeared.

I tilted my head back and heaved a deep sigh before mustering enough strength to climb to my feet again. As soon as I was up, the Void jerked his chin.

"Let's go then."

Not bothering to reply, I just walked over to him and let him wrap an arm around my back. Turning his head, he glanced over at me.

"Betrayed twice in the span of only an hour," he said. "What a rough night for you."

A humorless laugh bubbled from my throat.

Yes, what a rough night indeed. And it was about to get a whole lot worse because now I would have to go back to Prince Edric and tell him that I had the Dagger of Orias but then lost it to the Prince of Shadows.

There was no way that he would ever believe that I wasn't the traitor now.

The cabin disappeared around me as the Void worldwalked us back to the Court of Stone.

Gods and spirits help me.

CHAPTER 39

Morning light filtered in through the windows and filled the already pale throne room with a gray gloom. Courtiers chatted about politics, dresses, and other things that were of absolutely no significance to me. Drumming my fingers against my thigh, I waited for Prince Edric to arrive.

Since I couldn't very well barge into the royal chambers in the middle of the night, I had to wait until morning to tell the Prince of Stone about my failure.

Okay, so maybe it was because I had wanted to buy myself a little more time too.

But there was no way I could keep it a secret any longer than this, because as soon as Edric showed up, he would hear gossip about the break-in at the Court of Trees last night. And it was better that he heard it from me.

A short blast echoed between the shining white walls and announced that the Prince of Stone had arrived in the throne room. His blond hair flowed behind him as he strode across the marble floor. I kept my chin up as I slipped through the crowd and approached him.

My heart thumped in my chest as I waited for him to finish greeting various groups of courtiers. I could tell from his face the moment he heard about the break-in. Granite eyes flashed across the sea of people until they landed on me. Detaching himself from the cluster of nobles, he stalked towards me.

I sank into a curtsy as he closed the final distance between us. "My prince."

"Kenna." His voice was filled with barely restrained fury. "Care to explain?"

"Yes, my prince." Everyone else gave us a wide berth since they could no doubt feel the anger rippling off Edric too, but I still kept my voice low. "I went to the Court of Trees yesterday to investigate a tip about the dagger. I didn't think it would actually be there, so that's why I didn't tell you. But the dagger ended up being there and I managed to steal it." Breaking his stare, I dropped my gaze. "But then I was ambushed by the Prince of Shadows. He took it."

Edric was silent for a moment. "*Mordren* has the Dagger of Orias?"

"Yes, my prince."

Stone rumbled underneath my feet. I winced. All around us, the courtiers were moving even further away.

"Please," I said before Prince Edric could continue. "It was the Prince of Shadows. I didn't stand a chance. He used his pain magic on me until I couldn't even remember my own name and then he just took the dagger from me. Please, you have to believe me."

"It's a little too convenient, don't you think? We know for a fact that there is a traitor in our court and then you just happen to get a tip about the dagger that you go and investigate on your own without telling anyone. And then that actually leads you to the dagger, but then you just happen to be ambushed by Mordren Darkbringer who takes the dagger from you before you can give it to me. Tell me that doesn't sound just a bit too suspicious."

Glancing up, I found hard eyes staring down at me. "It's the truth."

"We'll see about that." Prince Edric jerked his chin.

Two guards detached themselves from the wall and started towards us. My heart hammered in my chest. I took a step towards Edric, which made him move out of reach. The guards picked up the pace. From across the crowd, people I knew watched the unfolding events. In the shadows by the corridor, the Void stared at me with unreadable eyes, while from the other side of the room, the blue eyes of my parents and siblings studied me. None of them made a single move to help me.

"Please don't do this," I begged. "I'm telling you the truth. Don't do this. I've only ever been loyal to you. I'm not the traitor."

The Prince of Stone only stared down at me with eyes of granite. I was about to open my mouth and spew some more half lies when two strong hands wrapped around my upper arms. Flicking desperate eyes between the two guards now flanking me, I made one last attempt to sway the prince in front of me before I was dragged off to no doubt be tortured until I told them what they wanted to hear.

"I didn't do this." I pulled against the iron grip around my arms. "Please, my prince. I didn't do this."

Ignoring me, he turned to the guards. "Take her to…" He trailed off as Ymas strode towards him.

Courtiers hurried out of the way as the tall and muscled spy plowed through the crowd. When he reached the Prince of Stone, he bowed low before straightening again.

"My prince," he said. "We have found the traitor."

My heart began beating wildly in my chest again.

Edric blinked at Ymas and then glanced at me before turning back to the black-haired spy. "Explain."

"The guards received an anonymous tip about a traveling book and then passed on that information to me." Ymas stuck a large hand inside his cloak and withdrew a small leather-bound book. "I went there to investigate and I did indeed find a traveling book. After looking inside it, I harbor no doubt that this is the traitor we've been looking for." His face was solemn as he handed the book to Prince Edric. "Please, read it."

Paper rustled as the Prince of Stone flipped open the small book and began leafing through the pages. "All this information about our court. All these arranged meetings. And this…" He motioned at the handwriting that appeared on every other page. "This is Mordren's handwriting."

"Yes, my prince," Ymas confirmed.

Prince Edric's face hardened as he snapped the book shut and clenched it in his fist. "Where did you find this? Who is the traitor?"

My pulse thrummed in my ears.

Ymas held Edric's gaze. "I found it in the private study of Lord Arquette."

"Lord Arquette?" Stone rumbled throughout the whole throne room as Prince Edric ground his teeth. "After everything I have given that man. This is how he repays me?"

With a flick of his hand, the guards released me and instead went on another traitor hunt. I rubbed my arms as I watched the two of them stomp through the crowd until they arrived in front of the brown-haired lord. Lord Arquette jerked up in surprise. When the guards moved to grab him, he jumped back and waved his hands in front of him.

Two more guards approached from behind.

A scuffle broke out as Lord Arquette tried to get away.

"Please, my prince," he called across the throne room as the four guards began hauling him away. "There has been some kind of mistake. Please. This is a mistake."

Surprise flitted over the Beaufort family's faces as they glanced between me and the falsely accused lord who they had owed a lot of money to. I gave them a brief nod before looking away. Standing out of sight behind Prince Edric's back, I watched the stern-faced elves drag Lord Arquette across the white marble floor. The smile on my face was pure evil.

That's what you get for messing with me and my family, I thought as wicked satisfaction coursed through me.

Setting this up hadn't been easy, but by all the gods and spirits, it had been so worth it.

Since I had needed to both solve the traitor hunt problem and my family's debt problem, I'd figured, why not do both at the same time?

The first step had been to convince Mordren that the first traveling book had been rendered useless. It had been a risky move, but since I had started plotting my revenge on Lord Arquette even before the assassins had showed up to kill me, I'd had a shot. My first move had been to write my final message to him in the very corner of a page, as if that was the only clean space left, and then I just had to deliberately not reply to any of his messages. And after that… well, let's just say that Mordren Darkbringer severely underestimated my ability to lie while under the influence of alcohol. Making him believe that the book had gotten drenched in blood had been a lot easier that I had expected, and as soon as he had given me a new one, I'd been free to use the old one in any way I saw fit.

Then, I'd had to visit Liveria Inkweaver and get her to forge the damning proof I needed. For that, I had required that particular traveling book that had already been used by the Prince of Shadows, as well as something that had Lord Arquette's handwriting. The latter had been easily obtained from the note he wrote about the remaining debt. Once I had both of those items, I simply had the Inkweaver erase my handwriting and everything written by the merchant who had used it first, and then I had her write the exact same thing in Lord Arquette's handwriting. It had been really expensive. But flawless work always was.

After that, I just had to plant the forged book in the unfortunate lord's study, which wasn't all that difficult for someone who can walk through walls.

Then came the next tricky part. I needed to set up the pieces to fall without my involvement.

Going to visit Stella to buy information about the guards in the Court of Trees had only been half my objective. When I strategically took out an entire stack of papers that I, oh so accidentally, knocked off the table, it had of course been meticulously planned. In my hunt for the scattered papers, I just so happened to miss one. That particular document just happened to be a little bounty note informing the reader that a hefty reward would be waiting for the person who could provide information about a missing traveling book. The fact that I had also scrawled Lord Arquette's name on it and circled it was of course very fortunate for Stella.

After that, I just had to give the money for the bounty to the captain of the guards, along with explicit instructions that if someone came to tell them about a missing traveling book, they were to pass on that information to Ymas straight away.

Then, all I had to do was wait for Stella's love of money to get the better of her.

The only problem with my plan had of course been that I couldn't control when that would happen. I had expected it to happen several days ago, but Stella had held out longer than I thought before she finally made her way to the Court of Stone to exchange more information for money.

Fortunately for me, it finally happened right as I was about to get arrested for treason. But now my name was cleared. As was my family's debt.

Who needed the help of spirits and gods when you could bring about the destruction of your enemies entirely by yourself?

"You weren't the traitor," the Prince of Stone stated as he turned around to look at me.

It was as much of an apology as I was about to get. But given that I actually *was* the traitor, I accepted it gratefully. Fortunately for me, I had also managed to wipe the rather villainous smile off my face before he saw it.

"No, my prince," I replied and inclined my head.

"Now, we need to…" Prince Edric trailed off once more as another figure hurried towards us.

A messenger with nervous green eyes skidded to a halt in front of Edric and bowed low. "My prince, King Aldrich has called an emergency meeting. He requests your presence immediately."

Stone rumbled throughout the throne room as Edric swore. "Mordren has made his move with the Dagger of

Orias." He whirled back to me and Ymas. "Gather the rest of the spies. We're leaving."

The two of us bowed before striding away to carry out his orders.

Nervous anticipation bounced around inside of me.

It was time to finally learn what Mordren Darkbringer had done with the Dagger of Orias.

CHAPTER 40

Anxious trepidation hung like a thick blanket over the throne room. The elven princes were standing in separate groups with their respective retinues clustered behind them. In the vast hall of gleaming marble, they looked like desolate islands in a great white sea. I flicked my gaze around the room. Nervous nobles glanced towards the empty throne atop the dais and stern-faced elves who most likely served their princes as bodyguards were scanning the crowd for potential threats. Both the king and Mordren were still markedly absent.

"Do you think the Prince of Shadows killed him?" Monette whispered next to me.

It seemed a bit at odds with what he had told me yesterday. But then again, with Mordren Darkbringer, you never knew.

"Honestly, I have no idea," I replied.

The clear ringing of trumpets announced the arrival of the King of Elves. A buzz went through the crowd. Prince Edric, who was standing at the head of our group, straightened and uncrossed his arms. I held my breath as I waited to see what would happen next.

A collective sigh of relief echoed from the gathered elves as King Aldrich strode onto the platform at the front of the room. It was quickly replaced by surprised intakes of breath when the Prince of Shadows followed him. Taking up position next to the king at the edge of the dais, Mordren squared his shoulders and stared out at the crowd. In his fine black suit, he stood out in stark contrast against the white marble around him and his whole pose dripped with authority.

Clothes rustled throughout the dead silent room as we all bowed and curtsied. It was meant for the king but I swore I could see a satisfied gleam in Mordren's eyes.

"Today, we gather for truly heartbreaking reasons," King Aldrich called across the sea of elves. "I have been informed of an assassination plot. Against me."

Shocked gasps echoed between the gleaming stone walls, and several people cast accusatory looks at the Prince of Shadows. He only stared back at them, entirely unaffected by their silent judgements.

"The Dagger of Orias has been found," King Aldrich continued, which drew more gasps of surprise from the courts that didn't already know about its existence. "And I was almost assassinated with it." He motioned at the black-haired prince next to him. "But thankfully, Mordren Darkbringer took it upon himself to stop this sinister plot and give the dagger to me for safekeeping."

Took it upon himself, huh? I was the one who had done all the heavy lifting in stealing that damn dagger and here he was, taking credit for it. Shifting my gaze to the Prince of

Shadows, I narrowed my eyes at him and I swore I could see a slight smirk tugging at his lips.

"I have asked you all here to bear witness to the arrest and confession of the traitor." The king lifted his arm and stabbed it straight at the group from the Court of Trees. "Princess Syrene, you have been accused of treason. How do you plead?"

Exclamations of utter shock rang out as the whole throne room whirled around to gape at the Princess of Trees. None so more than Prince Iwdael. He stared in open-mouthed horror at his wife. Syrene in turn pressed a hand to her chest while a mask of disbelief descended on her beautiful face.

"Treason?" Even her voice held that innocent tone of utter incredulity. "My king, you couldn't possibly believe that *I* would be some kind of assassin?"

"I didn't want to believe it at first, but Mordren made a very convincing case."

"Mordren?" She practically spat the name. "You would take his word over mine? The Prince of Shadows, the dark prince who is known for his ruthless and devious nature, over me?"

A look of sadness blew across the king's face. "He has presented convincing evidence, Syrene."

"Evidence that he has planted! In fact, he and Edric have been working together to set me up for this." Distress flashed in her violet eyes as she turned and pointed an accusatory finger at the Prince of Stone. "They are the ones who have been plotting against you, but then when they got caught, they pinned it on me instead."

"Have you lost your mind?" Prince Edric snapped. Stone rumbled beneath my feet. "You accuse *me* of this?"

"Yes, and I have proof. Last night, two of your spies tried to break into our court and plant the Dagger of Orias there."

"You said you had proof of that," King Aldrich cut in before Edric could level the whole castle. "What proof?"

Taking a step to the side, she motioned for an elf with short brown hair to step forward. Evander. Rage shot through me at the sight of him. His face once again had that earnest commoner look as he glanced around the room.

"A member of my court saw them break in and alerted the guards." Disgust blew across Syrene's face. "But they managed to get away before they could be apprehended."

"Is this true?" the king asked as his brown eyes slid to Evander.

"Yes, my king, it is true." His gaze darted to me before it returned to the king. "Would you like me to point out the two people who tried to plant the Dagger of Orias in the Court of Trees?"

My heart rate sped up. The Void wasn't here. He never attended public functions like this because it compromised his missions. That meant that the only one who was about to be accused of treason was me. Again. Keeping the calm mask on my face took more effort than I wanted to admit. I desperately wished that I had at least brought my knife.

"I've heard enough." King Aldrich snapped his fingers. "It is time for the truth."

Three servants in impeccable clothing materialized at the edge of the crowd and began moving towards the middle of the room. The black-haired one was holding a small white pillow. Something round lay at the center of it, but it was covered by a swath of pale fabric so I couldn't tell what it was.

"I didn't want to use this." Another sad expression blew across the king's face. "But it's not every day that I'm almost assassinated and I need to know the truth."

Stopping in the middle of the room, the black-haired elf

held out the small pillow while one of the two blond ones lifted the cloth.

Sharp intakes of breath bounced between the walls.

Across the floor, Princess Syrene's face drained of color. "My king, please, is it really necessary?"

"Yes." He waved a hand at the guards that had closed in around the Princess of Trees. "Bring her forward."

Dead silence hung over the room as she was escorted towards the crystal orb that lay perched on the white pillow. The final servant pulled out a needle and pricked his finger. Holding it above the orb, he let a single drop fall onto it. Red mist swirled inside it for a second before it returned to its original clear color.

"What is that?" Monette breathed next to me.

Not taking my eyes off the scene before me, I whispered back, "It's the Orb of Verity."

"Put your hand on it," King Aldrich instructed.

Princess Syrene swallowed and glanced at the guards around her but then placed her slender hand on top of the magical artefact. A soft glow began shining from within the crystal.

"Did Mordren and Edric try to plant the Dagger of Orias in the Court of Trees?" the king asked, his voice hard as stone.

Syrene was silent for a moment, as if trying to figure a way out of this, before replying, "No."

Relief washed over me. If she and Evander had outed me as a spy to the whole throne room, then I would have been as good as dead. But now, there was no reason for any of them to even try to point the finger at me.

"Have you been in possession of the Dagger of Orias?" King Aldrich continued.

"Yes."

"Did you attempt to kill me with it?"

Fear flashed in Syrene's violet eyes. "My king, please…"

His face could have been carved from the uncompromising mountain itself for all the sympathy it held as he raised his voice. "Did you try to kill me with the Dagger of Orias?"

"No."

A cry cut through the throne room. Red light beamed from within the crystal orb. Princess Syrene continued screaming in pain and yanked her arm but she couldn't get her hand off the orb. Tears ran down her cheeks.

"Yes," she finally pressed out between broken sobs. "Yes, I tried to kill you."

The red light faded and the Orb of Verity returned to its normal color. As soon as it did, two things happened. Princess Syrene snatched her hand back and the blond servant who had provided the drop of blood collapsed. His partner, the one who wasn't holding the orb, caught him in his arms and began hauling him away.

Magic was never limitless. And for something as powerful as an item that could compel the truth from people, there was always a cost. The Orb of Verity drained the user's energy which left them unconscious for days or even weeks afterwards. That was why it was only used when absolutely necessary.

"Take her." King Aldrich flicked his hand.

The guards grabbed Princess Syrene by the arms and started pulling her away, but something appeared to have snapped inside her. Digging her heels into the floor, she twisted towards the Prince of Trees.

"I should have at least killed *you* while I had the chance!" she snarled. "Did you really think that I would be satisfied being some second-rate princess to someone as weak as you? All you ever do is drink and dance and fuck anything that moves. No plans. No ambition." Her purple slippers slid against the white marble as she desperately tried to keep the guards from dragging her away. "Did you really think that would be enough for me? *I* should have ruled the Court of Trees!"

Harsh words spread through the grand hall at her scandalous declaration. The Prince of Trees, however, looked genuinely stricken. Tears gleamed at the corner of his yellow eyes and his face appeared to have gotten stuck between shock and devastation. I scanned the crowd for Evander, but the brown-haired spy was suddenly nowhere to be found.

"You see, Kenna?" Monette said under the cover of the buzzing audience around us. "This is a warning. This is what happens to people who reach for too much. Ambition is not a good thing." Stepping closer, she linked arms with me and glanced over at me with concerned turquoise eyes. "Please tell me you learned something from this."

Oh I learned something alright. If you're planning to overthrow a king... don't get fucking caught.

Thankfully, I was spared from answering because the king raised his voice again.

"This has been a truly heartbreaking ordeal, but I choose to find comfort in knowing that there are exemplary people in our lands as well." Twisting slightly, he motioned at the Prince of Shadows. "Mordren Darkbringer has once again shown that he is honorable, resourceful, and strong. A true leader. And I encourage you all to strive for those kinds of qualities too. They will be needed in the next King of Elves."

Mordren inclined his head to King Aldrich with a respectful look on his face, but I could see the satisfied gleam in his eyes as he turned to face the crowd. Out on the floor, the other four elven princes glared up at him.

So this had been his plan. He hadn't wanted the Dagger of Orias so that he could kill the king. Instead, his plan had been to be the hero of the story and gather further favor in order to strengthen his position as the next King of Elves. I had to admit it. It was rather clever.

Clothes rustled again as the gathered crowd bowed to their king before he strode away. His white hair flowed behind him like a curtain until he disappeared into a doorway by the dais.

As soon as he was gone, Prince Edric turned around to face his group of spies. I flinched as his granite stare locked on me. He might no longer believe that I was the traitor, but I had still lost the Dagger of Orias to the Prince of Shadows. And now Mordren had used it to solidify his position. The marble floor vibrated slightly beneath my feet. I swallowed. I might have to do some more groveling before this day was over.

Clamping his jaws together, the Prince of Stone stared me down for another few seconds before looking up and addressing all his spies. "I have some business to attend to. Ymas, you're with me. The rest of you, be down by the landing area in fifteen minutes."

We bowed while Ymas and Prince Edric stalked towards the Prince of Trees.

Before Monette could turn back to me, I slipped away and set course for the balcony, because after everything that had gone down today, I needed some air.

Since I was in public, I had to actually open the doors before going outside.

Crisp mountain air filled my lungs as I closed my eyes and

inhaled a deep breath. The morning sun beamed down from a bright blue sky and warmed my face. Leaning back against the cold stone wall outside the door, I tried to calm my thumping heart.

The Dagger of Orias had been found and dealt with, the traitor threat against me was gone, and my family's debt was cleared. All of my current missions were over. But the sense of closure and the sheer relief that I had actually pulled off all these crazy schemes were mixed with a small voice of panic. I was in so much shit.

Not only was my entire fortune gone, I was also out of favor with Prince Edric because I had lost the dagger to Mordren. And those two mishaps together put me as far away from my freedom as one could possibly get.

"I hear you kept your mouth shut about the Void."

Opening my eyes, I found the Prince of Shadows strolling towards me. His long black hair shone like obsidian in the bright sunlight as a breeze snatched it up before sending it cascading down his back again. I remained leaning against the wall while he stopped before me.

"That was the deal," I replied.

"Good to know that you honor your deals." A smirk spread across his lips. "Even when they're made under duress."

I snorted and rolled my eyes. "And I see that your little scheme worked out exactly like you wanted it."

"It did." Mordren closed the final distance between us. Raising his hand, he pushed a long red curl back behind my ear. His fingers brushed my jaw on the way back. "You played a good game, though. Too bad you were outmatched from the very beginning."

"Outmatched?" I arched an eyebrow at him. "I don't think so."

"No?"

"No." I straightened from the wall so that our faces were so close that I could feel his breath on my skin. Locking eyes with him, I let a wicked smile spread across my lips. "You see, I haven't even started playing yet. And once I do, you won't know what hit you."

His midnight laugh caressed my face. "Is that right?"

"Yes. When I'm done with you, you will be the one on your knees, groveling."

"Is that a threat?" His shadows glided out and trailed their way up my arms. Mordren's smile was nothing short of villainous as he stared down at me while a black tendril slid over my collarbone before encircling my throat. "You wouldn't dare threaten an elven prince, now would you?"

Grabbing the front of his crisp black suit, I pulled him towards me until his lips almost brushed mine. "I think I just did."

His dark laugh danced against my mouth. "Oh, this will be fun. Do it, then. Give it your best shot. Play your best game." Challenge glittered in his silver eyes as he drew soft fingers along my jaw. "It will still end with you on your knees before me every time."

"We'll see about that." I smirked up at him before adding, "My prince."

Another satisfied chuckle slipped from his lips but his shadows withdrew and he took a step back. Still smiling, he inclined his head. "I'll see you soon then, Kenna."

He waited for me to nod back before he strode away. I watched the muscles in his back shift under his shirt until he had disappeared completely into the throne room. Once he was gone, I let out an incredulous laugh.

Challenging the Prince of Shadows? Maybe I really did

have a death wish. But I was done letting people push me around. I was done doing everything for everyone else at the expense of my own health and happiness. It was time to start thinking about me and what I wanted. It was time to start putting myself first.

A strong wind swept across the balcony, making my long red curls billow behind me. Squeezing my hand into a fist, I stared out at the unforgiving mountains before me and drew a deep breath of cold air.

Having ambition was incredibly valuable when you wanted more from life.

I knew what I wanted. I wanted freedom. And power.

And I was going to get it.

An evil smile spread across my lips.

Even if I had to take on the Prince of Shadows to do it.

BONUS SCENE

Do you want to know what happens when Kenna attempts to steal jewelery at a party and Mordren Darkbringer suddenly shows up? Scan the QR code to download the **exclusive bonus scene** and find out what happens between the scheming spy and the Prince of Shadows.

ACKNOWLEDGMENTS

The world needs more kindness. It needs more people who are willing to lend a hand to their friends, family, and random strangers. So in that sense, helping people is of course an amazing thing. However, it is not such a good thing when it is continually at the expense of your own health and happiness. Not when people are just using you to get what they want while you have to sacrifice and put your own dreams on hold. So, to all of you who have spent your life doing everything for everyone else, remember to put yourself first too. Put your own health and happiness first for once. Your dreams matter too.

As always, I would like to start by saying a huge thank you to my family and loved ones. Mom, Dad, Mark, thank you for the enthusiasm, love, and encouragement. I truly don't know what I would do without you. Lasse, Ann, Karolina, Axel, Martina, thank you for continuing to take such an interest in my books. It really means a lot.

Another group of people I would like to once again express my gratitude to is my wonderful team of beta readers: Alethea Graham, Deshaun Hershel, Luna Lucia Lawson, and Orsika Péter. Thank you for the time and effort you put into reading the book and providing helpful feedback. Your suggestions and encouragement truly make the book better.

To my amazing copy editor and proofreader Julia Gibbs, thank you for all the hard work you always put into making my books shine. Your language expertise and attention to detail is fantastic and makes me feel confident that I'm publishing the very best version of my books.

I am also very fortunate to have friends both close by and from all around the world. My friends, thank you for everything you've shared with me. Thank you for the laughs, the tears, the deep discussions, and the unforgettable memories. My life is a lot richer with you in it.

Before I go back to writing the next book, I would like to say thank you to you, the reader. Thank you for joining me and Kenna on this mission. If you have any questions or comments about the book, I would love to hear from you. You can find all the different ways of contacting me on my website, www.marionblackwood.com. There you can also sign up for my newsletter to receive updates about coming books. Lastly, if you liked this book and want to help me out so that I can continue writing, please consider leaving a review. It really does help tremendously. I hope you enjoyed the adventure!

Printed in Dunstable, United Kingdom